Love's Image

Rosalyn Alsobrook

ZEBRA BOOKS
KENSINGTON PUBLISHING CORP.

ZEBRA BOOKS are published by

Kensington Publishing Corp.
850 Third Avenue
New York, NY 10022

Zebra and the Z logo Reg. U.S. Pat. & TM Off.

First Printing: July, 1996

Printed in the United States of America
10 9 8 7 6 5 4 3 2 1

One

Jenny Langford never felt closer to her famous great-grandfather, Tyler Dykes, than when she slid the treated dry-plate into the back of the large camera and heard it thud into place.

Eager to find out if the restored antique worked, she had spent most of that afternoon preparing three dry plates according to the instructions in a book she had bought. Her excitement grew to sheer euphoria as she stepped back to admire her handiwork. The polished wood and black metal gleamed in the overhead light of her small apartment. Within minutes, she would have the honor of taking a photograph with one of the very same cameras her great-grandfather had operated back in the year 1896.

A rush of pride washed over her when she glanced at the two other cameras she had inherited. Her favorite of the three was the Scovill and Adams, a smaller shutter-release camera camouflaged to look like a stack of three leather-bound books. It was a less cumbersome piece of equipment that used an amazing new flexible film developed by George Eastman. Just knowing how ultra-modern it was for its time gave it a mystique the other two cameras just did not have. She would have restored it first, had it not needed so much more work than the Rochester.

Even so, she knew the Scovill and Adams would not sit idle for long. She was too intrigued by the camera's history. Her great-grandfather Tyler had used the unusual book-camera to capture extraordinary photos of people who otherwise would never have been photographed. The camera's clever disguise had allowed him to take hundreds of candid shots of infamous outlaws, noted gunfighters, and shady politicians involved in tawdry love affairs. With the Scovill and Adams he had sneaked the famous photograph of the Dalton brothers just days before most of the gang was killed or captured. The picture showed the young men, along with two unidentified lawmen, sitting at a small table with their boots off, smoking long cigars, and drinking mixtures of milk and whiskey.

Along with earning him an unprecedented amount of money, shortly after the photograph's publication, Jenny's great-grandfather's popularity soared to new heights. One of her grandmother's yellowed newspaper clippings proclaimed that there was not a photograph Tyler Dykes couldn't or wouldn't take. "He'd take a picture of the very devil himself if he just knew where to find him," the article stated.

Having always been fascinated by the wild tales surrounding her most controversial ancestor, Jenny smiled as she reached for the black jar of flash powder she'd made earlier. Hearing all about his reckless nature and reading about his many photographical conquests had inspired her to become a free-lance photographer. That, in turn, had prompted Jenny's grandmother to will all of his photographs and photography equipment to her.

Jenny looked again at the treasured possessions scattered about her apartment. Until Grandma Victoria's recent death, they had been kept in the attic, lovingly stored inside several old wooden trunks that smelled of moth balls and cedar. The family brought them out and examined them during special occasions, usually in mid-July, on the anniversary of her great-grandfather's death.

Rarely were the items brought out for a stranger's eyes. No matter how much the collectors around the world offered, Grandma Vic had kept his possessions private—for family viewing only. Even her boyfriends, when she had time for them, had not been allowed to share such a private event.

Now it all belonged to her.

Jenny glanced around in awe of what she now possessed. Why, the unrestored Scovill and Adams alone was worth over eighteen thousand dollars. The restored Rochester was worth another eleven or twelve thousand.

But monetary value did not really matter. Like her grandmother—God rest her sweet, gentle soul—Jenny would never part with even one piece of her great-grandfather's photography equipment.

For now there was a part of her in this equipment as well. She had personally cleaned and polished the bulky box-style Rochester inside and out, had had the metal pieces replated, replaced a broken piece of glass, reset the large awkward portrait lens, repaired the broken tripod and replaced the rotting cape.

With the chemicals and paper necessary to develop the first of the three glass plates ready inside her darkroom, within an hour she would know if she had restored the camera correctly.

Painstakingly, Jenny scattered a measured portion of the black powder across the flash pan, then recapped the jar and set it aside before returning her attention to the camera itself.

As she picked up the box of long matches—since her great-grandfather's flash pan was not the type with a built-in flint—her excitement grew. The height of feeling was tempered by the awesome knowledge that just over a hundred years ago her great-grandfather's gifted hands had touched the very same equipment. She felt oddly insignificant in comparison.

Tyler Dykes had been a brave and adventurous man. How ironic was the manner of his death. Rather than being killed during one of his daring escapades to sneak one of those infamous couldn't-be-had photographs, he had been murdered in his own home. Right inside his own photography studio back in Black Rock, Oklahoma—doing nothing more exciting or more dangerous than developing family portraits he had taken earlier that day.

Jenny's stomach clenched. How senseless that the life of such a fascinating man had been cut so short. Story had it that the daring thirty-nine-year-old Tyler Dykes had been stabbed through the heart for the forty-eight cents his receipts showed to be in his cash box.

Forty-eight cents.

The equivalent of five hours of common labor back then.

He had lain dead on his own floor for half a day before a woman who had come to pick up portraits taken a week before discovered his body. Tyler's own wife, Janeen, was away in Philadelphia visiting family, and did not learn about her husband's murder until receiving a telegraph message hours later.

Sadly, because of an endangered pregnancy that kept Janeen bedridden in her parents' home where she was visiting when she nearly miscarried—a condition that had eventually landed her in the hospital for two weeks—she had been unable to return for her husband's funeral. A close friend had arranged Tyler's burial and packed up and sent most of their belongings to her.

Jenny's insides churned like they always did when she thought about the death. Because of what Grandma Vic had termed "a lazy, no-account sheriff," Tyler's murder remained unsolved forever. No one was ever brought to justice. *That* angered Jenny as much as it had her grandmother.

"I wish I'd been there," she muttered, double-checking the camera to make certain the base was securely bolted to the tripod. "I'd have made *sure* that sheriff found out who murdered him. You can bet on that."

Finally ready to take the first picture, Jenny glanced around for a subject.

"Ah!"

There was her ever-faithful pet tabby, Stillshot. Asleep, as always, on the topmost shelf of the small bookcase nearest the windows.

Dressed for comfort, and later for bed in a knee-length, white terry-cloth robe, a comfortable cotton nightie, and a pair of white slip-on canvas shoes, Jenny moved two flex lamps closer to the bookshelf to soften the effect of the flash against the white walls.

Next, she moved the frame with a photograph of her great-grandfather taken inside his studio closer to Stillshot so it would be in the picture, too.

The photograph showed Tyler wearing his usual wide-brimmed black hat with the front tugged down to a cocky angle and a dark-colored shirt, open at the collar. Although no smile peeked beneath the thick, drooping mustache, his dark eyes twinkled with obvious mirth—large, oval eyes, much like Jenny's.

Angling the frame so the glass would not catch the flash from the powder, Jenny returned to the camera then took out the still-protected glass plate so she could quickly check the pose. When she pulled the lens cap off and glanced through the viewer to make sure the cat and photo were positioned exactly where she wanted, she blinked in disbelief.

"What the—?"

The upside-down image reflected a room far different than her own. Instead of a modern living room with white walls and dark shelves, it reflected a darker room with an open door, paneled walls, and part of an old desk. Her cat, the bookshelf, and her great-grandfather's portrait were not visible at all.

"How weird." She ducked out from beneath the cape to see if she could figure out what caused the odd images.

Perplexed, she found nothing even remotely similar to the ghostly shapes reflected on the glass. Checking the large lens for possible smudges, she found only one tiny scratch off to the side. Not significant enough to cause a distortion of that magnitude.

"Stillshot, old age must be settling in early. I'm starting to see things that aren't there."

As usual, other than to twitch the tip of his long, striped tail, the cat ignored her.

Thinking perhaps poor lighting had caused the strange shadows on the view glass, she brought in another lamp and placed it at an angle different from the other two.

"Well, that sure didn't help," she muttered.

Next, she tried opening the windows. The humidity from cooking earlier might have affected the camera in some way, she thought. But no matter what she did, she still saw the false images.

Eventually, she gave up. It was late. She was tired. And the cough medicine she had taken earlier to knock out a tickling cough was already taking effect, making her drowsy. All she wanted was to take the one picture, see if she could develop it, and go to bed.

With book in hand, she checked to make sure the camera was pointed in the general direction of the cat and photo, then following the instructions, slid the dry glass back into place. Quickly, she pulled out the protective covering, set the book aside, and ducked back under the cape. Reaching forward, she plucked off the lens cap.

"Don't move," she told the snoozing feline unnecessarily. That was the whole reason she had named her pet Stillshot. Except early in the morning when suddenly he decided himself a predator, the worthless animal could easily serve as a hairy paperweight.

"Say cheeeese—"

Carefully, Jenny lit a match and touched it to the powder. *Hisss—flasssssh—sp-p-p-putter—KA-POP!*

Startled by the loud sound, Jenny jerked her head out from under the cape at the same time she slapped the heavy cap back over the lens.

What the—?

Jenny blinked hard, stretched her eyes to their limits, and blinked again.

The room had changed.

To the one she had viewed just seconds ago inside the camera.

But how could that be?

Dumbfounded, she glanced first at the camera, then down at herself, as if seeing her own body would somehow reassure her. It didn't. But observing herself and the camera unchanged baffled her more. Why were some things changed and others not?

Why was anything changed at all? It did not make sense.

She stared at the stub of the match still in her hand and wrinkled her nose against the acrid stench of burnt powder.

Both the blackened match and the flash pan still smoldered. Adding to that strangeness, the air around her felt decidedly warmer. Perhaps ten degrees warmer. Or more.

Puzzled, she glanced at what had once been a pair of small, open windows. In their place was now a solid wall covered floor to ceiling with photographs—some in frames, but most not.

A soft breeze against her cheek made her look in the opposite direction. She jerked with surprise.

Across the room, where her entertainment center had stood not five minutes earlier, she saw a half dozen open windows. These windows were large, with wooden frames, and brimmed with daylight.

Daylight?

Blinking again, she glanced around for a clock and spotted one atop a tall counter near the only door to the outside.

One o'clock?

How could it possibly be one o'clock?

More confused than ever, she looked again at the windows and frowned. It just did not make sense to see sunlight streaming down when the nightly news had just ended. Nor did it make sense to see tall, leafy bushes stirring in the dappled sunshine through windows that should open onto a covered breezeway.

Still searching for *something* familiar, she looked to where a large-screen television had once stood and saw several tall wooden file cabinets in its place. Where the cat had been asleep on his favorite bookshelf now existed a cluttered desk with twin frosted oil lamps at one corner. An antique-looking beverage set sat beside them.

Her heart drummed harder against her chest. Nothing was like before. Except for the camera. It had not changed. Except maybe the black cape. That did look to be made of a different material. But how could that be?

None of this made sense.

Hoping to find some answers, she took several steps toward the photograph-covered wall. When she did, the room started to feel oddly familiar—although she knew she had never been there before.

She stepped closer to the photographs. Some of those seemed oddly familiar as well. When she bent to examine them closer, it finally struck her where she was. Her eyes widened with yet more disbelief. Somehow she had entered her great-grandfather's photography studio.

But that couldn't be.

Her stomach twisted into a hard, tight knot while she lifted her fingers and touched the photographs. They felt real. As did the polished wall behind them and the wooden floor beneath her feet.

But they *couldn't* be real.

Grasping for a logical explanation, she decided the cold medicine was having some sort of strange side effect. She should not have tried that new brand. Something in it had caused her to hallucinate.

As comforted by that thought as annoyed, she turned to study the room as a whole again and noticed a wide-brimmed hat hanging beside a dark leather vest on a peg near the outside door. Both looked exactly like those items her great-grandfather always wore in photographs. She walked over and touched them. They, too, felt too real to be imaginary.

She pressed her hand against her arm, then her face. She felt both the warmth of her skin and the movement of her hand. She doubted an hallucination would allow her sense of touch to be so acute, a medically induced dream to feel so incredibly alert.

A tightness pulled at her chest as she pressed her hands together and rubbed them hard.

Whatever had happened to her was real. As incredible as it seemed, somehow she had been transported back in time and now stood inside the private studio she had seen dozens of times in photographs.

But how could that happen?

She looked again at the photographs. Some she had seen before. Others were unfamiliar. All were of people dressed in fashions popular in the late 1800's.

Photographs her great-grandfather had taken.

Bending closer to examine a newspaper article tacked to the wall, she wondered fleetingly if her being there had anything to do with the wish she had muttered just minutes before taking the picture. Could she have *wished* herself there? Preposterous. That would mean she had somehow willed herself through time.

And space.

Impossible.

She bit her lower lip at her next thought. What if the flash powder had been mixed incorrectly and had caused an explosion? What if she had been hurt in that explosion and didn't even know it?

But she would feel pain if that were the case.

Wouldn't she?

Her gaze moved again to the newspaper article. The date at the top read 1895. Yet the paper had not yellowed. A head shot of her great-grandfather was at the top of the article—a photo that again reminded Jenny how very much she looked like him. He had the same high cheekbones flanking a slender nose and the same dark, lash-fringed oval eyes so common to her grandmother's side of the family.

As much compelled as she was frightened by the odd situation, she leaned closer and read the first two paragraphs. They described a trip Tyler Dykes took to El Paso, Texas, to get a photograph of the infamous outlaw, John Wesley Hardin, for the Texas Townhall magazine. The third paragraph told of how Tyler had to settle for a photograph of a freshly dug grave and one of Sheriff John Selman, who had shot John Hardin in the back of the head only two days earlier.

Intrigued, Jenny looked for those two photos among the others on the wall. None showed a grave, but several had lawmen in them. Was one of them Sheriff John Selman?

Returning to the article, she read further to see if there was a description of the man. Caught up in a passage about the sheriff walking into a saloon with his pistol drawn, she suddenly heard a loud crash in the next room.

Instinctively, Jenny rushed toward the noise. As she neared an opened door, she heard a second shattering crash.

"Who's in there?" she called out, still several feet from the darkroom.

After a pause, a large, broad-shouldered man shoved past her, slamming her against the wall. He wore bulky gray clothes and had a dark brown hat pulled low over his forehead. A black cloth covered most of his face.

Knocked off balance, Jenny grabbed hold of the desk to keep from falling, and missed seeing more than a scuffed black boot disappear through a nearby window.

Remembering the circumstances of her great-grandfather's death, her chest wrenched tighter with each successive beat of her heart as she stepped on inside the small, unlit room. She smelled the fresh blood even before she spotted Tyler's body lying on the floor, already stabbed through the heart. Just enough light emanated through the doorway to allow her to sidestep several pieces of broken bottles and check his pulse.

None.

Trembling, she scanned the wall for a light switch, then remembering there would be none, she hurried toward a nearby wall lamp that looked similar to those she had seen in western movies. Finding matches in a pocket near the base, she struck two together and lit the thing, all the while fighting to hold back her panic and decide what to do.

The small porcelain lamp offered just enough light for her to see that half the room was in shambles. Pieces of broken bottles and dry glass littered the floor, chemicals puddled across a work table, and a half dozen cabinet drawers and doors stood open. Obviously she had caught the man searching for something.

But what?

Jenny pressed her cold hands over her cheeks, willing herself to calm down long enough to make sense of all the havoc. While studying the room, her gaze was again drawn to her dead great-grandfather, lying on his side, a pearl-handled knife handle still in his chest. His eyes were still open, his gaze eerie and distant. Blood ran in three shimmering trails across the uneven floor and pooled dark red beneath the largest worktable.

Suddenly, her legs felt too weak to hold her weight, causing her whole body to shake. Tears threatened when she remembered how warm his neck had felt when she checked for the pulse. He had been dead only minutes. A sick feeling washed over her. If only she had gone into that room first, instead of to the photos and newspaper clippings on the wall, she might have prevented the murder.

No, that was wrong. If she had arrived before the murder, she would have heard the struggle. The noises she had heard were not the noises of a life-and-death struggle. They were the noises of a careless search. Careless because the murderer had thought the house empty.

Unable to gaze at her great-grandfather's lifeless body any longer, Jenny pressed tight fists against her stomach and looked away. She had to tell someone. But who? She remembered from her grandmother's stories that the local sheriff would be of little help; and Tyler's wife, her great-grandmother, was still in Philadelphia.

Who could she tell? Surely there had to be someone.

There was. The friend who took care of the funeral arrangements. The man who had also packed and shipped all her great-grandparents' belongings back East so her pregnant great-grandmother would not have to come do it herself.

Tapping a finger against her mouth while her heart throbbed painfully hard, she tried to recall the man's name. She had heard him mentioned a hundred times during her youth. But for the life of her she could not remember it. All she could remember was he'd had a simple name, and he had been a close friend to both her great-grandparents.

Frowning, Jenny gave up trying to force the memory. She could not let her great-grandfather's body lie on that cold floor any longer. *Somebody* had to be told. And the only person she knew to tell was the sheriff—inept though he may be.

But first she needed to find clothing more suitable for the street, or she would never be taken seriously.

Hoping her great-grandmother, Janeen, had left something behind she could make do with, Jenny hurried toward the door that joined the studio to the main part of the house. A bedroom seemed the most logical place to find clothing from that time period. She needed to find something suitable and change into it as quickly as possible. Before her grandfather's killer made a clean getaway.

Tearing through the house at breakneck speed, until finally she found the master bedroom, she threw open a cabinet and found it filled with women's clothes. Glad Janeen had not taken all her clothes with her, Jenny pulled out several likely garments.

Quickly, she tried on an outfit made of what looked like a lavender-colored wool. Although not a perfect fit, the sashed waist allowed her to pull the garment snug around her middle, and the long pleated skirt was just short enough that it did not drag on the ground.

Having worn no undergarments under her cotton nightie and robe, and not about to venture out into the unknown without any, Jenny scrambled through the two drawers at the bottom of the cabinet, then snatched on a pair of the odd-looking underdrawers that bagged from her waist to her knees. She did not bother with a camisole or a corset. She did not have precious time to waste tugging in and out of the dress again. She also did not have time to put on the stockings and boots she came across. Instead, she shoved her bare feet back into her own canvas shoes.

Making sure everything was tied or buttoned that should be, and that her canvas shoes did not show enough to cause undue curiosity, she hurried to the vanity for a quick check in the mirror. She blinked at how odd she looked in the antiquated outfit, then noticed her long, wavy hair, layered away from her face. Not exactly a hairstyle of that time.

Working quickly, she found a small, stiff-bristled brush and a dozen or so flimsy-looking hairpins, then reached into her pocket for the rubber band she had left there. Using the mirror, she pulled her dark hair into a long ponytail near the top of her head, then hurriedly twisted and tucked the loose portion under and secured it with the hairpins.

With that done, she hurried back through the studio and out into the side yard, which was not much more than a small, fence-bound patch of grass edged in plush flower gardens. There was no front yard at all. The front of the L-shaped veranda butted right up against the sidewalk.

Reaching the street, she discovered herself at one end of a small, tree-dappled town that looked like something straight out of an old John Wayne movie. She scanned the many buildings, mostly wooden structures with elaborate false fronts, and glimpsed the steep, rocky hills beyond where short, stocky trees not quite as green as those in town dotted the grassy knolls. At the top of the largest slope lay the giant black boulder that had given Black Rock its name.

Turning again at the flourishing little town, it did not take long to figure out which of the three dozen or so buildings housed the local sheriff. Even across town, she could see the heavy bars over the windows.

Aware now she had been given something extraordinary—an opportunity to right a grievous wrong—Jenny's adrenaline pumped with such force she actually felt its heat coursing through her veins. Ready to take advantage of the bizarre situation and see family justice finally served, she lifted the lavender-colored skirt just high enough to avoid brushing the gravel- and sawdust-covered street and headed for the small brown-brick building at the far end of town.

Taking short, quick steps to avoid tripping over the cumbersome dress, she hurried along the sun-bleached boardwalk. Determined to see that Black Rock's lackluster sheriff did everything within his power to find her great-grandfather's killer, she had yet to worry about her own fate.

This time the murderer would be brought to justice. Even if she had to go out, find the culprit, and drag him in herself.

Why else would she be there?

Two

Jenny ignored the curious stares of the people she passed during her race down the worn-plank sidewalk. She wasn't sure if they gaped because she had dressed inappropriately or because she was in such a hurry and was a stranger in town. But none of that mattered anyway. All that concerned Jenny at the moment was her great-grandfather. She wanted his body off that cold floor and she wanted someone out there hunting for the killer. *Now.*

Noticing little about her surroundings other than it was taking her forever to cross over into the busier end of town, Jenny covered the distance between her great-grandfather's house and the local jail as quickly as she could. By the time she had crossed the final intersection, her heavy clothing had become a heat trap. Sweat trickled between her breasts and down the center of her back as she stepped up onto the boardwalk that butted the tall corner brick building on two sides.

"Wade Mack, County Sheriff." She read the sign out loud, through winded breath.

The door, set back and at an angle to accommodate entry from either street, stood wide open. So did most of the tall, guillotine-style windows. Peeking inside, she glimpsed a sparsely furnished room with dull wooden walls.

Jenny paused outside just long enough to shake the sawdust from her hem and make sure her long hair was still tucked into place before lifting a determined chin and entering the jail. Inside the drab building, she spotted a tall, heavyset man standing near a cluttered desk with his back to her.

She could not see his face, but quickly noted he wore low-slung gray trousers, a brown-leather gunbelt, and a faded green vest over a rumpled white shirt with rolled sleeves. The odd get-up and the way he stood with his weight shifted to one leg while he poured himself a glass of water made her think of John Wayne. So much so, she halfway expected him to whirl around, give his trousers half a hitch, and say, "What can I do for ya, pardner?"

But he did not turn around. Obviously, he had not heard her enter.

"Are you Sheriff Mack?" she called out. He whirled with surprise, and she was a little disappointed to see he bore no resemblance at all to the actor. The sheriff had ordinary-looking green eyes, skinny eyebrows, a flat nose, and thinning brown hair worn long enough to bunch against his collar in the back. His only distinctive feature was the long, heavy mustache that hid his upper lip and curled down to flank a receding jaw.

He was not an appealing man. But then, it really did not matter what he looked like. What mattered was his ability to help—if she could just convince him to do so.

"That's me." He gave a confirming nod as his gaze swept over her with obvious interest. "Can I help you, Miss—?"

"Yes, you can." Ignoring his hint for her name, Jenny pulled in a deep breath to keep her voice from faltering beneath tumbling emotions. "There's been a murder."

"A murder?" Straightening, he plunked the water glass on his desk then patted his holster as if making sure his revolver was still there. "Where?"

He appeared far more concerned than Jenny had expected. "Follow me and I'll show you." She headed immediately for the door.

"But where're we goin'?" He tugged on a high-crowned

gray hat kept with other hats on a tree by the entry while he followed her outside.

"Just down the street. To Tyler Dykes's place." She paused to allow a carriage to rattle past, then hurried across the gravel-strewn street, her long skirts swishing behind her.

"Tyler Dykes? Is that who's dead?" The sheriff caught up with her at the other side.

"Yes." She again swallowed back her anguish, not wanting to give rein to her emotions. *At least not yet.*

"And you think maybe he was murdered?"

"I know he was." In her haste, Jenny edged two paces ahead of the sheriff. "He's been stabbed through the heart."

"Through the heart? Must've been *some* knife." He sucked in a loud, wheezing breath, clearly not used to walking at a fast clip. "Did you happen to see who did it?"

"Sort of."

"Sort of? What do you mean by sort of?"

Despite his longer legs, Sheriff Mack fell another pace behind. Jenny spoke louder to carry the distance, which caused more of the locals to stop and stare at them. "I didn't get a look at his face, but I can tell you something about his size, shape, and I can tell you what he wore. That should help some."

"So it was a man? How close were you when you saw him?"

Again the sheriff caught up with her when she paused for traffic at the next intersection. "Close enough for him to knock me aside when he bolted away."

"That close? Why were you there?"

How much should she tell him? "I was there to see Tyler Dykes." The way clear again, she hurried on across the street, leaving the sheriff a step behind.

"Why? Were you plannin' on havin' a photograph taken?"

Not wanting to distract him with the strangeness of her situation, she nodded.

"So is that who you are?" He wheezed, barely able to get the words out. "Someone who came here to have your picture taken? Is that what you're doin' here in Black Rock? You just wanted Tyler Dykes to take your photograph?"

Again she nodded. "I heard he was the best photographer this side of the Mississippi."

"Yeah, I suppose he was."

With the house now in sight, the sheriff halted his questions until they reached the section of wraparound porch that stretched in front of the studio. There, he paused to catch his breath better.

"Wait out here, I'll go in and have a quick look and be right back out," he said, his expression intent as he reached for the doorknob.

"Why should I stay out here?" She followed close on his heels. "I've already seen the body. In fact, I've touched it."

"You touched him?" He skidded to an abrupt halt to stare at her, clearly startled.

"Yes, to see if he was dead."

"Lady, a man with a knife through the heart ain't got much chance of bein' anything but dead."

It annoyed her that he had such a valid point. "I wanted to know for sure."

He shook his head at her foolishness.

Once inside, he paused for another breath, then plucked his hat off and hooked it over a peg near the door, right next to Tyler's hat. "So where's the body?"

"In there." She pointed toward the small, windowless room now lit with one lamp.

Sheriff Mack walked to the door, peered in, then stepped cautiously inside. Jenny watched from the doorway while he bent over the body a moment, then stood and surveyed the disheveled room. "He was murdered all right. Tell me more about the man you say you saw run out."

Jenny told him everything she could remember about the incident, then stepped back when he headed through the door again. She watched curiously when instead of leaving as she feared he might, he walked over to the taller of the two desks, near the front door. "What are you doing?"

"Checkin' to see if his money is still here." He frowned when he popped open a small wooden box and peered inside. "And it is."

Originally robbery had been declared the motive, Jenny remembered. But now, she had interrupted the killer before any money had been taken. Robbery would not be so easily claimed. Good. Money was not what the killer wanted, not the way he tore apart that darkroom. If after money, he would have started in far more logical places—like one of those two desks. Or he would have gone on into the main part of the house to search the family's personal belongings.

No, whoever killed Tyler Dykes was searching for something. Something that logically might have been found inside that darkroom.

Had the sheriff reached the same conclusion? "So what do you think the killer was after?"

Sheriff Mack stroked his sloping chin, his face drawn into a puzzled frown. "Retaliation maybe."

That answer surprised her. *"Retaliation?* For what?"

"I don't know. Maybe for havin' taken so many pictures of people clearly outside the law. Maybe he was killed by someone he took a picture of he shouldn't have, maybe someone from the Dalton gang, or Ned Christie maybe. Could be any number of people angry at him."

Jenny had not thought of that. Those people were certainly the type to seek reprisal. "You think so?"

"I don't know." He shrugged, then looked again at the money box still in his hands. "Or maybe robbery *was* the motive. Maybe you interrupted the man before he could get on with that part of it."

"To me, it looks like the murderer searched for something else." Lifting the cumbersome skirt just high enough to avoid tripping, Jenny walked over to the darkroom door and looked in again, but kept her eyes averted from her great-grandfather's body, which already was losing color. "Something he expected to find in here, but didn't."

"Could be," the sheriff agreed, then came to stand behind her. When she stepped on into the room, he followed. "It does look like somebody might have been searchin' for somethin' all right." He scratched his chin and again scanned the room. "But then again, maybe that just means it *was* robbery. Maybe what the man was searchin' for was valuables he thought Dykes could have hid away in here. And again, it could be Tyler was murdered out of just plain meanness. There are some strange sorts out there."

Jenny shook her head, frustrated by that reasoning. "But that would not account for the open drawers and cabinet doors, or for the broken glass and scattered bottles. No, somebody was searching for something in particular. And searching for it in a hurry."

"Not necessarily. It could be Tyler left the drawers and doors open hisself to make it easier to get to them things he needed to make his pictures. And the glass could've been broken durin' a struggle. It's hard to say for sure what happened here." He stepped carefully over a rivulet of blood, headed to the untouched area of the small room. "I suppose what I'll end up puttin' down, though, is robbery. Chances are that's what it was."

Jenny thought the retaliation theory made more sense. She voiced her opinion to the sheriff, then glanced again at the broken glass, then at the bottles of chemicals lying on their sides. "Maybe whoever made this mess was searching for a particular photograph Tyler took." She looked down at several scattered across one of the counters. All were typical studio-type portraits. Nothing anyone would kill for. "And if that's so, and we could find whatever photograph he was looking for, we might be able to figure out who killed him."

"No, I think robbery was probably the motive here." The

sheriff glanced at her as he pulled out one of the closed drawers and poked at the contents with his finger. "It was probably some drifter passin' through who noticed this nice house or saw the fancy carriage Dykes drove. Probably decided there might be a little money lyin' around in such a fine house. I imagine the man who did this is long gone by now."

Jenny bristled. Her grandmother was right. This man had no intention of figuring out who murdered Tyler Dykes. All he wanted was to come up with something logical enough to write down for his records. "But what if it wasn't a drifter?"

He opened another drawer, then bent slightly as he peered toward the back. "Probably was, though."

"But what if it wasn't? What if it was someone from around here? Someone who knew Tyler personally?"

He frowned at her, clearly annoyed, then returned to the body where he knelt and pulled the knife out of Tyler's chest with one quick jerk. "Then maybe somebody will recognize this knife. I'll show it around and see."

He wiped the blade on Tyler's trousers, then ran his fingers over the ivory handle reverently. "Sure is a fancy thing, don't you think?"

"Is that all you plan to do?" she asked, so upset now she felt like screaming with rage. But didn't. Instead she drew in a deep breath and pressed on. "All you're going to do is show that one knife around?"

"What would you have me do?" He stood and faced her squarely. He obviously did not like her insinuation that he was lax in his duties. "Look, lady, it ain't like this is the only crime I have to solve around here. It just so happens I'm already hard at work tryin' to take care of two others. One of them *very* important."

"And *this* isn't important?" Angry, she pointed at her great-grandfather's body. "A man has been murdered in his own house and you don't think it's very important?"

"You don't understand. Last week, right in the middle of the big July Fourth doings, our bank was up and robbed by the Craig boys. Over a hundred thousand dollars was stole." His eyes brightened at the memory. "This time we know it was the Craig boys, because the bank president himself happened in on them while they was there and tried his best to fight them off, but he couldn't do much alone. By the time I got there, they had the money and was practically out the door."

He waved the knife to emphasize his words. "Lance Maze is just darned lucky all he got was a bump on the head for his efforts to save that money. Those Craig boys are a mean bunch. Why, they are so wanted that last week Black Rock was crawling with Federal men and newspaper fellows. We even had us one honest-to-goodness bounty hunter pokin' around. But everybody cleared out just a few days later when they learned the Craig boys had already hit another bank in Oklahoma City." His expression dulled. "They must have took those fifty-some-odd miles without hardly stoppin' to rest. But then men like that don't need much rest. They thrive on pure meanness alone."

He frowned and shook his head, but his voice did not sound particularly grim when he continued. "That robbery left this town in a bad way. A lot of our local merchants kept their money in that bank. So did the sawmill and some of the ranchers. Why, old man Rutledge, who owns the largest ranch and cattle company around these here parts, lost thousands of dollars. It's gonna take him quite a while to make up that kind of loss."

Jenny felt a disgusted tug inside her midsection. Clearly the bank robbery and the national attention that followed had been the sheriff's big moment of glory. Her great-grandfather's murder paled in comparison. "So you're just going to let this man's killer go free?"

The sheriff studied her a moment, then suddenly smiled. "Well, if it'll make you feel better, little lady, I'll ask around to see if anyone else saw anything of this big man in gray clothes and a black mask." His gaze dipped when he stepped closer, as if appraising what lay beneath Jenny's bulky lavender-colored dress. "But I don't really understand why it should be so important to you. He was just some photographer you wanted to take your picture."

"He was also my—brother." That would be easier to believe than the truth.

"Your *brother?*" He studied her first with surprise then doubt. "Well, I suppose you do look somewhat like him. But I've been sheriffin' around here a good, long time. If you were Dykes's sister, how come I never met you before now?"

"Because this is my first visit to Black Rock. I arrived from back East just this afternoon." *Well, everything about that particular statement was true.*

"Yeah, seems I remember Dykes saying something about a sister living in either St. Louis or Philadelphia." He nodded. "And to think you arrived here almost in time to witness his murder. That must've been hard on you, findin' him lyin' in here like that."

Jenny quit fighting an urge to cry. As Tyler's sister, emotion was not something she had to hide anymore. The tears forming were real, for the man lying on the floor was the father her grandmother adored but never knew. "It still *is* hard."

Awkwardly, the sheriff slipped the knife through a loop on his gunbelt, then took Jenny by the shoulders and led her into the adjoining room. As he pulled a chair out from behind one of the desks, a smaller, much younger man wearing an oversize western-style hat and a bright red shirt poked his head in the door.

"Wade? What's going on in here?"

"There's been a murder." The sheriff nodded toward the other room. "Someone killed Tyler Dykes. He needs to be

taken over to the undertaker's. Go find some men to help
you carry him over there."

The deputy scowled, then scuffed a worn boot across the
doorjamb. "But I was on my way to go eat. Deborah's been
waiting lunch on me for nigh on an hour now."

"Not until you see the body over to Joe's."

Hunching his skinny shoulders and muttering, the disgruntled young deputy stomped off to do as told.

The sheriff waited until his helper left, then gestured
again to the wooden chair. "Why don't you sit down while
I see to it that your brother's body is taken care of."

"Thank you," she replied, sinking awkwardly onto the
small chair. She found it difficult to sit in such a long,
bulky skirt, and gathered as much of the excess material
around her as she could.

The sheriff knelt in front of her and took her hand in his.
Not having expected that and not being the type of person
who liked being touched by strangers, Jenny fought the urge
to jerk free.

"I sure am sorry about your brother, Miss—" He lifted
a hopeful eyebrow. "Pardon me, but I never caught your
name."

"Dykes," Jenny answered, remembering only that the
great-aunt she hoped to impersonate had married later in
life, and that her first name was something short that began
with an R. "Ruth Dykes."

"You're not married?" His expression brightened when
she nodded. "I sure am sorry about your brother, Miss
Dykes. He was a good man."

"But you said he was *just* a photographer," she reminded,
meeting his gaze straight on.

He shifted uncomfortably. "But he was also a good man."

Not wanting to make an enemy of him, she decided to
let him off the hook for his callous remark. "I know he
was."

Her grandmother had told her that plenty of times.

Suddenly aware of his appearance, the sheriff let go of her hand long enough to slice his fingers through his thinning hair and readjust his collar. "We haven't been properly introduced, have we? My name is Wade. Wade Mack. And if there is anything I can do for you in your hour of need, don't falter in askin'."

Jenny's heart rate quickened at such a noticeable change in his attitude. "Actually, there *is* something you can do for me, Sheriff Mack."

"Wade," he corrected, clearly hoping she would offer the use of her first name in exchange.

But she ignored the hint. "There is something you can do for me, *Wade*. Find the man who murdered my great——" she stopped in time to correct the mistake—"brother."

He let out a disappointed breath, then spoke with obvious reluctance. "I'll do what I can."

"I'd be forever grateful," she replied just as the deputy returned. When he did, the sheriff dropped her hand and quickly rose.

Several other men followed. They all nodded politely to her, some removing their hats while they walked in unison into the other room. Before long, a second group of men, then a third, came in and followed the first on into the darkroom. Soon a dozen or so men packed that other room, many talking at once, some louder than others.

"Man, Pete, look at him. Did you ever see so much blood?"

Jenny cringed at the heartless comment.

"No. Not ever. Not even when we slaughtered my wife's prize pig last fall."

"Check those eyes. Looks just like he's staring straight into hell, don't it? Try to close them, Jack, will you?"

"They won't stay closed. Maybe if we twisted his eyelashes together or something."

"Goodness, look at the size of that hole in his chest. How deep you figure it goes?"

Hearing the comments, too, and sensing her resentment, the sheriff frowned, then excused himself.

Jenny sat with hands clutched, trying not to listen while the sheriff chastised the group for being so insensitive. "That happens to be Tyler's sister in there, and here you men are actin' as if this was some sort of side show. Why can't you just grab hold of that body and haul it on out of here without makin' all those rude comments?"

Not wanting to hear their complaints to that, Jenny had to escape. She headed for the porch and nearly ran headlong into a tall man with burly shoulders, long brown hair, and dark-fringed blue eyes just as she rounded the door. A quick look up revealed he was a handsome man with strong facial features who looked to be about thirty-two or thirty-three years old. The sort who, in any other situation, might have caused her a major adrenaline rush.

"What's going on over here?" he asked, already scanning around the room.

Figures. *Yet another gore-loving spectator.*

Although Jenny's first thought was to tell this thrill-seeker it was none of his blasted business, she instead gestured to the other room with a flagrant wave of her arm. "There's been a murder. Please, do join the crowd."

"A murder?" He took a step in the direction she indicated, but then turned to face her angrily. Apparently, the handsome stranger did not care for her scornful behavior. "Who's been murdered?"

Before she could respond, Sheriff Mack emerged from the other room. "Jordan? What are you doin' here? I thought you were still out of town."

The lean-hipped man called Jordan gestured toward a window with a wave of the dark-brown hat he carried. "I was just riding in when I noticed everyone rushing over here. I came to find out what was going on."

Sheriff Mack paused, then cut his gaze to the room he had just left. "Your friend's been murdered."

The word friend caught Jenny's attention. She studied the newcomer again, then realized the anger glinting in those huge pale-blue eyes was not so much directed toward her as it was toward the situation as a whole. "You were a close friend of Tyler Dykes?"

The man nodded, the muscles in his well-defined cheeks taut with bottled emotion, but he paid her little heed. His interest lay with the sheriff. "Who murdered him?" His voice cut cold as ice.

"Don't know. I think maybe it was a drifter." The sheriff glanced at Jenny, then frowned and pulled the knife out of his gunbelt and showed it to the newcomer. "This was the weapon used."

He held out his hand, and the sheriff reluctantly laid the knife in his palm. Jenny watched the handsome man study first the blade, then the handle, his expression as hard and dark as the huge black rock this town had been named after.

While the others' attention remained on the weapon he held, she placed hers with her great-grandfather's "friend." He was about half an inch shorter than the lumbering sheriff and not as burly in size. His hips were a lot leaner, and he didn't appear to be quite as wide through the back and shoulders. Even so, he was clearly the more formidable of the two men.

Although both men were considerably stout, with brawny, sun-browned arms protruding beneath rolled shirtsleeves, the newcomer's body looked to be the more solid of the two, his stance more confident. He also had a stronger chin, a narrower nose, and a lot more hair. His grew thick, dark, and full where the sheriff's was thin, dull, and flat across the top.

Who was this Jordan?

Taking an unsteady breath, she lowered her gaze from his still-intent expression down to where his gray-cloth work trousers hugged long, well-muscled legs, then slowly up again to where open-collared dark-blue shirt hung from a solid upper torso. A glimpse of dark curly body hair peeked out where the soft material parted. Dark, springy hair also covered the muscular arms that flexed as he turned the knife over in his strong hands.

What did this guy do for a living?

Punch cattle?

Break horses?

Move mountains?

She focused again on the smooth, firm lines of his face, her attention drawn to the endearing slant of his jaw then back to his incredibly long eyelashes. Her heart fluttered at the overall effect. She could not help but notice that her great-grandfather's friend was what most would call drop-dead gorgeous and exuded the ultimate in masculinity. Just being in the same room with him made her libido do fascinating but highly inappropriate cartwheels.

Why couldn't she meet someone like that in her own time? Most the men she knew barely caught her interest, yet here was one who had set her heart to tearing through her like an Indy 500 racer.

"Did anyone see it happen?" Still not noticing her, he handed the knife back to the sheriff at the same time he hooked his hat over a small, unlit lamp that sat on a nearby table—as if by habit.

"No. But this woman thinks maybe she got a glimpse of the man who did it."

Suddenly, she had his attention.

Her pulse stirred beneath the unexpected scrutiny of those liquid-blue eyes while she awaited the chance to speak to him. Obviously, this was a man who might know something.

"Who's she?"

"Oh, I forgot to introduce you," the sheriff stated with a clear lack of enthusiasm as he slid the white-handled knife back through the leather loop on his gunbelt. "Chad Jordan, this is Miss Ruth Dykes, Tyler's sister. She arrived here just minutes after the murder took place."

Chad's steely gaze narrowed until his long lashes nearly touched each other when she stuck her hand out in what was meant to be a friendly gesture. An ominous chill skipped across her shoulders.

"You're wrong, Sheriff."

"How's that?"

"Tyler Dykes has only one sister still living, and that's *not* her."

Three

He was on to her. Jenny's heart plunged to the pit of her stomach. She had recognized the name the moment it rolled off the sheriff's tongue. Chad Jordan was the friend who had originally packed up all her great-grandparents' belongings then sent them on to Janeen. His was the name she had tried so hard to remember earlier.

She swallowed at the tight knot lodged in her throat. If anyone in that town had a reason to think her an impostor, Chad Jordan did. According to Grandma Vic, Chad was the only person who had tried in earnest to find her great-grandfather's killer. It was unfortunate he hadn't had enough clues to work with. Chad had been one of Tyler's closest friends for years and, as such, knew a lot about him.

Somehow she had to make that fact work for her instead of against her.

"You're calling me a liar?" Ah, well, attack *was* a better form of defense. "You don't even know me." If she acted outraged enough, she might plant just enough doubt that the sheriff would believe her over Chad. Maybe even *Chad* would think himself wrong. "How can you do that?"

"If you told the sheriff you're Tyler's sister, you're nothing but a liar," he responded with maddening calm. A tiny twitch at the back of his left cheek was the only indication of his rage.

"Well, I did tell him that, because I *am.*" Wanting to keep her tale as close to the truth as possible, she pinched her arm through the pleated sleeves of her great-grandmother's lavender dress. "Some of the very same blood that flowed through Tyler Dykes's veins flows through mine." She planted her hands on her hips, daring him to dispute *that*.

Chad studied her a moment, but showed not even a glimmer of uncertainty. "I applaud your performance, but you're *not* his sister. I've seen a photograph of Tyler's sister. Except for all that dark hair and those big dark eyes, you don't look anything like her."

"Oh? And in what way do you find me different from my photograph?" She lifted her chin, pleased with the way she had worded that. Maybe she could confuse him into submission.

"For one thing, you're far too pretty to be the woman in those pictures. Tyler's sister has a thin face, an extremely long neck, a small mouth, and more what I'd call a boy's figure. You, madam, have none of those."

"A boy's figure?" She did her best to sound insulted and gave herself a quick glance. "How can you say that? I do not have a boy's figure. And I do not have a thin face."

"That's true. You don't." His gaze dipped briefly to the curved lines that could in no way be considered boyish, then lifted again to her face. "But Tyler's sister *does*."

"Show me this photograph," she challenged, praying he would not know where Tyler kept it. If he did, she already searched for some quick, logical excuse for not looking like the sister pictured there. "I have never seen a single photograph that made my face look skinny."

"The photograph isn't of you," he reiterated. His muscles bunched down his arms and across his shoulders. "It's of Tyler's sister. And I don't know where he keeps it. Probably somewhere in the main part of the house since it's a picture of family. But if it'll help settle the matter, I'm sure willing to go look for it."

Aware Chad still had no doubts that she was an impostor—although the sheriff looked totally confused—Jenny chose a different approach. "There's no point looking for it, because if it wasn't a photograph of me, then it was *not* a photograph of Tyler's sister." Reminded again of Tyler's living sister and feeling a need to explain away the person in the photograph, she paused, then added, "Unless, of course, it was one he may have had taken of Christina."

Chad's head jerked back slightly as if having taken a small, invisible blow to the chin. "Christina? Who's Christina?"

Uncertain if she was digging her way out of the ticklish situation or further in, Jenny gave a challenging glare. "I thought you said you're a close friend."

"I am—*was*." His jaw tightened. "And still would be if he hadn't just been murdered."

"Then why is it you don't know who Christina was?" she asked accusingly, hoping to put him on the defensive yet.

Chad's eyes narrowed into a harsh glower that bore right through her, but it was the sheriff who finally asked, "And just who *was* Christina?"

Thank heavens *someone* took that phony bait. Having forgotten the real name of the sister, she had pulled that one right out of thin air. Hopeful again, she turned to the sheriff, "Christina was our older sister who died eight years ago."

"And Tyler had a photograph of her?"

"He may have." She gave Chad a quick, skeptical look, then returned a sweet, guileless smile to the sheriff. "But *I* don't remember seeing it. The only photograph I ever saw with her in it was the one with most of the family, the one taken out in my mother's rose garden when my sister was still quite young and we all still lived back East." The one that had hung in Grandma Vic's living room all of Jenny's life, and one Chad possibly might have seen. By mentioning a photo he had seen, she might create that tiny doubt she wanted.

If *only* she remembered the little girl's real name.

For good measure, she thrust her chin forward, then added, "But I do find it odd that Tyler would show a picture of Christina to anyone, when it was always so hard for him to talk about her. He and Christina were *very* close. Her death struck him hard."

The sheriff's expression remained thoughtful while Chad's grew darker still. Chad wasn't buying a word of this.

"Did this sister of yours have a skinny face?" Sheriff Mack asked.

"Thinner than mine, but not what I'd call noticeably *skinny*." Jenny cut Chad an insulted look. "Crissy inherited her slender features from our mother. I inherited a more oval face from our father."

"Then that must be what happened," the sheriff said with a sudden smile, clearly pleased to have the matter resolved. He slapped Chad on the shoulder. "He must've showed you a photograph of his dead sister and you misunderstood and thought it was his alive sister he was showin' you."

Chad continued his glower, first at the sheriff then at Jenny. "She's lying. The only other sister Tyler had was Elizabeth, and she died while still a child."

"That's not altogether true," Jenny put in, aware Elizabeth was the name she had forgotten. *Figures he'd know it.* "There was Christina, who also died young, and there still *is* me."

"She's *lying*," Chad repeated, so angry now his cheeks looked like they had been sculpted from granite. Even in anger, he was incredibly handsome. "She is not Tyler's sister."

"How can you keep sayin' that?" the sheriff asked, coming readily to her defense. "Just look at her. She has the same eyes, the same mouth, even the same nose and cheeks Tyler had. Why, if it weren't for the obvious age difference between the two, you'd think they were twins."

"I don't care. I still *know* she's lying."

Sheriff Mack let out an impatient huff. "Look, I think you're bein' a little unreasonable here. All it takes is one good look to see that this woman has to be Tyler's younger sister. Besides, why would she lie about somethin' like that?"

"I don't know." He tossed his hands, frustrated not to have an answer for that. "Maybe she hopes to get her hands on some of Tyler's property while Janeen isn't here to say what items would or wouldn't go to his sister. She could sell it then for a quick profit. Why, Tyler's horse alone could keep a woman like her in pretty petticoats and fine lace for the next ten years. And I imagine this photography equipment of his is worth a pretty penny, too."

"It ain't like you to be so irrational."

"I'm not being irrational. I'm being sensible. Tyler would have told me if he had another sister still living, especially if she planned to visit. He never said a word." Again, Chad spoke to the sheriff, but kept an accusing gaze on Jenny.

The sheriff shifted his weight to one leg in disgruntled fashion. "But how could he tell you anything? You've been out of town."

"I've only been gone a few days. He'd have known before then, and would have told me before I left."

Jenny knew by the sheriff's scowl that he had run out of arguments. It was time again to take up her own defense.

"Not if I was planning to surprise him," she put in quickly. "Which is exactly *what* I'd planned to do. Tyler had no idea I was coming. Nor did anyone else."

"How convenient that you told no one." Chad crossed his arms into a solid stance, one meant to intimidate her. And to a degree, it did. "And why wouldn't you at least tell his wife so she'd be prepared for a guest? Or were you planning to surprise her, too?"

"No. Of course not. She's not even here right now." *Good try, though,* she thought, pleased with herself for not having fallen into *that* one. Janeen had already been gone for weeks.

"And where is she?"

"At her sister's house. In *Philadelphia*." She tried to look more annoyed than apprehensive over all these questions. Eventually, he would ask something she should know and didn't. She never had been too talented when it came to out and out lying. "And the reason I didn't write to tell her I was coming out here is because I don't know her sister's address and Philadelphia happens to be a very large city." *Thank goodness.*

The sheriff smiled, apparently satisfied again. "See? She knows all about Janeen Dykes being back East."

Clearly out of arguments, Chad curled his hands into rock-hard fists and headed for the room where Tyler's body still lay, then suddenly spun around again. "How did you arrive here?"

The guy wasn't giving up. At least not yet. Jenny considered the century, then gave the best reply she knew. "On a train."

"Guess again, stranger," he commented, looking oh so pleased with his oh so handsome self. "The train doesn't come here. The nearest depot is in Perry, over six miles south."

Jenny's stomach knotted. She had just entered the unknown. Transportation during that time was not something she and her grandmother had discussed at any length.

"And that's exactly where I took the train to," she answered, amazed at the conviction her voice held. "To get from there, I hired a buggy."

Even that did not satisfy him. He gestured to the window. "And where *is* that buggy?"

Determined he not best her, even if she *was* lying, she leveled her gaze. "I had no more use for it, so the driver I hired drove it back."

He didn't give an inch. "What livery did you hire from?"

"I don't recall the name." Her heart continued its hard, frantic rhythm while her thoughts darted ahead. If he asked to see her baggage or a return train ticket, she'd have none. But the sheriff obviously was not interested in hearing any more of their argument.

"What difference does it make where she hired a rig from?" he interrupted. "All that matters is that when she got here, she saw a man rush out that window, then when she went in the other room she found her brother had just been murdered. Can you imagine how shockin' that was for her?"

"He wasn't her brother," Chad restated, still not yielding. "And I wouldn't be too surprised to learn that this woman is somehow linked to the murder."

"Linked to it?" Jenny cried, this time truly outraged. "Me?" She stared at him dumbfounded. Did he really think her capable of murder? Or was there *another* reason he wanted to put the blame off on her? A more personal reason.

She eyed him suspiciously. Perhaps he'd never found Tyler's killer because he had never truly wanted to. Were his attempts to help merely a smokescreen?

"Jordan, I think you're gettin' out of hand here," Sheriff Mack cautioned. He rested a tempering hand on Chad's tensed shoulder. "Now, I understand why you're so upset. After all, your best friend was just killed. But that's no reason to take it out on this pretty little lady. Besides, where that knife punctured the body, there is no way someone as small as her could have done it. It takes brute strength to shove a knife straight through a set of ribs."

He looked at Jenny with an somber expression. "Sorry, ma'am, I know you don't want to have to hear something like that. It's just that he needed to know that before he said something more he would later regret."

Though obviously still unconvinced, Chad stalked off into the other room without another word to either of them.

Jenny's insides quaked by the time the sheriff bent toward

her and spoke in a voice that wouldn't carry into the next room. "Please don't be too offended by what all he said. He's just not thinkin' straight right now."

Glad she had not yet lost credibility with the sheriff, she forced another smile. "I understand. And, to tell you the truth, for a moment there—when he acted so quick to put the blame off on me—I wondered if *he* might not be involved in the murder somehow. I guess suspicion is a normal reaction in a situation like this. Until someone is caught, everyone's suspect."

"It's good of you to be so understandin'," The sheriff let his gaze wander about her face, clearly smitten. "Beautiful *and* understandin'. That's a mighty fine combination in a woman."

Knowing the sheriff was still her main hope for catching the killer, Jenny fought the urge to look away. Instead, she smiled prettily, her insides still thrashing wildly from all that had happened since her untimely arrival.

First, she had found her own great-grandfather dead, which was quickly followed by the realization she had somehow been tossed back into the past, which was promptly followed by having to run all the way across town in an impossibly long dress to find the inept sheriff, and just now, the angry incident with Chad. When would she get a little breathing space? "Why, thank you, Sheriff."

"Wade," he prompted and reached for her hand. But he stopped just short of taking it when a loud, male voice sounded from the other room.

"Comin' through."

The sheriff grasped her by the shoulders and turned her toward the wall.

Reminded of the horror that had caused her situation, Jenny held on to the edge of a filing cabinet while she listened to the shuffling of feet across the wooden floor and to the clamor of muffled voices. She was glad she did not have to watch the men haul away her great-grandfather's body. The image of him lying on the floor in a pool of his own blood was hard enough to bear.

If only he hadn't looked so very much like the pictures she had come to love and admire. Then maybe she could remove herself from the gut-wrenching emotions tearing through her. But he'd looked exactly like she had envisioned him.

Straightening her shoulders, she vowed not let the painful emotions have their full rein again. She could not be as effective in helping find the murderer if she allowed herself to remain so emotional. To battle the pain, she conjured thoughts of the man in gray who had knocked her against the wall in his haste to escape. By doing so, she tried to convert her feelings of sorrow back into anger—an emotion that could more easily be put to her advantage.

It worked. When she realized how close she had come to seeing her great-grandfather alive—how close she had come to being able to warn him of the danger—her anger did return. In force.

She waited until the clomping, scuffing sounds had shifted outdoors before turning to the sheriff with renewed vigor and conviction. She could not forget her mission. "Sheriff, I want to see the man who killed my brother hang."

It surprised her to find Chad had returned, this time looking visibly shaken. Was that because he had just viewed his best friend's body, she speculated, or because of what she had said about hanging the culprit? Again, she wondered if he had acted a bit too eager to put the blame on her as his way of making sure the blame was directed away from himself. Was Chad Jordan not quite the good friend of her great-grandfather he pretended to be?

She looked down at his right hand twitching at his side. He knew what happened to a man whose neck was snapped by a good, strong rope. "Sheriff, until that killer's caught and hanged, I'll do what I can to keep busy here."

"Doing what?" Chad asked, coming quickly out of his shaken state. He glowered again.

"Cleaning up the mess." She pointed to the trail of bloody footprints coming from the next room. "After that, maybe I'll get started packing a few things away. I doubt Janeen will continue to live here now that Tyler's gone, especially since she'll have that new baby to care for. I imagine she'll stay right there in Philadelphia where her sisters can help her through the rough emotional times ahead."

Chad's mouth tightened. "How do you know about the baby?"

Jenny sighed. He still did not believe her. "Everyone in the family knows about the baby she's expecting."

When he did not respond immediately to that, she returned her attention to the sheriff. "It *is* okay for me to stay here, isn't it? I really have no place else to go right now and I can't afford to pay for a room at the hotel."

That was all true enough, but what she wanted most was the opportunity to conduct a little investigation of her own. She had no intention of leaving everything to such an incompetent man as this sheriff. Wade Mack took matters at face value far too readily.

"Aren't you worried the murderer could come back?" the sheriff asked, clearly undecided.

"No," she answered honestly. The murderer never returned. "Knowing that you are on to him, the man who did this wouldn't dare come back here. Besides, I'd like to help out however I can."

"I guess that's okay with me," Sheriff Mack told her, one eyebrow arched, his tone still hesitant. "But are you sure you're up to cleanin' the sort of mess that's in there?"

"I'm a strong woman, Sheriff." Plus, she had spent two years as a candy striper in a hospital, where blood was a common sight. "And I'd really like to do something useful while you're out there finding that killer—something to help Janeen. Besides, I'll want to be here when the killer is finally brought in."

The sheriff shifted uncomfortably at the non-too-subtle reminder of the job he had cut out for him. "I see no problem with you staying here, especially since the rent's probably paid up through next month anyway. I'm sure Mrs. Dykes won't, either. I'll mention you when I wire her about what's happened."

Jenny's heart skipped a double beat. "Are you sure you should do that?"

"Do what?" He looked at her, uncertain. "Wire her about her husband's death? Why wouldn't I?"

"Well, she *is* in a very fragile state right now, what with the baby coming and all. She might not be able to handle such horrible news."

"Uh, I never thought of that." The sheriff scratched his head while he considered the situation further.

"Don't listen to her," Chad said, stepping in. "Janeen has a right to be told. There are decisions she will want to make—about the burial if nothing else. Janeen is also a very strong woman, and she has both her sisters with her to help her adjust to her loss."

"You're right. She *should* be told of her husband's murder. I'll wire her this afternoon."

Aware Chad had made a valid point, that Janeen had every right to be told, Jenny did not continue the argument. All she could do was hope Janeen would be so shocked by the news of Tyler's death, nothing else would register.

"Try to be as quick and delicate as you can," she suggested, knowing how painful the news would be. Janeen's love for Tyler was such, she would never remarry. Jenny's eyes teared at the thought. She had always longed to know such a love, but never had.

"But do be sure to mention that Tyler's 'sister' is here,"

Chad put in, his gaze narrowed with intent. "I'm sure she'd want to know that, too."

Jenny nodded, hoping the sheriff would word it just that way. If the real sister wasn't where Jenny could reach her easily, she wouldn't think it necessary to notify her for now. After a few days, Janeen would be unable to notify anyone because she would be in the hospital, where her grief coupled with her difficult pregnancy would keep her for several weeks. "Yes, tell her I'll take care of what I can here."

Chad clenched his hands in frustration. "Sheriff, I really don't think it is a good idea to let this woman stay and have a free hand in packing Tyler's belongings. No telling what will disappear before anyone from the family has had time to arrive."

"That's enough!" The sheriff let out an exasperated breath. "She stays here as long as she wants. Or until I get word from Janeen asking that she leave." He narrowed his gaze. "And that's all there is to say on the matter."

Chad's face smoldered with rage as his glower traveled from the sheriff to Jenny. "You're making a serious mistake," he stated forebodingly, then quickly turned and stalked hatless out of the house.

Jenny watched through a window until his dark head and broad shoulders disappeared from sight. Then, feeling both relieved and yet vaguely disappointed, she turned away.

"Well, Sheriff, I guess I'd better get started."

She looked at him questioningly when he made no move to leave. With Chad now gone—and along with him the worry that the sheriff would be convinced she was indeed a fraud—Jenny could again concentrate on matters at hand. She wanted to explore that other room. "Shouldn't you be off finding the man who killed Tyler?"

The sheriff blinked, then nodded. "Of course I'll do what I can, but keep in mind I have other crimes to solve, too. Plus, I got me two more telegrams to answer. We've been havin' lots of inquiries and the like comin' in from back

East. So many it's hard to keep up with them all." He sighed. "It sure would be nice to be able to write them all back and tell all those newspaper and magazine men that we managed to get the Craig boys caught and put away in our jail. It'd sure make the folks around here happy."

Already making excuses. Not wanting to hear all about his concern for the townsfolk, or of his heroic deed having faced the Craig boys—happening in on them while out looking for the bank president—and lived to tell the story, she said, "Just don't forget about *this* crime while you take care of those others. After all, we're talking about murder here."

He nodded again and headed for the door, pausing long enough to plunk several items out of his pocket onto a table near the door. "Here's what Tyler had on him. You might want to put them in a special place. And since he probably doesn't have any crates for packin' around here, I'll send over a couple I got stored back of the jail."

He grabbed his hat off the peg and slid it over his thinning hair. "If you need me, you can probably find me at the jail or over at the Stover House, where I room. I'll stop back by later to see what you want to do about a funeral, in case Tyler's wife doesn't respond in time. After that, I'll take you over to the Silver Spoon restaurant for a good hot meal. You should be gettin' mighty hungry by now."

Jenny's mouth flattened. That's all she needed—to spend valuable hours dining with the town's idle sheriff. That would certainly slow down her investigation.

"We'll see."

When the sheriff still did not leave, she became more annoyed. She had things to do, things that could only be accomplished after she was alone. Faking another pretty smile, she gestured toward the door. "Keep me informed of any progress you make."

Finally, he took the hint and left.

Jenny waited until he cleared the yard, then hurried to

latch the door. She did not want anyone coming in while she carefully searched the place for whatever it was that killer had wanted.

But before launching her search, she needed to do what she could to cover some of the lies she had told. Chad could return at any minute to retrieve the hat he absently left behind and resume right where they had left off. The man might be incredibly handsome, but he was also incredibly stubborn. Not the best combination.

Hurriedly, Jenny packed a valise she had noticed earlier with some of Janeen's clothing, then hauled it into one of the unused bedrooms to make it look as if she planned to sleep there.

She returned to the studio, gathered several of her great-grandfather's personal belongings and carried those into the master bedroom. Wanting it to look like her intent truly was to pack Tyler's things, she then scattered the bed with some of Tyler's possessions: his black hat, his leather vest, several books of poetry she had found on top of the file cabinets, the apron he used in the darkroom. She included the pocket watch and other items the sheriff had left on the table near the side door.

After that, she made a quick search of the house for the picture Chad had mentioned, located it, and hid it at the bottom of Janeen's underwear drawer. Next, she carried a gold-plated dagger she had found inside one of Tyler's desk drawers and hid it in the bedroom where she had placed the valise and extra clothing, just in case she needed protection later on.

Seconds after she returned to the studio, at last ready to begin her search, someone knocked on the door. Fighting a very real urge to scream aloud her frustration, for she was not ready to face Chad again, she answered the knock. To her surprise, she was greeted by a woman about her own age, who stood dressed fashionably for the era in a long blue dress tucked at the waist with most of the material flowing behind her. She also wore a dark-blue hat with white ostrich feathers and had a white, knitted handbag dangling from the wrist of her white cloth gloves.

"Is Mr. Dykes here?" she asked, looking at Jenny with obvious surprise. "I'm Beth Donner. I've come for my photographs. I was told they would be ready this afternoon."

"Come in." Jenny stepped back to let the young woman enter. She tried not to appear quite as annoyed as she felt by the untimely intrusion. "I guess you haven't heard. Tyler Dykes was murdered a few hours ago."

"Murdered?" Beth pressed a gloved hand to her ivory throat, then looked as if she were about to swoon. "No, I had not heard."

Aware this was probably the woman who originally would have found her great-grandfather, and knowing the woman *had* indeed fainted, Jenny quickly led her to a chair, then explained what had happened. Once told Tyler's body was gone, the woman relaxed noticeably.

"Did you know my . . . brother very well?" Jenny asked, hoping to find out something more about her great-grandfather. Something perhaps Grandma Vic had failed to tell her.

"Not well. But I knew him. He was a nice man. Always had a friendly smile. Like his wife."

"What about his good friend, Chad Jordan?" she probed. Already, she had started her investigation. "Do you know him, too?"

Beth looked away, as if embarrassed by the question. "Why, everyone knows Mr. Jordan."

"And is he also a nice man?"

"Oh, one of the nicest I've ever met." Beth dared a quick glance at Jenny, her cheeks flushing. "And one of the wealthiest, and most handsome, too. It's a true shame he has no desire to marry again, not even after all these years. A decade is long enough for a man to be without a wife, and he would certainly make one of the women around here a fine husband."

I doubt that, thought Jenny. Even if he wasn't a murderer, the man was far too temperamental to be suited to marriage. If he really had been married, as Beth had just indicated, then the ex-wife clearly knew what she was doing when she left him. "So you don't find anything odd about him?"

"No. Nothing."

Jenny frowned. She had hoped to gain deeper insight than that, but obviously this woman didn't really know Chad at all. She hadn't bothered to look beyond those gorgeous blue eyes. "Let me see if I can find your pictures. They have to be around here somewhere. Are they portraits of you alone?"

She nodded while Jenny shuffled through the dozens of photographs scattered across one of the two large desks.

"How did Tyler act while you were here last week?" Jenny asked, stacking the photos as she searched through them. "Did he seem nervous about anything?"

"Nervous? No. A little distracted, maybe, probably by all the hoopla going on because of the bank robbery in town while he was away on one of his trips, but he appeared to be in good spirits. He even teased me about the position of the two quail feathers in the hat I wore that day. Said they looked just like devil horns."

Jenny smiled, pleased to know her great-grandfather had had a sense of humor. She continued to search for the pictures. "Are you wearing the hat in the photographs?"

"Only in one. For the others he had me take it off." She blushed. "Said my hair was too pretty to hide under a silly old hat. Said my fiancé would like the photographs much better with the hat off."

"Oh, you're getting married?"

"Yes, next month."

Jenny continued to search the photos on the desk until finally she came across a folder labeled Donner in a deep scrawl. Opening it, she found a half dozen black-and-whites of Beth, some smiling, some not, and one of her wearing the notorious "devil's" hat. She wanted to laugh at the dilemma her great-grandfather had faced. It really was an ugly hat.

She handed the photos to Beth, glad to soon be rid of her. Although she had liked hearing a little more about her great-grandfather, she wanted to get on with her search. The longer it took to find any clues, the better the killer's chances were of getting away. "I hope your fiancé enjoys them."

"Thank you." Beth reached inside her handbag and started pushing things around. "Those will cost me seven dollars and twenty cents, won't they?"

"No, they'll cost you nothing," Jenny said, already guiding her toward the door. "Consider them a wedding present from my brother. He'd be happy with the kind things you said about him today."

As happy she was.

The warm feeling the woman's words had kindled stayed with Jenny long after Beth had left. Calmer now, Jenny returned to the darkroom and started sifting through the rubble in systematic fashion. While searching for clues, she came across some of the oddest-looking gadgets, objects that obviously were used in 1896, although she could not fathom what those uses were. Finally, she took the time to appreciate the true weirdness of her situation. She stopped her orderly prowling and gave her surroundings a critical look, not at all sure how she had come to be there.

And even less sure how she would ever get back to where she belonged.

Her heart lurched at the mere thought of being stuck there forever. She had not wanted to think about being unable to return when the time finally came, but now she could not help worrying about it. What if there was no way for her to return to her own era? What if she was stuck in this past century forever?

What if this wasn't just some passing event?

Her insides twisted into a tight knot. What if the time change proved to be permanent? What if she was stuck there in the wrong century for the rest of her unnatural life?

Although exhilarated to have the chance to find her great-grandfather's killer and finally right that terrible injustice, she had no desire to stay in the year 1896—much less in a small town the size of Black Rock.

She tugged at the collar of the impossibly heavy dress, her neck prickling with more than the mid-July heat while she thought back to the events that had led to her being there. She recalled the wish she had made—almost a prayer. But that was nothing out of the ordinary. It was one she had made often through the years. Then she remembered the ghost images in the camera. Images of her great-grandfather's studio.

Putting aside the search for now, she returned to the main part of the studio, her entry point to this century.

Fearful of what she might find, her blood flowed fast and furious while she moved toward the Rochester camera. Slowly, she lifted the black cape, now made of a different material, and peered again into the view glass.

Amazement poured over her, leaving her both hyped with hope yet at the same time weak with relief. There was the upside-down image of her apartment she had hoped to find—sleeping cat and all. Surely that meant all she had to do to get back into her own time was duck back under the cape, touch the camera in some way like she had before, and take another picture.

But no sooner had she breathed that sigh of relief than a tiny tentacle of fear returned to niggle at her. She wouldn't know for certain until she tried it.

Eager to prove the theory valid and get back to her own world, she hurried to gather the necessary supplies but stopped just inside the darkroom door. If she went back now, who would solve her great-grandfather's murder? Certainly not that lazy, indifferent sheriff. And certainly not Chad. Those two had both proved how ineffective they were the first time around.

No, if she truly wanted the murder solved, she would have to stay and see to matters herself. It was up to her to effect a change.

Unwittingly, it was what she had wished for. Even so, she continued to stare at the camera a long moment. It was so tempting, knowing her own time period was probably only one quick flash away. But as tempting as it might be to return to the safety of her own time, and despite having that big photo shoot early the following week to get ready for, she resumed her search.

She would wait before using that camera.

At least until the killer had been caught.

Four

Still believing retaliation had something to do with her great-grandfather's murder, Jenny continued her methodical search of the hot, stuffy darkroom. She had no idea what clue she looked for, but whatever she found, it would have to be something solid enough and convincing enough to haul the idle sheriff further into the investigation.

After several more frustrating hours of examining the contents of drawers and cabinets, she had stopped to sweep up more of the blood-splattered broken glass when Sheriff Mack returned. The loud knock startled her from her morbid task.

"Why'd you lock the door?" he asked when she opened it to find him standing outside, holding two large empty crates. "Are you havin' second thoughts about how safe you are here?"

Jenny let out a silent, annoyed breath, not needing yet another interruption. Not while she was so eager to find out who had killed her great-grandfather, see him arrested, then get back to her own time before her cat discovered the open window and made mincemeat out of the neighborhood.

"No. I haven't thought about my safety. I just didn't want any more visitors. I've already had one of my brother's customers stop by wanting to pick up photographs. I was afraid more might follow, and I'm not in any mood to talk to anyone right now. I really just want to be left alone for a while." She hoped he would take that as a direct, personal hint.

But obviously, he didn't think she meant him. "Don't worry. By now most folks around here have heard about what happened so they shouldn't be stoppin' by to pick up photographs, or to try to have new pictures made. But if you really want to avoid any company, you might put a sign out on the door statin' such." He glanced at the broom still in her hand as he walked across the room and set the crates down near the smaller of the two desks. "Here are a couple of boxes, so you can start packin' whatever you think needs to be packed first. How's it comin' in there?" He took a few steps more to have a look. "Slow, I see."

"I know." She did not bother closing the outside door, wanting it just as convenient for him to leave as it had been for him to enter. "I've had a lot of things on my mind."

"I don't doubt that after what's happened. But it's good that you're keepin' busy. I don't suppose you've found anything that might interest me in there, have you?" Again, he cut his gaze toward the darkroom door.

"Not yet," she admitted, annoyed at how relieved he looked by that. Obviously, he did not want a reason to have to expend any more energy on her great-grandfather's murder than was absolutely necessary. "But, like I said, I've had things on my mind and, because of that lack of total concentration, I'm not making much progress yet."

"That's understandable." Looking away, he patted first one shirt pocket, then another, finally pulling out a folded piece of paper. "And that's why I thought maybe you'd like to know Mrs. Dykes has already wired back what to do about the death of her husband."

"Oh?" She tried to guess by looking at him whether that was good or bad news. Had Janeen exposed her for a fraud? Or was she still safe for now? "What did she say?"

"She's asked that Chad Jordan be the one to take care of the burial arrangements and see to it that her belongings are shipped to her sister's house in Philadelphia," he told her, then smiled. "I reckon, that means less for you to have to worry about."

"She's leaving everything up to Chad?" Her stomach tightened. The one man who did not believe a word she said had been put in charge. Obviously, Janeen hadn't readily accepted the news that Tyler's sister was in Black Rock.

What would happen if the sheriff stopped believing her because of Janeen's obvious reluctance to accept her presence there? Did he mention her in the telegram by actual name? Was that why Janeen hadn't accepted her offer to help? Was it because she had guessed the sister's name incorrectly. "Did you explain to her that I was here?"

Sheriff Mack gave the paper an extra fold, as if uncomfortable with that question. "No, I was in a hurry to get the message off and sort of forgot to have Andy put that in. But I'll be sure and mention you when I send a wire back tellin' her Chad's answer. That is, as soon as I have it."

"You haven't spoken with Chad about the telegram?"

"Not yet. I was too busy when I first got the message. But I stopped by his feed store a little while ago to tell him about it. It's not my fault he wasn't there." He shrugged and pushed his hat further back. Then, as if suddenly realizing he was inside a house, he snatched it off his head. "Doesn't really matter, though. I already know what his answer will be. He will do exactly what Mrs. Dykes asks of him. He's just the type of person who always does what's right. Which I figure should take a big load of worry off of you."

No, what it did was worry her more. Chad would now have authority over her.

She gripped the broom handle tighter to still the flutter inside her stomach. "Does that mean he now has the right to toss me out of this house? He's already made it pretty clear what he thinks of me staying here."

The sheriff shook his head. "No. Don't worry. Unless I get word direct from Mrs. Dykes tellin' me she doesn't want you here, you can stay on right in this house while you're tryin' to come to grips with what all has happened. You are family, and I see no reason why you shouldn't have a hand in helpin' Chad Jordan get matters squared away here."

"Even if he doesn't want my help?"

"Now, don't you be lettin' how he acted earlier bother you." The sheriff tucked the telegram back into his pocket, then rested a supportive hand on her shoulder. "He was just reactin' to the news that his best friend had been murdered. Hearin' something like that had to have been a terrible blow to him. Once he's had time to get over the initial shock, I think he'll change his mind about not wantin' you here. After all, packin' and cleanin' is women's work. Chad isn't much of a one to put up with doin' women's work."

"I hope you're right," she said, fighting the urge to pull away from his touch. She did not want to do anything to alienate the one man in a position to help her. "As I told you, I don't have anywhere else to go right now, and I really do want to be here when you finally figure out who murdered my brother and bring him to justice. How is that coming?"

The sheriff shifted his weight to one leg, then took his hand back. "I haven't had time to do much yet." His mustache twitched. "When I went to the telegraph office to send the wire to Mrs. Dykes tellin' her about your brother, I found out I had two telegrams waitin' on me askin' for special sheriffin' information. One was from a real important magazine back East." He straightened proudly.

Jenny stared at him in disbelief. Did this man really think responding to a magazine's telegram more important than solving a murder? It took all the restraint she had not to tear into him. "Oh?"

"I did find time to show that knife to a few people, but nobody has recognized it yet. And with the description you gave of the murderer fittin' at least a dozen or so men in this town, that doesn't really give me much to go on, either. But I'll keep askin' around to see what I can find out."

"As long as you don't give up." She wrapped her hands tighter around the broom, more determined than ever to find the information herself.

"Oh, I'm not givin' up. But keep in mind, there are lots of other things I have to take care of, too. I'm a very busy man."

Although Jenny had yet to see much evidence of that, she still did not want to cause bad feelings between herself and the only person willing to help at all. "I realize that."

"In fact, I'm off right now to see if I can find out where Chad ran off to so I can tell him about this telegram, then I'll have to see to it an answer is sent." He slid his hat back into place as he headed toward the door.

Not about to do or say anything that might keep that man there a moment longer than necessary, she walked with him as far as the taller desk where Chad had left his hat. Hoping to take away at least one reason for her lone adversary to return there and get in her way, she reached over and picked it up, noting the color when she did. Dark brown. *The same color the murderer wore.*

An eerie feeling crept through her as she again remembered how quick Chad had been to accuse her of involvement in the murder. As if trying to shift the blame. Should she tell the sheriff of her suspicions? Or wait until she had more to go on than just the color of his hat, his general size, and his eagerness to create suspicion where none could be found?

Proceed with caution. The sheriff would want a lot more to go on. Maybe the darkroom would provide the swaying evidence.

"Since you're heading out to find Chad anyway, would you please take him his 'brown' hat?" She emphasized the color, hoping the sheriff would realize the link on his own. "He left it here earlier."

"Sure thing." He took it from her, then gave her a friendly wink, as unconcerned with the color as she had expected. "Anything for you, Miss Dykes."

Chad's mouth flattened with further annoyance when he came out of his office and spotted Sheriff Wade Mack across the building, headed for the front counter. Part of him wanted to pretend he hadn't noticed him and slip on out the back door as planned, while another part of him was curious to find out if anything significant had occurred during the last few hours.

J. C. had mentioned Wade was by earlier asking for him. Had Wade also gotten a telegram from Janeen? If so, then he already knew the situation, and was probably there to discuss it with him. This was not something the good sheriff would care to confront alone. Wade never had been one to face a difficult situation of any kind, at least not willingly.

How the man continued to be elected sheriff was a mystery to Chad.

"Chad, I've been lookin' for you," Wade called out, already headed in his direction carrying the hat Chad had left at Tyler's earlier. Was that all he wanted? To return his hat? Why hadn't he just left it with J. C. earlier?

"I know. J. C. told me you'd stopped by over an hour ago asking where I was." He took the hat from him with a nod of thanks and put it on rather than set it aside. He was headed back out anyway.

"I need to tell you about the telegraph message Janeen sent back." The sheriff answered Chad's unspoken question. Reaching into his pocket, he came out with a multifolded piece of paper, then held it out. "She says she can't make it back here in time for a funeral because of the comin' baby and has asked that you take care of the burial arrangements. She also wants you to see to it that all her belongings are packed up and shipped to her at her sister's."

"I know." He reached into his own pocket and brought out a similar paper. "She wired me, too. I got mine about fifteen minutes ago. So, how do you think we should handle this?"

"Handle what?" Wade asked, clearly not following that question. "She said *you* are to make all the arrangements. I'm just a messenger. I got too much to do to make time for anything like that."

"No, I mean about that beautiful impostor inside Tyler's house. Are you planning to arrest her, or just toss her out because you're attracted to her and you want her to have a reason to like you?"

"Why do you still insist that she's an impostor?"

"Because of what Janeen said in her wire." He waved the paper, thinking that might help jog his memory.

"Why? What did she say?" He snatched the paper out of Chad's hands and unfolded it.

Aware there was a confusion, Chad then snatched up the telegram Wade had, and the two read each other's missives to find out what Janeen had told the other.

When Chad saw that the sheriff's telegram had been sent hours ago, he understood the problem immediately and waited for the sheriff to finish reading.

Wade's lips moved while he slowly took in the first few sentences. "I guess Mrs. Dykes hasn't heard yet that our bank has been robbed, not if she's asked you to take the money she and Tyler have in their account and use part of it to pay the undertaker and another part to ship her belongings to her. I wonder what she's going to do when she finds out that money's gone?"

He sighed, then continued reading. "I guess I'd better tell her about that when I wire her back. Oh, I see she's already gone to the trouble to wire Tyler's sister, Ruby Dykes, about the death." He glanced up to explain that. "I reckon I was in such a hurry to get a telegram off to her, I forgot to mention the sister was already here."

Wade turned the page over as if expecting to find more scribbled on the back. "But I don't understand——" He pushed his hat to the back of his head to scratch what little hair he had. "You said something about the woman in Tyler's house being an impostor. Where does it say that?"

Exasperated, Chad jabbed at the bottom of page with his index finger. "Right there. See? Where it says she has wired Tyler's sister, *Ruby* Dykes, about the death."

The sheriff continued to look down at the page, still clearly baffled. "So, how does that prove the lady is an impostor?"

Unable to believe this man's lack of reasoning, Chad shook his head. "It tells us right there in plain writing that Tyler's sister's name is Ruby. Not *Ruth*. See? I was right about her all along. The woman is not the heartbroken young sister she pretends to be. That's why I think we should get over there right now and tell Ruth, or *whoever* that stranger is, to stop trespassing and get out of Tyler's house. And we need to make darned sure she's empty-handed when she goes."

In a way, he hoped she'd put up a fight. He'd love a reason to have to remove her physically. As beautiful and curvaceous as she was, it would be a pleasure to grab her up into his arms and carry her outside.

His body ached at the thought. If the woman wasn't such a liar, and probably a cheat, too, he would be quite tempted to seduce her.

"Let's not act too hasty here, Jordan. It's more than possible the name Ruby bein' on here is just a mistake. You know as sure as I do how often old Andy slips up and makes a blunder. Remember that time he sent a message over to the Widow Stover telling her that her grandson had lost his leg in a county fire, when the message should have been was that the grandson had sold his pig at the county fair. It took two hours to revive that poor woman."

"But what if it isn't a mistake? What if Ruby really *is* Tyler's sister's name?" Chad continued, not as ready to accept the possibility of an error as the sheriff obviously was. "Seems to me the name is Ruby and not Ruth."

"But what if you're wrong? What if it isn't Ruby? What if I'm the one who's right here, and the woman you keep wanting me to toss out of Tyler's house really is his sister? Haven't you looked at the woman to see how convincin' the resemblance is? Those two have to be related somehow. No, I think the message came in too quick, and Andy just got in too much a hurry tryin' to get it all down so he wouldn't have to have it repeated. By doin' so, he made another one of his mistakes. Besides, even if it turns out true—though I don't think it will—how much harm could a sweet little gal like that cause?"

"Plenty." Beautiful women were always trouble, but beautiful, *conniving* women were sure-fire disaster.

"Not when all she's doing is helpin' clean up some of the mess and helpin' get everything ready to pack. But if you're really all that worried about what's goin' on with her, and want to go on over there and help her get things ready to send, that's fine. It'll just make her job that much easier. The poor thing has enough worries at the moment. Why, she isn't even up to visitors right now. In fact, I'm not too sure she'd want to see you over there. But if your mind is made up in that direction, you might as well be doin' something useful to help."

Aware there was no changing the *sheriff's* mind, Chad gave up arguing with him. "Yes, I think that's exactly what I'll do. I'll go over there and 'help' all I can." He'd do so by keeping a close watch over every little move she made— until he could find some way to prove she was not at all who she said she was.

"Suit yourself, Chad. Meanwhile, I need to get back over

to the telegraph office and let Mrs. Dykes know you've agreed to take care of the arrangements as asked, and also that Tyler's sister is already here helpin' to pack her things away. When you go over there to the house, tell Miss Dykes I'll be bringin' by those two barrels I promised her later on this evening. Probably when I stop by to see if she's ready to go eat."

Chad scowled. He was short an employee. As badly as he wanted, he could not go over there, not just yet. "First, I have to deliver an order I promised to have out at the Rutledge Ranch before dark." He had already put off delivering the load as long as he could—wanting to hear back from Janeen first. "Still, that shouldn't take but a couple of hours. As soon as I'm back from that, I'll be able to head straight over there."

And stay.

Too determined to realize yet how tired she should be, Jenny continued her methodical search of the darkroom, looking for anything that might identify the man who shoved her aside after murdering her great-grandfather.

At the same time, she wanted it to look like she was indeed cleaning and straightening as promised should Chad or the sheriff return unexpectedly. Therefore, she carefully put the room back in order while she prowled through the different drawers and cabinets.

Not yet having declared her search hopeless, she came across what looked to be a set of unprocessed dry plates wrapped in a black cloth inside one of the drawers the sheriff had poked around in earlier. Hoping she might finally have found a clue, she quickly gathered the materials she would need to process the unearthed plates. Before actually starting the work, she again bolted the door to the outside, then closed the door to the darkroom and turned the lamp low so as not to affect the light-sensitive images on the plates.

Disappointed when the pictures proved to be nothing more than portraits of a young girl holding a puppy, she opened the door again to let in some fresh air. Feeling a trifle defeated now, she resumed her search of the darkroom, hoping to come across yet more unprocessed plates or already-developed prints of something damning in nature. It was not until she had finished searching the entire room and had stepped back out into the studio that she noticed the Rochester pointed in her direction.

Remembering the smell of burned powder and the still-smoking flash pan when she first came out from under the black hood, she checked, and, to her delight, found a plate inside.

Her heart raced with renewed hope as she gave the clock a quick glance. Did she have time to process one more photograph before the sheriff returned with those blasted barrels of his?

Checking again to be sure the door remained bolted, she wrapped the exposed plate in a black cloth, returned immediately to the stuffy darkroom, and closed the door. Working as quickly as the chemicals and her tiring body allowed, she transferred the image to paper and was pleased, and a little surprised, to find the shadowy silhouette of that same man who later shoved her aside while he still stood over the body of her great-grandfather.

With hands trembling and her heart hammering at a painful rate, she tried to decide just how valuable the picture might be. All she could really make out in the dark, grainy photograph was the overall shape of the murderer, but it proved he was indeed the large, broad-shouldered man she remembered. It also confirmed another earlier thought. *The man wearing bulky clothes and the wide-brimmed dark hat was shaped very much like Chad Jordan.*

With no way to make reproductions of the photograph,

Jenny hurriedly sealed it, then, as soon as it was dry, hid it under a developing tray, where it would be less likely to be found. She wasn't really sure what to do with it yet, knowing the photograph yielded little in the way of solid clues, but at least it was *some* form of evidence. Something she might be able to use in the future, perhaps by coupling it with other evidence. At any rate, it was well worth keeping.

Turning up the oil lamp again, she made sure no telltale corner protruded before heading to the door to let some fresh air into this windowless room. Just as she placed her hand on the painted knob but before actually turning it, she detected noises in the studio. Her stomach knotted. With the outside door bolted, there was no logical reason for anyone to be in that house.

But then again, there was no logical reason for *her* to be inside that house either—other than the vague possibility she had been sent back in time to resolve her great-grand-father's murder.

Had someone else been sent back in time to help her?

Dumbfounded, she parted the door just a crack and watched in stunned horror while two men rummaged through her great-grandfather's belongings, clearly looking for something.

She leaned closer to the narrow opening she had made to get a better view, but late evening had fallen, filling the studio with shadows. Plus, the two men had on dark hats pulled down low and wore dark cloths over the lower halves of their faces, making it impossible to get a good look at either of them. All she could tell was that one was built much like Chad Jordan, tall and powerful, though cloaked with extra layers of clothing, undoubtedly to make him look larger still in case someone happened to see him.

The other man also wore extra clothing, but was clearly smaller in stature, with a slight forward hunch to his skinny shoulders, and moved with short, nervous jerks.

While jerking papers out of a large file cabinet and tossing them haphazardly to the floor, the larger man kept glancing toward the door that opened to the main part of the house, as if expecting her—or someone—to appear there at any moment. The smaller man seemed more concerned with the door to the outside.

Aware two against one were not the greatest odds, especially when they both had handguns strapped to their waists and she had not thought to bring a weapon of any kind into the developing room with her, Jenny decided not to confront them. Instead, she eased the door closed again and nearly died when the latch popped into place with a resounding click.

With her heart hammering out of control, she listened for footsteps. When it was clear the noise wasn't going to bring them running, she quietly turned out the lamp. She did not want them noticing a light under the door in the growing darkness.

Feeling her way in the blackness, she hid as best she could in the tiny room by climbing up under the smaller of the two worktables where a jutting wall cabinet helped conceal her. There, she waited in the sweltering heat for the noises to stop. Noises that included a lot of angry mumbling, a dull thud, and two loud crashes as the two men became increasingly more daring in their search. Moments later, one of the two voices sounded just the other side of the closed door, causing Jenny to panic.

Were they searching there next?

"We've looked everywhere I can think of. Maybe the camera was empty when she took the picture and she didn't know it. Or maybe you imagined the whole thing and she didn't take no picture at all."

An answering mutter rumbled in the distance, the voice too far away to make out words, followed by, "So now there's two things missing that should be in this house. Both vanished into thin air as if they never existed. Think maybe this place has ghosts? Maybe that's why we can't find what we need to find. There really *could* be a ghost working against us here. After all, the man was *murdered* right in that next room. Maybe his spirit is still here lurking around, watching over things, making sure we get our comeuppance for all we've done. Come on. Let's get out of here. Before that sister of his comes back from wherever she's gone. The thought of there being a ghost here gives me the willies."

There was more muttering from across the room, followed by more shuffling, then suddenly the sounds stopped.

Not about to come out from under that table until absolutely certain it was safe, Jenny waited several minutes before she emerged from the darkroom to find the studio in shambles.

Her great-grandfather's treasured photos were scattered everywhere. Angry and heartsick, she lit a nearby lamp to have a better look at the debris and spotted the Rochester lying on the floor; the tripod broken in the same spot where she had earlier repaired it.

Panicked, she hurried over, picked it up, and while praying it wasn't broken, laid it on a nearby desk. Fearing they had wrecked her only real chance of returning to the twentieth century, she lifted the hood out of the way, took a deep breath, bent forward, and peered into the view glass. Relief flooded her, leaving her shaky and weak when she saw the upside-down image of her apartment still there.

The camera remained intact.

Afraid something like that might happen again, and fearing next time the camera itself might not fare so well, she decided to hide it from further danger until she was finally ready to use it. But where could she hide it? Not having had time to explore the house fully, she knew of very few places large enough to conceal such a bulky thing.

For lack of a better choice, she carried it into the bedroom she had used earlier to change clothes and slid it carefully under the high-centered bed, far to the middle so it would not be seen from a distance. The bedroom was the same one where she kept the valise filled with the rest of the clothes she now claimed for her own—still waiting for Chad to wonder where her things were, eager to prove she was still one full step ahead of him.

With the camera safely stashed, Jenny returned for a flash pan, powder, the broken tripod, and an unused dry plate in case she needed the whole set-up to be able to return to her own era. Pausing long enough to make sure the bed skirts hid everything, but without taking the time to change out of her sweat-soaked clothes, she headed off to tell the sheriff what had just happened.

Maybe now he would believe there was something in that house someone wanted— and wanted enough to be willing to murder someone to get it.

With hands still trembling, Jenny closed all the windows and twisted the latches to lock them in place, making it harder for the two men to get back inside. Having no key to lock the door, she pulled the curtains and lit two extra lamps to make the room seem occupied, then stepped quietly out onto the side porch.

By then darkness had settled over the small town of Black Rock, but no one had yet bothered to light any of the street-lamps. Not taking time to prepare a lantern to carry with her, though several hung on the porch, she grabbed a stick someone had used to prop a plant and started immediately across town, hoping the prowlers were not out in the shadows somewhere waiting for her.

Five

Sheriff Mack entered from one of the back rooms just as Jenny burst through the front door. She had run most of the distance across the nearly deserted town and now had to wait until she caught her breath before she could possibly tell him any of what she came to tell him.

"Miss Dykes? What's wrong?" The sheriff's face registered immediate alarm as he hurried toward her. He slid a key he carried into his pocket. "What happened?"

She patted her heaving chest with the flat of her hand, indicating she still could not speak. After a few more gulps of air, she managed to rasp, "More trouble. The man came back. Brought a friend."

"What?"

She bent forward and drew in several more needed breaths, each one less crucial than the one before "it. "The man who killed my brother came back. Only this time he had someone with him."

"He *did?* What did they want?"

"To search the place again. For whatever it was he had hoped to find the first time but never did."

The sheriff's eyes stretched wide. "You saw them?"

She nodded. "I was in the darkroom with the door closed when I heard their noises and opened the door just enough to peek out. I saw both of them. But they didn't see me. I'm sure of that."

The sheriff wet his lips with the bulk of his tongue,

clearly dumbfounded by this latest turn of events. "Did you get a good enough look to recognize either one?"

"Not by face. They both had their hats pulled down low and wore dark cloths for masks. But I might be able to recognize the smaller one. He was a skinny, nervous man with a noticeable slouch."

The sheriff frowned and looked down at the floor, as if making a mental note of that description. "And you're sure they were searchin' for something?"

"Yes. Not only did I see both of them scrambling through drawers and cabinets, I heard one of them state right out loud that they were there searching for two different items but had little luck finding either one."

A skinny eyebrow lifted.

"Did they say what the items were?"

"No. But I think I know what *one* was. If I'm right, I'd already found it before they came."

That admission definitely interested the sheriff.

About time.

"What? What did you find?"

"Come with me. It'd be better if I showed it to you. Then you could see the mess they left, too."

Not yet having completely caught her breath, she headed again for the door. She did not want to leave the house unguarded for too long. Those men hadn't found what they wanted. They would try again.

Hearing the urgency in her voice, the sheriff took just enough time to strap his gunbelt back on and grab up his hat before he followed her out into the dimly lit street. By then a tall, skinny man with long arms and bowed legs worked his way down the street, lighting the streetlamps one at a time with some long torchlike apparatus.

He paused to watch as the two passed in an obvious hurry.

Within minutes Jenny and Sheriff Mack arrived back at Tyler's house. Because of the possible danger, Jenny let the sheriff enter first, pistol drawn. His shoulders drooped when he surveyed the cluttered room, proof foul play was still at hand. "Is there anything missin'?"

Remembering where the money was kept, Jenny checked the box and discovered it gone. "Looks like they pocketed that forty-eight cents you'd found."

"Anything else?" He walked over to the desk and poked around at the photos and papers scattered there.

"I don't know." She followed him to the desk. "I haven't been around here long enough to know if anything else is missing."

"And I'm not all that familiar with Tyler's belongin's, either." He pushed his hat back and scratched his head just above his thinning hairline. "But I reckon I know someone who is."

Jenny felt a gradual tightening at the base of her stomach. "Who?"

"Chad Jordan. He'd be able to look this mess over and tell pretty quick if anything important besides that little bit of money is missin'. You wait right here and I'll go see if I can find him." He glanced at the clock and frowned. "I wonder what happened to him. He told me he was headin' over here directly after work. That was hours ago. Looks like maybe somethin' changed his mind."

Not necessarily, she thought. Chad could very easily have been the larger of the two men. Should she mention that to Sheriff Mack? Or wait until she had put together enough evidence to prove that theory true. She *could* be wrong about Chad. All she really had to go on thus far was body size, body shape, and a dark-brown hat. She could not even rely on the gray color of his trousers, since it appeared both men had put on extra clothing over their regular clothes as a means of disguise.

"If he's not at his store, he might be at his house. Either way, I shouldn't be gone too long. Bolt the door behind me."

Jenny did exactly that, *gladly*. But within minutes the sheriff knocked, wanting back in.

"Chad was already on his way here," he said in way of explanation, gesturing into the darkness behind him.

Jenny's heart jumped when seconds later, the tall, handsome man she suspected of murder appeared on the porch, his eyebrows pulled low over glittering blue eyes. "What did you two want with me this time?"

Before either answered, he stepped inside and caught his first glimpse of the room. "What happened?"

Although he sounded strained, his face registered no emotion as he scanned the cluttered room, taking in every detail.

"Miss Dykes had herself a little company." Sheriff Mack gestured unnecessarily to the destruction around him. Desk and cabinet drawers stood open, some now empty, others with papers sticking out, while three chairs and an inkwell lay toppled on their sides. Strewn photographs, papers, and magazines blanketed every flat surface as if it had literally rained clutter inside that room. "They paid her a call while she was hiding in the darkroom."

"They?" His gaze cut to the now-open door of the darkroom, then again to the debris scattered across the furniture and floor. Careful not to step on any of the photographs, he moved further into the room. "More than one?"

"Two." Jenny told him.

"Men?" His expression remained darkly unreadable when he finally looked at her with those probing blue eyes of his; it caused tiny shivers to skitter across her arms. Were the questions ones he already knew the answers to? Or was he truly at a loss to see such a mess? A tiny part of her hoped the latter proved true, but a larger part refused to find him innocent until all proof was in.

Nodding in response to his question, she glanced down at his boots, not too surprised to find them black and scuffed. But then so were the sheriff's, so that might be common for this part of the country.

"And these two men did all this with you right there in the next room?" His eyebrow cocked questioningly, he nodded to the clutter around him. "Is there any chance you got a good look at them this time?"

There was an grating undertone in Chad's voice Jenny could not quite decipher. Was it anger? Frustration? Guilt? Or merely annoyance? "No, I didn't. It was getting dark and they both wore masks."

"So you have no idea who might have done any of this. No clue to who would have a reason to tear apart your 'brother's' studio?" He sounded as skeptical as ever.

So, we're back to that, are we? Rather than protest the questioning emphasis he had placed on the word brother, Jenny met his accusing gaze with one of clear determination. "None I want to admit to just yet."

Chad's eyebrows perked as he and the sheriff exchanged curious glances.

"But' you just said you didn't see those two men," he pointed out.

Now Chad looked as if he didn't know what to believe. *Good.* "I didn't."

The sheriff frowned, clearly as baffled as Chad, if not more so. "If you think maybe you have something on the two of them, you have to tell me. Otherwise, I can't do my job right. You said something earlier about havin' found something you thought maybe they wanted. I want to see it."

Jenny glanced at Chad, who was still glowering at her, and decided to keep the photograph she had developed secret a while longer. She certainly did not want Chad finding out about it—not just yet. "I said that to get you to come with me."

"Are you sure? Because I really do need to see anything you may have found." He sincerely wanted that evidence.

Perhaps the fact the murderer had not left town yet caused him a change of heart.

"Yes, the only real information I really have is what you already know. One man was large and muscular, like the two of you." She cut a meaningful gaze to Chad. "And the other wasn't much bigger than I am."

Chad stared at her a moment longer, a tiny muscle at the back of his jaw pumping rhythmically, then turned his attention to the cluttered room again. "Do you at least know if they left here with anything they came for?"

"I can't say for sure," she admitted honestly, for she had not watched them leave, "but I don't think they did."

"That's why I was headed out of here to find you, Chad. Other than the change in his money box, Miss Dykes doesn't know what, if anything, is missin'. I figured you'd been around here enough to know if anything of any real value was gone. Something that would account for them havin' come back here a second time."

Chad bent over the shorter of the two desks and started straightening the items into neat piles, studying the room while he worked. "Tyler's hat is missing." He waved a hand toward the pegs near the door. "So is his vest." He then pointed to the smallest file cabinet. "So are some of his books. And one of his cameras. The big one that used to be right over there." He pointed to where the Rochester had stood.

Jenny was impressed with his powers of observation. "No, none of that is missing. I carried those items into the other part of the house so they'd be among the first things I pack."

He glanced at her curiously, but returned his attention to the room. "It's really hard to say for sure, as cluttered as the place is, but I really can't tell that anything else is gone." He slid open the top drawer of the larger desk and peered inside. "I don't see that little silver match box that U.S.

marshal gave him a couple of years ago. But it could very well be somewhere in all this clutter."

The sheriff leaned forward to look over his shoulder. "Anything else missin', you think?"

Chad glanced around again, then shook his head. "Not in here. I'll go check the rest of the house."

"There's no need to do that," Jenny told him, not wanting him finding out she had hidden the camera he had noticed missing up under the bed. That would seem a peculiar place to put something she intended to pack. "They never went back there."

He frowned, annoyed for some reason with her for having said that. "Why not? That's where most of the items worth stealing are."

"I can't say for sure why, but the way the larger man kept his eye on that door, I think since there were no lights burning in the studio itself but one left burning in one of the bedrooms, he figured I was off in that part of the house. I don't think it ever occurred to them that I could be in the darkroom."

"I can understand that, especially not with the door closed like you said it was—not as hot as it was today." His blue eyes studied her a minute longer, as if trying to decide her reason for having been in there with the door closed in the first place. "Has anyone bothered to check on Tyler's horse. Is Champ still out there or was he perhaps stolen, too?"

The sheriff glanced to the curtained windows and frowned. "I hadn't thought about that. Guess I really ought to go check."

"And you might also want to feed the animal. If he's out there. I doubt Miss *Dykes* here thought to do that."

"I didn't know to," she argued in ready defense of herself. She remembered Chad having mentioned there being what sounded like an expensive horse, but it had never occurred to her the animal would be somewhere on the premises. Wasn't that what liveries were for? In every old western movie she ever saw, the people in town either had their horses tied up to a rail out front or else they had to go to the livery to get one. "Had I known to, I would have."

"There's no problem," the sheriff put in quickly, clearly eager to get in his Brownie points with her. "I'll go take care of Champ right now."

Chad watched Sheriff Mack leave, then turned to face Jenny with an angry glower. "I just want you to know, you may have Wade Mack fooled with your sweet little act of innocence and charm, but you don't have me fooled one bit. I don't care what you say, or how much you seem to know about matters here, you are *not* Tyler's sister."

"Then who am I?" she challenged, knowing he would have no answer for that.

"I don't have a name for you yet, but I think you are probably the same person who spent the last couple of hours ransacking this room. I think you wanted ready vindication after having decided to take a few things for yourself. There's more than a silver match box missing. There's Tyler's gold-plated dagger and a half dozen gold coins missing, too."

Knowing exactly where the dagger was, for she had confiscated it to use as protection for herself, she asked, "If you knew that, why didn't you tell the sheriff?"

"I will. Eventually. That is, if you don't put the items back and leave here of your own accord."

"And thus prove to you that I am indeed the little impostor you thought all along?"

His expression hardened. He stepped closer, making her more aware of him than ever. "Among other things."

She lifted a hand and pressed it against his chest to keep him from coming any closer. Big mistake. She was better off not knowing for certain that he was every bit as solid as he looked. She dropped the hand quickly. "Among *what* other things? You don't think I'm the one who murdered Tyler Dykes, do you?"

"No. The sheriff's right. It would take considerable strength to put that knife where it was. But I do think you know who *did* kill him and are carrying that secret."

"And that worries you? Why?" Absently, she rubbed the hand she'd used to touch him to remove the odd, tingling sensation that lingered there. "Do you think I plan to black-mail the killer? Is that the reason you think I'm keeping such a secret?" Aware he watched her nervously rubbing one hand with the other, she stuck them both behind her.

"I don't have a clue what your reasons are, but it's hard for me to believe that you just fell into this situation. Also, I never saw you go through the normal period of disbelief a real sister would have gone through had she *accidentally* found her brother dead. You accepted it all a little too quickly. I think Tyler's murder was expected by you."

Expected maybe—after all, she had known about this murder all her life—but it was not something she had par-ticipated in.

Enraged that he thought her capable of having anything to do with any murder, Jenny stiffened.

With hands balled at her sides and teeth clenched, she met his accusing gaze with defiance. "You have some nerve coming in here and trying to put blame on me." She leaned closer still until practically nose to nose with him, a move that clearly surprised him. His eyes rounded briefly before narrowing again with continued caution. "I'll have you know, Mr. Chad Jordan, I wasn't even *here* when it hap-pened. I didn't arrive until after Tyler was already dead."

"Can you prove that?"

A ripple of apprehension skittered over her skin. Why was he trying to drag her into this? They had already ad-mitted she could not have possibly been the one to shove that knife through Tyler's ribs. "No. There was no one around to see me arrive, except maybe for the killer."

"How convenient."

For you maybe. "Look, you can try if you want, but there is no way you can involve me in this. I wasn't here when the murder took place. If I *had* been here I certainly would have done something to stop it."

He continued to look at her questioningly. "How very noble. And what would have done?"

"I don't know. But I'd have done something," she said, though something told her there was not much she could have done against such a large, strong, determined man.

She eyed Chad for size and might, very glad the sheriff was still right outside. If Chad *was* guilty, and he *did* mean her bodily harm, a scream should bring help immediately.

"So you aren't going to cooperate?" he asked, though clearly not surprised.

"I *am* cooperating. If I could cooperate any more, believe me, I would." She would tell all if she just knew something substantial to tell. Was he testing her to find out how much she *did* know?

Chad studied her a moment more, then shook his head. His dark hair fell forward across his forehead, forcing him to rake it back with a strong hand. "Whatever you are up to, you won't get away with it. I'll see to that."

Not certain if she should read that as a threat not to get in his way, or if he really was innocent and sincerely thought her the bad guy, she lifted her chin. "And how will you do that?"

"By watching your every move until you finally leave town."

Another chill skittered across her skin, this one so intense it caused her take a tiny step back. It was hard to remain confrontational when suddenly you were the one being confronted. "Oh?"

"And also by doing what I can to prove that you are not who you say you are." A semblance of a smile appeared on his face, one that caused a shadow of a dimple to form and his pale eyes to glitter with rancor. "Take note that I have just this afternoon sent a telegram to Janeen asking her to describe Tyler's family in detail, including names and ages. I could easily have a response by early tomorrow."

Jenny swallowed and hoped the wire he sent would not arrive until after Janeen had gone into the hospital for special care. Janeen would be less likely to send a prompt answer once that happened. But what if a response did make it through? Would the response be one to mark her an impostor? What then?

"Good," she replied with far more conviction than she thought possible. "Then maybe you'll believe me."

"Either that, or I'll finally have the proof needed to have you thrown out of this house."

"So I'll finally be out of the way?" she surmised aloud, thinking it obvious. If he was the killer, and he had killed to get whatever might be hidden in that house, then he needed another clear shot at searching for it.

He ignored her last comment. "I've also wired all the liveries in and around Perry to see if they can remember anyone of your description hiring a buggy. And should it turn out that really *is* how you arrived here, I've also asked what name you used when arranging for the rig. Somewhere, somehow, you must have slipped up with all the lies you've told—if you haven't already, *Ruth*. Or should that name be Ruby?"

Jenny's eyes widened. Maybe it should be Ruby. She wasn't sure. But *he* didn't need to know that.

"It's Ruth."

"Well, you'd better hope I don't prove otherwise, because once that one major slip-up of yours finally surfaces and I catch it, you are as good as out of here. You are *not* Tyler's sister."

The sheriff reentered the studio a minute later to find the two staring at each other angrily, but he didn't ask what had happened while he was gone. Clearly, he did not want to put himself in the middle of the dispute. "Good news," he announced. "The horse is still out there. So's the carriage and all the tack as far as I could tell. I fed Champ enough to last him through tomorrow night and made sure he had plenty of fresh water. He definitely was thirsty."

"Thanks," Chad responded, yielding his angry gaze only a second. It was as if he thought being the first to turn away would be construed as an admission of defeat. "I'll take over feeding him from now on, since I'll be staying here for the next several days."

Jenny's stomach lurched. "Staying here?" She tried to show none of the alarm that statement caused.

"That's right." His expression took on a triumphant quality. "Except to go get my clothes, I'm not leaving this house until you do."

The sheriff sounded as concerned as Jenny felt over that news. He moved closer to the pair. "But what about your store? Who's goin' to run that?"

"The same person who runs it whenever I take a trip." He divided his attention between the sheriff a few yards away and Jenny, directly in front of him. "I've already told J. C. he'll be in charge of the store part for a while longer, and Marge will take care of the office part as usual. If something important comes up that they can't handle alone, they already know where to find me." His expression filled with disgust as he raked his gaze over Jenny's tense form. "Until she leaves, I'll be making this house my home, too."

Unnerved by the thought of being left alone with the tall, handsome, overbearing man who just might also be her grandfather's murderer, Jenny argued, "But both of us can't stay here. Not alone. It would be inappropriate." She looked to the sheriff beseechingly. "People would talk."

"About Chad? People *already* talk about him," Sheriff Mack informed her, clearly amused, his attention wandering to the areas of her body where her sweat-dampened clothing clung in a provocative manner.

She crossed her arms self-consciously as the sheriff cut Chad a far less appraising look.

"I realize that such talk may be a problem for you, but it certainly has never been one for Chad. He doesn't care what other people say. He has his own way of doing things." He shrugged, then frowned as he turned to face Jenny again. "Most folks already know that about him, and will figure you are the victim of circumstance that you are. Besides, I can't very well run him off. Remember? Because of your wantin' to make your visit a surprise, Mrs. Dykes didn't know you were comin', so she sent me that wire askin' for Chad here to take care of matters for her. Turns out she sent him one, too, statin' that was indeed what she wanted him to do. So, if he wants to stay here and help square things away, he has every right to. I have no authority to stop him."

"Isn't there *anything* you can do to help me?" She swallowed hard, already aware she fought a losing battle. Like it or not, she was stuck with the man. "Anything at all?"

She looked at Chad again and had the oddest thought. If it weren't for the nagging fact he might really be her great-grandfather's murderer, coupled with her need to be alone to continue looking for clues, she just *might* like being stuck in that house with such an attractive man.

The sheriff joined her in looking at Chad before answering her question. "I can't do anything except maybe take you out to dinner with me like I promised earlier. You've been here since early on this afternoon. You're bound to be gettin' awful hungry by now."

It had been fourteen hours since she had eaten, but for some reason the lack of food had yet to affect her. "Thank you, but I'm not that hungry. I'll just see what I can find in Janeen's kitchen." She was not about to leave Chad there alone to look for whatever clues might have been left behind. No telling what kind of evidence he would destroy, if he was the guilty party. "I'd rather keep working."

"But you have to eat," Sheriff Mack argued. "And I'm not too sure Tyler has much food here in the house. I know he's been having a woman come in and cook since his wife left, but I think she pretty much would bring whatever she planned to fix that day with her."

"Just the same, I'll get by," she said, knowing she would rather starve than let Chad have the opportunity to destroy her chance of ever finding out who murdered her great-grandfather. No, if Chad had honestly intended to help find the killer, he would have done so the first time around. "Don't worry about me."

Sheriff Mack looked at Chad, then at her again, scowling with annoyance. "Well, Miss Dykes, maybe by the morning you'll have changed your mind. I'll stop in to see if you'd like to go over and have breakfast with me. I'll even give you your choice of places to eat."

Aware she had struck his pride by refusing to dine with him, she smiled sweetly. "Thanks. You are a kind man. I appreciate your concern." But rather than make promises, she bent and picked up a handful of clutter and started work, separating the photographs from the rest. To her, the photographs were Tyler's most prized possessions.

"I'll see you in the morning then."

Chad walked with the sheriff as far as the porch, then returned minutes later to stare silently at her while she continued sorting through the rubble. Intimidated by Chad's presence, she stopped her work in the studio and went off into the other part of the house, where she planned to stay long enough to gather her wits. To her dismay, Chad followed.

Thinking the sheriff right, she really should eat something, she went on into the kitchen. There, she found bread, but no meat, and not much else in the way of ready food. Not about to take the time to cook, and not certain she would even know how to prepare anything on such an odd-looking stove despite her years cooking over a campfire, she cut a couple of fat slices off the bread loaf and headed off to find a comfortable spot to eat. Again, Chad followed.

For the next hour, no matter where she went, or what she did, Chad stayed with her, giving her no time to explore like she wanted. Finally, she'd had enough. "I thought you said you were going to return home and get your clothes. It's getting late. Don't you think you should go ahead and go do that before it gets any later?"

While he was gone, she would have another opportunity to look the place over.

"It's hours yet until bedtime," he said, without bothering to check a clock. "I have plenty of time to do that if I want."

If I want? Had he changed his mind about having fresh clothes? Was he never going to leave? "Just so long as you realize you have no clothes here."

Rather than continue a conversation with a man who made her pulses race with as much with awareness as uncertainty, she headed back into the studio. There, she picked up the two crates the sheriff had left her and carried them into the main part of the house where the windows had screens and could be left open without fear of someone climbing through. Besides, if she worked in the studio and came across whatever it was Chad might be after, he would surely take it from her before she could show it to the sheriff. That would never do.

Not wanting Chad accusing her of having lied about wanting to help, she set the crates down on the kitchen table and started packing some of the items inside the drawers. Having no newspapers, she used dish towels and tablecloths to cushion the breakables, very much aware that Chad sat the whole time, tilted back in a nearby chair, watching her every move.

Exactly like he had threatened to do.

But he still hadn't bothered to tell the sheriff about the missing items. Did that prove he had no intention of letting Wade know the items were gone? Because he was the one who had taken most of them?

Finally, the heat, the heavy clothing, and Jenny's growing exhaustion got the better of her. Tired of his intimidating behavior, she marched over to where he sat and confronted him with the fact he had yet to lift a finger.

"You told the sheriff you were here to help," she reminded him, narrowing her gaze. "I guess that was an out and out lie."

"Guess again, stranger. I *am* helping." Except for a slow, sensual blink, he did not move. Instead, he continued to lean lazily back in the chair, staring at her with those unnaturally blue eyes.

"How can you say that? You've done nothing but sit there."

"Watching you," he appended, as if that explained it all, then qualified, "Making sure you don't do whatever it is you've come here to do."

"And that's a help?"

Clearly not pleased with the snap in her voice, he sat his chair forward with a clap and met her angry glower. "Yes, I'd call that a great help."

He stood, forcing her to look up at him now instead of down. Her stomach knotted at the reminder of how tall and powerfully built he was.

Clearly, he was angry with her, but for some reason she wanted him angrier still. Maybe because *she* was so upset. "Well, you may call it helping, but I call it being lazy."

Eyebrows leaping skyward, he moved closer, forcing her to tilt her head back. His gaze dipped to take in all of her as he reached out to touch her cheek with his open palm, causing an unexpected shock wave of warmth to shoot through her body.

His pale-blue eyes glinted with amusement at how quickly she had stepped back. A devilish smile lifted his firm mouth. "Just what is it you'd have me do?"

Six

Not having expected Chad to try to use his own strong sexuality to intimidate her like that, Jenny swallowed hard and looked away. Absurdly aroused, it was all she could do to speak in a normal tone. "You could start by taking the items off the top shelves and placing them on the counter where I can get to them more easily."

His glittering gaze cut toward the cabinets, then again to her body, boldly letting her know where his interest truly lay. Another shiver of awareness swept over her, cutting off her next breath. *The man was impossible.* Surely, he didn't think she was interested in him. Just because he was so incredibly good-looking and had the body of a Greek god?

Suddenly, it was impossible not to imagine what he would looked like draped in nothing more than a skimpy sheet.

"I'd rather just watch." He shifted his weight to one well-muscled leg and crossed his strong, suntanned arms, letting her know he planned to do his watching from right there.

That would never do. It was bad enough she had been forced to waste several valuable hours packing her great-grandmother's belongings just to keep these people from questioning who she was, and thus her right to be there. She did not need the added aggravation of having this provocative, overbearing man ogle her while she worked. "So what you're telling me is that you lied to the sheriff about wanting to help get matters squared away here." Maybe she could goad him into doing something besides making a close study of her.

"Look, stranger, I never once said that was my intention," he pointed out sternly but calmly. "The sheriff did. All I promised to do was feed Tyler's horse, starting tomorrow."

"So you don't plan to help inside the house at all. You've decided to let your promise to Janeen go ignored."

"Again, I'm not the one who promised Janeen anything." A taunting smile stretched his mouth wide, revealing the rounded tips of a perfect set of white teeth. An undeniably sexy dimple sank into his suntanned cheek, for he clearly thought himself clever. "The sheriff did."

"Oh?" she asked, refusing to be distracted no matter how attractive he was. She had a mission, and this man was not part of it. Unless, of course, he did turn out to be the murderer. "Then I'm sure Janeen will understand when she finds out you didn't lift as much as one finger to help."

The taunting smile flattened. She had struck the very nerve she had gone after. How would it look to others if he didn't at least pretend to care about the needs of Tyler's widow? He was supposed to have been Tyler's best friend after all. He should act the part.

Aware of her success, her chin came up in triumph. It was a small victory, but a victory nonetheless.

Chad glowered a long moment before turning abruptly away. Snatching up the chair he had just sat in, he stalked over to the kitchen cabinets. Without speaking again, he slapped the chair down, stepped into the seat, and started jerking items off the top two shelves, slamming them down on the counter.

Proud to have turned the tables so quickly, Jenny stood watching him for several minutes, admiring what she saw despite her misgivings. Undeniably attractive, he stood tall, broad-shouldered, narrow-waisted, and wore his long thick dark-brown hair brushed softly away from his well-sculpted face. The lightly haired, sun-bronzed arms exposed below tightly rolled shirtsleeves rippled with lean precision while he worked, reminding her he was also a powerful man. One who did not normally shy from strenuous work.

She shuddered, remembering how easily he had tossed her aside when he burst out of her great-grandfather's dark-room earlier that day. Like she was little more than a rag doll.

If that person had been Chad.

Despite every clue thus far pointing toward him, and despite his cautious, almost fearful treatment of her—as if deeply worried about what she knew—she still had doubts niggling at her. Chad Jordan just did not seem like the type of man who could kill a man in cold blood. No matter what the prize.

But what did she know about men? In her twenty-eight years of dealing with them, except for her father, she had never been able to judge their true worth. Which had a lot to do with why she had never married. The men she had chosen to date had been far from wonderful. Good-looking? Yes. Successful? Often. But wonderful? *Hardly.* Their appeal always proved surface only.

"Now who's not getting any work done?" he asked, looking back with an arched eyebrow.

Embarrassed to have been caught staring, especially knowing how much she had admired what she saw, she hurried back to the crate and resumed stuffing it with Janeen's belongings. Hard work was the best way to work off sexual stress.

Odd that she could want and yet not want a man all at the same time.

After filling the second crate, and while Jenny searched for something else to use for a box, a loud knock sounded at the back door, startling her.

Chad, being closer, stepped down and answered it.

"Thought I'd find you two back here," the sheriff said, entering uninvited. "I don't know why, but women always

want to start their packin' with the things in the kitchen."
Rather than take off his wide-brimmed hat, he pushed it to
the back of his head, allowing the lamplight to fall full
across his mustached face. "I got hold of the wagon and
brought you those two big barrels I promised you. Where
should I put them?"

Chad turned a grim expression to Jenny, essentially ad-
mitting she had taken charge of the actual packing.

"In here will be fine," she replied, finding certain pride
in being the one to answer. Chad might question who she
was, and rightfully so; but he didn't question her ability to
get things done. "Like you said, we've decided to start with
the kitchen items first." Simply because she did not want
Chad with her when she worked again in the studio.

The sheriff studied her a moment, then Chad. "Everything goin' all right here? No problems?"

"None," Chad answered stiffly. *"Yet."*

The sheriff stared at him a moment longer, then blinked.
"No, I don't mean between you two. It's obvious you'll
never get along with each other. I meant with anyone else
tryin' to break in here. Any trouble on that front?"

"None that I'm aware of," Chad answered before Jenny
had time to respond. Clearly, the only authority he had re-
linquished to her was that over the general packing. "I noticed she'd already shut and latched all the windows in the
studio, which should pretty much keep anyone from slipping through them again." An eyebrow arched as he cut an
accusing blue gaze at her. "But she left the side door unbolted, so I stepped over and bolted it myself before coming
back here. The rest of the house has wire window screens,
which should keep anyone from just lifting a glass and
crawling through. The screens were put in at Janeen's in-
sistence as I recall." His glower turned pointed. "To keep
out all *manner* of pests."

"Just remember, screens can be torn out pretty easily,"
the sheriff cautioned, temporarily drawing Chad's attention

back to him. "All it takes is a good sharp knife to get through them. You both still need to keep a close watch on what's going on around you."

Chad nodded, then smiled a most fascinating smile. One that flanked his sensuous mouth with a double set of long, narrow dimples and sent an unexpected burst of tremors through Jenny's body.

"Oh, I've already been keeping a very close watch on what's going on here," he admitted, his tone sinister. "And I've found some of it to be quite intriguing."

The sheriff pushed his hat back further, frowning. "How so?"

Also curious to hear that answer, thinking he was about to accuse her of yet something else when she had been careful to do nothing condemning, Jenny stopped work long enough to study his expression. The devilish glimmer beneath his long dark eyelashes caused a quick catch in her throat. *What was he up to now?*

"Well, look at her." He spoke to the sheriff, but kept his glittering gaze locked with Jenny's. "Even though she's not who she says she is, and is undoubtedly here hoping for some form of personal gain, you have to admit she's a desirable woman. What man wouldn't enjoy keeping a watch over something like that, what with that long brown hair and those big, dark eyes? And look at that body. Nothing missing there."

Not have expected him to say something so bold, especially about her, Jenny stared at him a moment, unblinking, then turned back to her work. She had no idea how to respond to such a brazen comment.

Part of her liked knowing he found her attractive, while another part of her was terrified by the thought of what that might drive him to do.

"You're right. She is desirable," the sheriff agreed, albeit begrudgingly, clearly not pleased by Chad's observations.

"But keep in mind, she is also Tyler's sister. And Tyler was your close friend."

"No, I'll keep in mind that she *says* she's Tyler's sister, but that's as far as it goes with me. I'm afraid it's just a little too convenient that a sister Tyler never mentioned suddenly appears out of nowhere *after* he's dead."

Tired of Chad's continued accusations, and tired of the two men standing there chatting about her as if she had no ears, Jenny stiffened her back, hoping they didn't notice how that lifted her breasts when she then faced them again. "Sheriff, I appreciate being considered desirable, but we aren't getting any work done by standing around here talking about such matters. Why don't you bring those two barrels inside and help us fill them with Janeen's things?"

She prayed he would agree to do just that. She would feel so much more comfortable having a third party there. Especially after hearing about Chad's reaction to her. If he really was the killer, then he was a man with no principles, which meant he would have no qualms about acting on the fact he found her desirable, whether she wanted him to or not.

"Sorry, but I can't stay. I'm due at the Alley saloon for my regular Wednesday night game of cards." He glanced at all the utensils and gadgets scattered across the counter. "Besides, it appears you two pretty much have matters in hand here."

"But we could always use more help," she persisted. She did not want to be left alone with Chad again. Not even for a little while. His presence was far too nerve-wracking. If she couldn't have the house to herself, she would much rather have both men there with her.

"Sorry. The others are expectin' me. I can't let them down." He frowned, then his expression brightened quickly. "But I'll be by tomorrow mornin' to take you to breakfast just like I promised."

Aware the sheriff had no idea how unappealing he was

with his receding chin, unkempt hair, and wiry mustache, especially to a woman of the twentieth century, and also aware he had taken her interest in him staying the wrong way, she quickly changed tactics. "Whatever. I just thought you'd like to help. You being the sheriff and all." She shifted her attention to the crates again, tucking in stray corners of the towels and cloths she used for padding. "But we'll do fine without you."

He hesitated a moment, frowning again when he returned his attention to Chad. "Just remember. There's still every chance she's Tyler's sister. And until you can prove otherwise, it would be a darned good idea for you to treat her as such."

Uncertain if the sheriff's protectiveness stemmed out of genuine concern, or because he had mentally staked her for himself, she thanked him. "I'm glad that at least *someone* around here is willing to believe I just might be who I say I am."

Chad did not respond to either comment, though both were directed at him. Instead, he offered to go out to the wagon and help the sheriff with the two barrels.

The moment the pair stepped out into the darkness, Jenny let go of the breath she hadn't known she had been holding. Her nerves taut, she leaned against the counter, clearly needing its support. She could not take much more of having to be on guard all the time. She had to get rid of Chad.

Watching the now-empty, clattering wagon, Chad waited until the sheriff had driven off before returning to the house. After entering the kitchen from the outside, he went immediately back to removing the last of the items Ruth—or *whoever* the hell that stranger was—had tricked him into pulling off those top shelves. It was not until he had finished with the last of it, and had climbed down from the rickety wooden chair, that he returned his attention to the woman herself.

Although he had said it only to intimidate her, he had not lied when he admitted to the sheriff he found the stranger desirable. Wade was right. It would take a blind man to have missed that fact. No. It would take a *dead* man, for even a blind man would be able to sense beauty as breathtaking as that. Her perfume alone was enough to drive a man to total distraction.

Moving closer, he stared at her appraisingly while she continued to work, now filling the largest of the two barrels Wade had brought with various-size pots and pans, using bed clothes found in a chest at the end of the hall to cradle the breakables. It was already after nine o'clock, well past bedtime, and she had yet to offer an excuse to quit work.

That surprised him.

In the past hour, she had worked without stopping. From bending so often, the ends of her dark hair had come loose from its pins hours ago but remained gathered high on her head by some sort of tiny blue band. Even so, the majority of it cascaded past her shoulders where it divided into thick waves of dark brown tinged with gold.

With all but the shorter hair near the front kept back from her face, it was easy to notice the perfect shape of her nose, cheeks, and chin, as well as the long, incredibly thick eyelashes that surrounded huge, almond-shaped eyes he remembered to be the most vivid shade of brown.

He could well imagine a man becoming lost in those dark eyes. Lost enough to do whatever she beckoned, whether in or out of bed.

Aware of the danger, he shook that last thought and resumed his appraisal of her overall shape and size. She was tall—but then he preferred taller women, especially when put together with a shape like *that*. His gaze dipped to the way the still-damp lavender dress adhered to her womanly curves. Too bad the material didn't cling quite as adeptly as it did earlier, when it had left little to the imagination.

His body ached with the memory. The woman was perfection physically. Too bad she had the manipulative soul of the very devil himself.

Still appraising her from several yards away, he noted again that her skirts were about two inches shorter than the length the women he knew wore theirs and were the same soft shade of lavender that Janeen loved to wear. Her shoes, when he glimpsed them, appeared to be made out of a hard white cloth, though he was not sure what. Twice now, while studying those shoes, he had caught sight of her ankles and knew she wore no stockings beneath her skirt.

The knowledge of bare legs had aroused him originally. But when closer inspection had revealed she was undoubtedly not wearing much in the way of the other undergarments women should wear—for earlier the bodice of her sweat-drenched dress had clung to her like a second skin— he had caught himself trying to picture what she must look like completely without clothes.

Despite knowing she was an impostor, and possibly a woman involved with a murder, he envisioned what it would be like to remove those clothes ever so slowly then carry her off to bed to seek out her pleasures. His body ached at the mere thought. She was a full-bodied woman, every curve just the right size to fill a man's hands to overflowing. Just the right sort to enjoy ravishing in every way possible.

But he wouldn't feel comfortable doing that. Not with a woman like her. Not with a woman he didn't trust.

If only he believed she was Tyler's sister, then he would feel freer to pursue his interest in her. But he didn't believe it. Not for a minute. He and Tyler had been too close. They'd had no secrets.

Except maybe one.

His gut wrenched when he remembered Tyler sending word to come by the house last Friday afternoon, that he wanted to talk to him about something important. But Chad was already on his way out of town by the time he had learned of the message, and because he had planned his purchasing trip to Oklahoma City for months, he didn't bother turning his horse back around. He was already late and had thought that whatever Tyler wanted to tell him could wait the few days until his return.

He had instructed the young man who had caught up with him to give him Tyler's message to tell Tyler he would come by to see him just as soon as he returned. Then, not giving it another thought, he rode on.

Never to see Tyler again.

Never to keep his promise.

Blinking back tears of guilt and frustration, he turned away, unable to continue looking at the woman he believed harbored some clue to Tyler's murder. He turned his gaze to a blackened window instead, allowing his memories a moment to torment him.

Some friend he had been. He should have turned that horse right around and gone to see what Tyler wanted to talk to him about. But how could he have known the message wouldn't wait?

He closed his eyes against the twisting ache. Did whatever Tyler hoped to tell him have anything to do with the reason he was murdered? By ignoring Tyler's plea, was he just as much at fault as the man who plunged that white-handled knife into his chest? Had he gone right then to hear what Tyler wanted, would things have turned out differently? Would talking to Tyler have given him insight into what was about to happen? Enough so, he might have done something to prevent Tyler's death?

Where had his head been? Why hadn't he rushed right over? Tyler was his friend, for heaven's sake. His very best friend.

Well, he had let Tyler down once. He would not do so again. He would take care of Janeen's interests here. He would personally see to it this woman, *this impostor,* did not get her hands on whatever it was she was after. He would make sure she left there just as empty-handed as she had been when she arrived—and if he did finally break down and carry her to bed, it would be to wheedle information out of her.

And no other reason.

Jenny worked until she had one of the two barrels filled to its metal rim. It was nearing eleven o'clock and she was fed up with Chad having refused to leave her side for the past several hours. The only place he had allowed her to go without him was to the privy, and he had stayed close by even then.

The only way she would finally free herself of his watchful eye would be to stop work and go to bed. Surely he did not plan to sleep with her, too.

Her insides fluttered at the thought. What if he did? How would she convince him to let her sleep alone?

"There," she said, as she stepped back and admired her handiwork. With careful planning, she had managed to pack an amazing amount of kitchen gear into that one fat barrel. "That's a good stopping point."

Chad did not say anything as he stood nearby waiting to see what she did next.

"We can start filling the other barrel first thing in the morning." She bent her shoulders back to stretch her aching muscles, but when that caused the front of her bodice to pull tight against her damp skin, she tugged at it with her fingers, as much to allow air to circulate as to prevent him from getting another eyeful. "I could sure use a nice cool bath before going on to bed. Where exactly do I go for that?"

She waited for his reply, afraid to guess. If the restroom

facilities were out in the backyard, no telling where the bathing facilities were.

Rather than answer, he gestured to the back door.

"Outside?" She blinked at the thought. She had not seriously believed that would be the case. "You people actually do your bathing outside?"

His frown was immediate. "No. Of course not. The tub is stored out on the back porch, but you bring it inside to have your bath. Do you want me to get it for you?"

She hesitated. "That depends on if you plan to allow me any privacy for a bath. There'll be no need to bother with it if I won't be afforded any privacy. I will not bathe with you staring at me like some sort of lecher."

"I suppose I could turn my back long enough for you to have a bath, if you really think you need one."

"Of course I need one," she stated, thinking that should be obvious. With no air-conditioning, she had sweated buckets that day—unlike Chad, who had not so much as formed a sheen across his brow. "But none of this turning your back business. I'll want you to leave the room entirely while I bathe. In fact, while I'm taking my bath would be a very good time for you to go get those clothes you never went to get."

"I'll get them tomorrow. For now, I'd rather just turn my back while you bathe," he restated. "That way I don't have to worry about what else you're up to."

Stubborn. "Fine, then I won't have a bath at all." There was no way she trusted this man not to turn around and take a gander once she was in the water. "I'll just use a wet washcloth for now." She walked over to the sink, pumped out a bowl full of water, picked up a sliver of what she had been told earlier was soap, snatched a small cloth off the counter, then headed toward her bedroom.

"Where do you think you're going?" he asked, his voice deep and commanding.

"To bed. To get some sleep. I suggest you do the same. I plan to get an early start tomorrow."

"Wait a minute—"

Too tired to deal with him even another minute, she whirled on him, sloshing part of the water out of the bowl. "And don't you dare suggest sleeping in the same bed with me. Or even in the same bedroom. I've had to put up with you staring at me all evening. I'm not putting up with it all night, too."

"But——" He took a menacing step in her direction, the muscles in his arms knotted.

"But nothing. Find another bedroom. There are others." She headed off again, took two steps, then whirled back, sloshing yet more water out of her bowl. She frowned at her now-soaked hem. "And don't let me catch you up later sneaking around the house, either."

"Me? Why would I be the one sneaking around?"

Not falling for the innocence in his voice, she tapped her foot, realizing that the ogling Chad was just the type to wait until she was asleep, then finish tearing the studio apart looking for whatever was hidden there. She certainly couldn't allow that.

"Forget what I just said. I've decided we are going to share the same bedroom after all. As it turns out, I don't want you out of my sight any more than you want me out of yours. Give me just enough time to wash off and change out of these filthy clothes, then you can come in and climb into your side of the bed where you will sleep without touching me."

Chad stared after her confused. He had understood her reason for wanting him to sleep in another bedroom. It would give her the opportunity to slip out during the middle of the night and resume her prowl for valuables, then steal away unnoticed with whatever she found. What he did not understand was her sudden reversal of that decision. Why did she suddenly request they share the same room? To throw him off guard?

It had certainly done that.

Or was her plan to seduce him into working *with* her instead of *against* her? Did she think by luring him into her bed, she would be able to lure him into helping her do whatever it was she had come there to do? Did she really think him that shallow?

Well, the plan would not work because, although he would gladly share her bed, if for no other reason than to keep her from prowling the house later that night, he was not about to let her seduce him. No matter how much she intrigued him.

If anything, he would use the opportunity to seduce *her*.

His eyes widened with that last thought. If it looked like her plan had anything at all to do with seduction, he would turn it around and seduce her instead.

If anyone bent to someone else's will that night, it would be her.

Not him.

Jenny hurriedly bathed, using the damp cloth and crumbly soap. She did not want Chad entering, thinking she had had enough time for a bath, before she could change into her nightie and robe—the same short nightgown and knee-length robe she'd had on when she had somehow been tossed into this century.

She had already had a look at the long, burdensome nightgowns Janeen obviously wore and was not about to try to sleep in anything so cumbersome. Still, she wasn't about to sleep in just a thin, short, cotton nightie, either. Not when Chad had already admitted finding her desirable, and not when her nightgown reached only to mid-thigh and was thin enough to see right through in a good light.

That meant sleeping in her robe, too. Still, she would rather sleep in both her nightie and robe than wear a garment that would not allow her to turn over or put her arms up around her pillow as was her habit.

"You can come in now!" she called out as soon as she had cleared the bed, checked to make sure the dagger she had taken from the studio desk was where she could get to it, then slid beneath the bed covers. Which she had done carefully, not wanting the sides to ride up and expose the camera hidden beneath.

While waiting for the door to open, she secured her robe sash with an extra knot, then turned the oil lamp flame brighter, for it had dimmed considerably since she had first entered. When there came no immediate response to her call, she worried he had gone into the studio to try again to find whatever there was to be found. Thinking to catch him in the act, she hurried to the door and flung it wide, only to find him just reaching for the knob, still fully dressed, but his hair damp on the ends as if he had just taken a sponge bath similar to hers.

His eyes widened, then narrowed when he caught sight of her attire.

"That's what you wear to bed?" A muscle at the back of his iron jaw pumped rhythmically when his gaze fell to her bare legs and feet.

Insulted by his disapproving tone, she crossed her arms and faced him squarely. She'd had enough of this man constantly judging her. Anger replaced her apprehension. "No, this is *not* what I wear to bed."

For some reason, she had a strong need to shock him. Even more than he had shocked her earlier when he had so unexpectedly touched her cheek with his palm. She would show him she could be just as intimidating as he could be, and that she did not care one bit what he thought about her.

Looking down, she reached for her sash, worked with it

a moment, then tossed the terry robe to the floor. Though the cotton nightie was modest by twentieth-century standards, it wasn't by those of the nineteenth century. It covered all the twentieth century essentials, but not nearly enough of the nineteenth century ones. And she knew that. *"This* is what I wear to bed."

Emboldened by his startled expression, she took a step in his direction, then arched her shoulders back, letting her breasts push proudly against the soft fabric. "And if wearing something like this to bed hurts your sensibilities, then too bad. *You* are the one who insisted on staying here when you have a perfectly fine home of your own to go to."

Rather than climb back under the covers where she could hide from his view as she had planned earlier, she sat down on the edge of the bed, hooked her heel on the bed support, crossed her legs at mid-thigh, then idly trailed a finger up the side of her leg, then back down again.

Seeing the muscles in his arm visibly bunch, she offered a perverse smile. For the first time since her arrival, Chad Jordan was speechless. "Does this sort of thing bother you? Then perhaps you should know that I'm the type of person to wear whatever I please, and I behave however I want in the privacy of my own bedroom. If you don't like it, then go home and sleep there."

His eyes narrowed more, until they were but two hardened slits of blue steel when she bent her toes down to flex the muscles along the back of her leg in provocative fashion.

"I wouldn't be so bold if I were you," he cautioned in a deep, meaningful voice as he reached for the buttons that held his shirt. His lithe fingers freed the tiny disks one at a time as he moved toward her, his unyielding gaze darkening more. "Not unless you're prepared to suffer the consequences. Or have you forgotten that for tonight this is my bedroom, too?"

A fresh wave of apprehension washed over her when she realized what she had done. Instead of sending him running like she had hoped, she had lured him closer. Foolishly, she had just baited the very man who might have killed her great-grandfather. And baited him well.

Time for a radical change in plan.

"Then go to bed," she said, standing abruptly as if suddenly dismissing him. Turning her back to him, she bent over to straighten the covers she had folded back earlier, letting out a frightened gasp when he grabbed her from behind and spun her to face him again. An electric jolt shot through her when he held her firmly in his grasp, her body only inches from his.

"That's exactly what I plan to do," he informed her, his voice deep and sultry as one hand went around her back and the other to her breast, where he sent yet another electric charge through her system. Staring intently, he bent to kiss her parted mouth with a fervor that frightened as well as amazed her. Desperately, she tried to wriggle out of his grasp, but the arm holding her in place was far too strong.

Seven

Unable to break her mouth free of Chad's, Jenny shoved a hand between them to try to push him away, startled to find her palm flattened against warm, taut skin instead of cloth. He already had his shirt pulled open and the hem tugged out of his trousers. How'd he do that so quickly?

Her heart hammered wildly while she tried to figure out what to do to stop him from taking this fit of passion any further. She was extremely aware of her vulnerable state. She was alone in a strange bedroom with a powerful, handsome man while she wore only a thin nightgown with nothing underneath and he was already half out of his shirt.

Screaming would not alert the neighbors since the nearest house was half a block away and the insects outside made enough noise to cover even a small sonic boom. And there would be no calling 911. Heck, she had seen no telephones in Black Rock at all.

This was not good.

She would have to save her own skin.

Using all her might, she pressed both hands against his hard chest and shoved as hard as she could, this time breaking his grasp easily. Too easily. Not expecting it, she lost balance and fell backward onto the bed, her gown rising precariously high.

With eyes gone black with emotion, Chad tugged out of his shirt, revealing a masterpiece of muscles and suntanned skin as he bent to yank off his boots with two hard, fast jerks. Watching the rippling movements beneath his sleek, tanned skin, she could not help noting that if he weren't possibly a killer, she would easily be aroused by him. His body was perfection plus, as was his strong, handsome face.

But the odd moment of fascination proved short-lived when he reached for the buttons of his trousers and unfastened them with several quick, agile movements.

"What do you think you are doing?" Her gaze went immediately to the springy dark hair trailing down his flat sun-browned stomach into the opening of his trousers, dipping beneath the stark white fabric of his underdrawers. Pushing against the mattress with her arms, she started scooting away from him, only to realize that was pointless. There was no real chance for escape. The windows were partly open but had screens, and the door was too far away. He would catch her before she had cleared the bed. And the dagger she'd hidden behind the dresser was nearly as far in the opposite direction, though she was not all that sure she could use it against him even if she had it in her hands.

Her only hope was to reason with him.

So why wouldn't her tongue cooperate? Why was she suddenly unable to utter a sound? Had he truly struck her speechless?

"I'm doing exactly what you suggested," he answered in such a low, husky voice, it sent a whole new kind of shivers through her. These not all that unpleasant, but just as frightening. "I'm getting ready for bed."

Gazing into her unblinking eyes, he slid his thumbs beneath the waistbands of both his trousers and drawers, slowly nudging the material downward until the trail of hair fanned back out into a thick, dark patch against stark white skin. Mesmerized, despite her fear, she watched as he paused a moment, then gave the material another push.

His desire sprang forth, letting her know she had fully aroused him with her shameful behavior. She gasped as his clothing hit the floor. She had never seen a man more magnificent. Still, she was not about to let him take her.

She looked again at the door. How'd it get so far away?

"This is what *I* wear to bed," he said, taunting her with words similar to her own as he crawled onto the bed with her. He straddled her with his strong, muscular legs and arms. "Does it bother you that I am also the type of person to do whatever I please in the privacy of my own bedroom?"

She looked at him again, riveting her gaze to his, and nodded. For the life of her, the words she so desperately wanted to speak refused to burst past the constriction in her throat.

How had her plan to run him off for the night backfired so completely? Obviously this man was far better at intimidating than being intimidated. Why hadn't she taken that possibility into consideration?

Gulping, she tried to catch her short, shallow breathing up with her racing heartbeat, but the attempt was useless.

"So, beautiful lady, are we about to share more than just this bed?" he asked, dipping his head to tug lightly on her lower lip with his teeth. His thick hair fell forward to tickle her cheek.

She gasped but still could not find the sanity needed to answer. This simply could not be happening. But then again, she had thought the same thing about being tossed into a different time period, and look where she had ended up!

"What about sharing a few secrets, too?" He lowered his body to hers, covering her with a heat so provocative and profound, she found concentrating on his next words almost impossible. Already her body ached with a rebellious need, one that was not all that familiar to her.

True, she was not a virgin, but in what experience she had, she had never felt anything so overwhelming.

"Why don't you tell me the real reason you are here?" He ducked lower to nip lightly at her neck at the same time he slid his hand down to cup her breast where his thumb played lightly with the sensitive tip. A shaft of white-hot need shot through her, startling her with a realization somewhere deep inside her that she wanted Chad. Wanted him in a way she shouldn't—not when it was possible he had killed her great-grandfather.

Still, the desire he had created inside her was there, growing with each tiny stroke of his thumb and each glitter of his translucent blue eyes.

Her thoughts took a new turn.

What if she allowed him to make love to her? It was not as if she loved him or would be making any sort of lifetime commitment. True, she had never before made love to a man simply for the sake of making love, but there was always that first time. And she had so much tension and so many emotions inside her needing release. It would be good to rid herself of them. She would be able to think clearer and, in the process, it might soothe some of Chad's hostility.

Having convinced her mind what her body already knew it wanted, she lifted her hands and ran them up the length of his strong, corded arms until her fingers met and locked behind the solid muscles of his neck. Never had she touched a man so virile. So masculine. It aroused her more.

Her touch must have also set him over the edge, for after one deep moan, he suddenly quit his masterful play on the outside of her gown. Eagerly, he lifted his body enough to jerk her gown up out of his way, then lowered himself again, flattening hot skin against hot skin.

While he kissed her hungrily, his hand returned to bring her more sensual pleasure, only this time without the disadvantage of a thin covering of cottony material. Never having been quite this aroused by a man, for in truth her experience was rather limited, she moaned at the exquisite sensations developing inside her as he manipulated the hardened tip between his fingers and thumb. All the while he worked this mastery on her, she purposefully ignored the tiny little voice that niggled at her conscience."

This was not a man she should make love to.

But something inside her refused to listen. She was too tempted to find out what other pleasures Chad could give her, for he definitely knew what it took to arouse a woman.

Giving in to her own body's desires, she writhed beneath his masterful touch while his hand manipulated her breast with a skill that had to have come from years of practice and the kiss deepened into something so sensual it melted her insides. Her eyes drifted closed of their own accord, allowing her to enjoy every tiny sensation as his tongue dipped lightly to stroke the sensitive areas of her mouth. Never had she been kissed so expertly.

Immersed in a swirling need more powerful than any she'd ever known, she arched her back to give him easier access to the areas that interested him most, areas in which no other man had evoked that much sensation before.

Still, the tiny voice nagged at her.

Unable to free herself of that tiny inkling of guilt and shame, she broke her mouth away, expecting to bring this madness to an end. Before the unthinkable happened. But a scant second after his mouth left hers, his warm, pliant lips found their way to the same throbbing breast he had teased so deftly with his hand.

Weak with the sizzling sensations that shot through her as he suckled hungrily on that same breast, she was barely able to moan the word stop. But with no conviction behind the word, and losing any desire to back the command with action, she arched higher still, allowing him to taunt the other breast at the same time he suckled this one into a frenzied need for more. With him centered on top of her, her knees came up, almost as if commanding themselves, allowing her to wrap her legs around his back so she could better feel each powerful movement of his body atop hers.

Hands she had originally planned to use to push them

apart now groped and pulled at his shoulders, trying to break the hungry torment long enough for him to satisfy her needs. She needed him inside her.

But he refused to bring the blissful torture to an end. Instead, he moved his body rhythmically against her while continuing to manipulate both breasts, prompting her to match his rhythm with one of her own. He waited until she had pressed her head back into the soft mattress, teeth buried into the sensitive flesh of her lower lip, then asked again, "Why are you here?"

It was not a question she could answer. She herself had no idea why she was there, unless it was to solve her great-grandfather's murder. It was the only explanation that made sense. "To help."

"To help who?" Although he remained controlled enough to ask his questions, his voice ran ragged and his breath came in short, rapid gasps.

"To help the sheriff," she answered, frowning. Why did he bother with that *now?* Why couldn't his questions wait until after? "To help him find out who murdered Tyler."

"Help him how? There's no need to keep secrets from me. Tell me why you're here." He continued to work his magic over her body, continued moving rhythmically as his fingers tugged and twisted her throbbing nipples. "Tell me what you know."

Those words fell over Jenny like a cold splash of water. All he wanted was to find out what she knew about the murder. What she knew about *him.* She'd been right about him all along. He *was* involved in the murder. Why else would he be asking her such questions? And in his attempt to get information, he was using her own body against her.

Her stomach coiled to realize that she had become so physically exhausted, and so in need of releasing some of her caged emotions, that until a few seconds ago, she had let him do just that.

Mortified by her own foolish behavior, she finally gathered the strength needed to push him to one side. Her body still throbbed with unfulfilled passion when she rolled off the bed, pulling the gown back down when she did.

Refusing to look at him, not wanting to be reminded of just how far she had allowed him to carry his subterfuge, she snatched her robe off the floor, stuffed her arms inside, and tied it securely in place. With that done, she reached for his clothes and tossed them in the general direction of his ragged breathing.

"Here. Get dressed. I've changed my mind about stopping to rest for the night. I've had a renewed burst of energy." *Putting it mildly.* "I'm going back into the kitchen to work a little longer. Of course, you're free to stay right here and catch some sleep if you want," she offered, knowing he would never do that for fear she would find whatever was hidden in that house before he did. He still thought of her as the impostor who had stumbled in the way and learned things she shouldn't.

"Well, I'm not tired, if you're not," he said, reacting just as stubbornly as expected.

She moaned silently. This all was like a badly written B-movie. First, she had made a wish out loud, one she and her grandmother both had uttered many, many times before her grandmother's death and with no result—but now look at her situation. Not only was she suddenly cast back in time to the very day her great-grandfather was murdered, but the man who very well might have killed him suspected *her* of equally sinister motives. Because of that, he refused to leave her alone long enough let her get on with what she needed to do to prove him—or whoever—guilty so she could see an arrest made and return to her own time.

She thought about her poor cat, by now surely quite ticked because his supper dish hadn't been replenished. Then she thought of the window she had left open, and of her neighbor's beautiful new potted plants, probably all slaw by now. Well, at least she could trust that same neighbor

to feed her cat once she realized her gone—if for no other
reason than to save the neighborhood from ruin, for when
Stillshot's energy came, it came in destructive bursts.

She moaned again. His last rampage had cost her nearly
two hundred dollars in plants and broken pottery.

With legs trembling from the force of emotions still reel-
ing inside her, Jenny hurried on out of the room, not once
looking back at Chad. But within minutes, he had joined
her, redressed and immediately set out helping her fill the
second barrel with kitchen items.

No words were spoken while they systematically worked
at packing away a set of gold-rimmed china and Janeen's
better drinking glasses. They were both too lost to their
thoughts to bother with conversation.

Angry with herself for what she had allowed to happen,
and with Chad for having found a weakness she had not
known existed until now, Jenny worked on pure adrenaline
for the next several hours. Even after they had filled the
second barrel and had it ready to cap, she continued to
work by wiping out the cabinets and drawers they had emp-
tied and sorting some of the remaining items into more
logical groups.

It was nearly three o'clock before the adrenaline wore
off, leaving her suddenly too exhausted to think. Needing
rest to continue, and still irritated that she had found no
opportunity to do the one thing she had wanted to do most,
search her great-grandfather's studio for more clues, she did
not bother announcing her intentions to quit for a while to
Chad, who continued to work nearby.

When she could go no further, she simply laid down her
rag, walked back to the bedroom, and crawled on top of
the rumpled bed with her robe still on and her back to the
center of the bed, glad when Chad did the same. Again,

neither spoke, and within minutes she heard Chad's heavy, even breathing.

Too tired to get up and make a decent search of the studio while he slept, she decided she would doze long enough to gain her senses back, then sneak off to see what she could find. But the moment she closed her eyes, she fell instantly into a deep, long sleep.

When she awoke hours later, it felt like coming out of heavy sedation. The morning light hurt her eyes enough to keep her from opening them right away and her thoughts proved slow to collect. When they finally did, her first thought was how totally bizarre her night's dream had been. Imagine, being tossed back in time like that.

Yawning, she rubbed her cheeks and eyes to stimulate the blood flow to her face, but when her hands fell away and she caught her first look at the bedroom around her, her heart froze in mid-beat.

It was no dream. She really had wished herself back to her great-grandfather's time. The memory of all that had happened since that wish came to her in a mad rush. Recalling Chad, his determination to accuse her, and her near seduction the night before, she sat bolt upright. Still putting her thoughts together, she glared first at the blanket covering her, then at the empty half of the bed.

Chad was gone.

Shoving her feet into her canvas shoes, she hurried into the other part of the house, expecting to find him in the studio tearing the place apart. Surprised, she instead found him sitting at the kitchen table, staring intently at a metal coffeepot on the stove. *Waiting for his first cup of the day, no doubt.*

Knowing how vital coffee was to some people, Jenny backed out of the kitchen, unnoticed. Safe again from his sight, she returned to the bedroom to dress. Working quickly, she donned yet another of her great-grandmother's dresses, this one pink with elbow-length sleeves, then hurriedly brushed her long hair and tucked it up again.

With no makeup to worry about, she pinched her cheeks for color, made sure the camera was still hidden from view by carefully making the bed, then returned to the kitchen just as Chad filled two cups with coffee.

"I heard you up so I poured you a cup," he said in way of explanation as he set one of the steaming cups in front of her. He eyed the scoop-necked dress she wore with a somber expression but said nothing to reveal his grim thoughts as he slid into the chair across the table from hers.

Never having been much of a coffee drinker, Jenny sat forward while she blew across the surface several times, then took a tiny sip of brew that was so strong it set her back in her chair with a jolt. By the time she drank half a cup, she was wide-awake. By the time she finished the entire cup she was wired for a full day of work, but decided to wait until he had finished his second cup before starting.

So far, no hostile words had been spoken that morning, which gave little reason to hurry away from the table. In fact, other than the mention of the coffee, no words were spoken at all. It was as if a truce had been called. Just as willing to put off the next round of arguments as he seemed to be, she watched quietly while he held a mug cupped in his two strong hands and took another long drink.

Jenny tried not to remember the way those hands felt caressing her, or the way his mouth felt kissing her. She did not want to be attracted to this man. Did not want to be physically drawn in any way to the very person who might have murdered her great-grandfather. Even if he turned out to be innocent, it was not a smart idea to be tempted by him. Not when she would be leaving just as soon as she had completed her mission.

Without looking up from his cup, though obviously aware he had her attention, Chad broke the silence first. "I found four eggs and some more bread and thought about cooking a little breakfast for us but then remembered you would probably be having your breakfast with the sheriff, since you say you're here to help him."

Giving her no time to respond, he pointed to what looked like an upright wooden box with an extra-thick door. It wasn't too much larger than her microwave, and with its rounded edges, reminded her of a tiny, stand-up coffin. "There is some cheese and a little milk in there, too, but not much."

Jenny's stomach literally growled at the thought of real food. Not having worked in that area of the kitchen yet, she hadn't realized the wooden box held food. "You're right, I *am* here to help the sheriff in any way I can, but I don't plan to have breakfast with him. I don't have time for that." She stood, already headed across the room. "Why don't I make an omelet out of those eggs."

"Omelet?" He watched her, his solemn expression lifting. He raked his hands through his long hair, which fell perfectly back in place. "You know how to make omelets?" He sounded as if he hadn't expected her to be quite that domestic. "Need any help?"

The offer to help surprised her. As much because of his earlier treatment of her as because of the fact he was from the 1890's. Did men from the 1890's really offer to help women cook? She had thought them too macho to do "women's work." Why, even some of the men from her own time period were still too macho, or in truth too lazy, to do women's work.

"No, I don't need any help," she answered honestly, having cooked enough over a campfire while out on nature shoots to make preparing something on an old iron wood-stove that was already hot enough to brew coffee a cinch. She quickly dug a heavy skillet out of the barrel, glad it was near the top.

Within minutes she had browned five fat slices of bread in the skillet, and ate one while she cooked the eggs to fluffy perfection using the oven closest to the fire Chad built to heat the coffee. By the time the sheriff stopped by to escort her to a local restaurant, they were half finished eating and in a much better mood than the night before.

"But I thought you were goin' to have breakfast with me," Sheriff Mack said, frowning to find them already eating. He stared pointedly at their plates after he placed a large wooden box he carried on the floor.

"Sorry." She hoped to make up for disappointing him by offering one of her sweetest smiles. "But I didn't want to have to stop work long enough to go somewhere else to eat." She gestured to the area of the kitchen where they had worked until the wee hours of the morning. "As you can see, we got a lot done last night and hope to get a lot more done today. So far, we've made great headway here and don't want to lose our momentum."

Chad neither agreed nor argued with that. He merely sat watching the sheriff, his solemn expression returned.

"Maybe by noontime you two will be ready for a little break," he said, again hopeful as he pushed his hat back and surveyed their work. "They have a real fine meatloaf on Thursdays over at the Stover House. I'll stop back by and see if you're not hungry again by then. Chad can join us, too, if he likes."

Chad did not respond. He merely continued to stare at the sheriff, as if gauging him somehow.

The sheriff shifted his weight. "I was plannin' on havin' him come with us this morning, too. Unless he would rather have used the time goin' home to change clothes and have a shave. But I see he's already shaved."

Chad ran a hand over the smooth lines of his lean jaw, but gave no mention of where he had located a razor. Or a hairbrush, which he had also obviously found, too, for his dark mane lay in soft, neat waves swept away from his face. Except for his rumpled clothing, he looked all set for a new day.

More so than the sheriff did, with a day's stubble on his receding chin and his thinning hair tousled beneath his hat.

Jenny noted how intently the two men scrutinized each other. Were they silently battling over her? Or were there deeper problems between them? They had seemed cordial enough to each other the afternoon before. What had happened since then to cause such friction? Was it because the sheriff had refused to think ill of her? So much so, he let her stay in the house, and was even willing to provide her with a hot meal?

Until one of the two voiced the problem aloud, there was no way for her to know. Should she encourage an argument so she could get a better handle on was going on here? Or should she follow her gut instinct and stay out of it?

Finally, the sheriff twitched his flat nose and pulled his gaze away from Chad's. A feat she knew from experience was not easily done.

"I'll be by for you two shortly after noon. We can go have us some of that meatloaf then."

"We'll see" was all Jenny would say, not about to commit so much of her time to doing something as frivolous as eating. Now that she'd had her fill of omelet and toast, food held no interest again. All she wanted was a chance to get back into that studio—*alone.*

If only Chad would leave. Maybe he would do what the sheriff suggested and go change clothes, since he still had on the same ones he had worn the day before. She'd certainly suggested it again and again.

Just as anxious for Sheriff Mack to be on his way as she was for Chad to be gone, she started toward the door. "But for now I guess we really should get back to work here. Thank you for bringing us another empty box."

"Well, I had it sittin' in the back room doin' me no good." The sheriff followed reluctantly, but stopped just as he was about to step back through the same door he had left open upon entering.

He turned to look at Chad again. "Oh, when I wired Mrs. Dykes back, tellin' her you'd take care of everything for her, I didn't bother mentionin' that the bank had been robbed. I changed my mind. Thought I'd give her a few days to digest the fact her husband's been killed before hitting her with the fact their savings is gone."

Chad shrugged, unconcerned when finally he spoke. "There'll be no need to tell her about the bank robbery at all. I've already decided to take care of the funeral costs and the shipping charges myself."

The sheriff arched a skinny eyebrow, as if not quite believing Chad's generosity. "Oh, that's right. You didn't have any money in our bank when it was robbed. You're still sittin' pretty in this town."

Jenny detected a hint of resentment in Sheriff Mack's voice. Or was it suspicion? Could Chad also be involved in the robbery? Evidently the sheriff thought so.

"I'm doing well enough," Chad agreed.

"But are you doin' so well that you're sure you want to take care of those costs yourself? It's not as if you couldn't sell something of Tyler's to pay for everything you'll owe. Maybe even sell Champ. That horse would sure bring a pretty penny, and I know for a fact that Lance Maze has been eyein' that animal for over a year now."

"I'm not selling Champ." Chad finally stood and leaned indolently against the table's edge, his muscular arms crossed. "Not unless Janeen instructs me to do so."

"Well, if you change your mind, or if part of what Mrs. Dykes tells you to do is sell Tyler's horse, just keep Lance in mind. He'd pay a fair price. And he'd pay in cash."

Chad waited until the sheriff had strode across the street while headed back toward the jail before muttering, "It'll be a cold day in hell before I'd sell Lance Maze that horse."

Jenny looked at him, surprised by the hostility in his voice. She remembered from an earlier conversation with the sheriff that Lance Maze was the heroic banker who, along with the sheriff, had taken on the entire Craig gang and had lived to tell about it. Why did Chad resent the town hero? Jealous, perhaps? Or did this Lance Maze have something on him? "Bad blood between you two?"

He cut her an angry look, then bent and took his last gulp of coffee. "Maze is the whole reason I never put my money in that bank." He set the cup back down with a clack, then looked out the window again. "I guess I should thank him for that, though. Had we been more prone to see matters eye to eye, I wouldn't be one of the few people in this town who didn't lose money in that robbery."

She studied Chad's rigid stance. Did the man have problems getting along with everyone? Evidently. "Were you serious when you said you planned to take care of Tyler's funeral expenses and the shipping costs to send Janeen's things to her?" She could not imagine him being quite that noble. Not this man who had not performed one redeeming act in all her time there. Perhaps guilt was driving him to help. Or, could it be he hoped to throw suspicion off himself by proving just how true a friend he really was?

"Yes, I was serious. I can afford it. Janeen can't." Clearly it wasn't something he wanted to talk about. He was probably afraid she would question his motive before he had one quite figured out. Instead, he reached for the empty box the sheriff brought and set it on the table. It was a little over a yard long and both two feet wide and tall. "I won't take long to fill this thing. After that, we'll have to go find more boxes and crates. Either that or go buy the lumber needed to build our own."

Jenny started wrapping empty jars in the last of the bed sheets and tucking them inside. "Well, since you are the one with all the money, and know where to go and what to buy, I think you're the obvious choice for that."

Her heart raced with the thought of being alone while he left for more packing supplies.

"Why does that suggestion not surprise me?" He walked over to hand her more empty jars, his strong hands gripping them by the mouths in fours. "We'll go just as soon as we've finished filling this one."

"We?" Her stomach knotted as apprehension crept back in. "Why we? Why should we both go?"

"Because I don't trust you to be here alone," he said honestly. "No telling what would disappear while I was gone."

She tapped her foot, insulted. "Do you really think I'm the type who could steal from the dead?"

"Liars are often thieves."

She bristled. "Then you can search me and my things when you return."

"If you are still here."

"And where would I go? You said yourself the only way out of this town is to hire a buggy."

"Or ride over to Perry on one of the freight wagons. Or hitch a ride with someone traveling through."

"Still, you'd be able to catch up with me. How far could I get in the short time you'll be gone?

He considered that a moment. "How do I know you don't have a horse stashed out somewhere?"

She sighed. "If I did, it'd be a mighty hungry horse by now, don't you think? I've hardly left this house in nearly twenty-four hours."

"You could be planning to steal Champ."

"Then take the gear I'd need with you or go hide it where I can't find it."

Still eyeing her carefully, he stroked the strong lines of his jaw with his hand, then finally dropped it to his side, his decision reluctantly made. "Just remember, I *will* be coming right back. And the moment I return, I *will* be searching you, your things, and every space that looks large enough to hide anything."

"Fine," she said, making a mental note to pull that camera out from under the bed. She would have a hard time explaining why it was hidden. She also needed to put the stolen dagger way up between the mattresses so it could do her more good if needed to protect herself at night.

If he found those items, he would think she planned to steal them and would have immediate reason to have her expelled. He would decide he had proved his theory she was a thief. "You do that. Search all you want when you get back." Meanwhile, she would take advantage of the chance to return to the studio and resume her search. Perhaps by the time he returned, she would have whatever the sheriff needed to make an arrest.

Chad stared at her a moment longer, then walked just inside the hall, toward the closed door that led to the very studio she so longed to search.

"Where are you going?" she asked, her heart pounding with the fear he had somehow read her thoughts and planned to be the one to search the room first.

"To get my hat. I'll be back as soon as I can. It shouldn't take long to do what I need."

She followed him into the studio, which looked even messier than she remembered, although no one could have gone in there while they slept, not without having broken a window or splintering the door.

"While you're gone, see if you can get hold of some old newspapers or something else to use for packing. We are about out of towels and sheets. And you might go ahead and get those clean clothes you never went after last night."

"The clothes can wait." He snatched his hat off the wall peg where he had left it, then headed back the way he had come. "I'll be right back."

Obviously Chad had no intention of leaving her there

inside the studio. Instead of unbolting the side door and exiting the house that direction, he escorted her back into the kitchen and waited until she had resumed packing before using the back door.

Within minutes, Jenny was headed right back into Tyler's studio to resume her search.

Eight

Jenny had no time to continue being orderly in her search for evidence. Instead, she went ripping through what few places the two men had missed with trembling, fumbling hands.

There had to be something there the prowlers had overlooked. Something to help identify the man who had killed her great-grandfather—other than that one vague photograph she had developed. Something Chad clearly did not want her to find.

He hadn't fooled her for one minute with that bit about worrying she would steal something of Tyler's while he was gone. No, the only reason he did not want to leave her there alone was because he worried she would find whatever clues were still hidden inside that house. He knew if she found them, she would then turn them over to the sheriff. With positive proof, the sheriff could make his arrest. In a time when men were still hanged for murder, it was not something he would want done.

A tiny disturbance surfaced inside her after that last thought, but she forced herself to ignore it. She refused to picture Chad swinging from the end of a rope. Or any man.

For she still wasn't certain *who* was responsible.

Which is why she continued her search.

With no idea yet what she looked for, but certain something more incriminating than that one dim photograph had to be hidden there somewhere, she kept an eye turned to the windows while she hurriedly sifted through the mess.

She had barely made a dent in the area she had hoped to search when she glanced outside and saw Chad already on his way across the street.

Disappointed but hoping since he was empty-handed and only fifteen minutes had passed that he was just stopping in long enough to check on her, she hurried back to the kitchen. She quickly took platters out of a cabinet they had yet to pack and stacked them on the counter, as if getting them ready to pack.

"For someone moving so fast, you sure didn't get much done while I was gone," Chad said, tossing his hat aside as he entered the back door. He pointed to the still half-empty box.

Wanting him to think he had surprised her, she tossed her hand against her throat and gasped before glancing toward the box he indicated. "Oh, that? I was tired. I took a short break."

"But you'd just started," he pointed out.

"Still, I was tired. I'm having a hard time finding enough energy to do anything this morning."

"You didn't seem to be having any problem yanking those platters out of that cabinet with lightning speed."

He had her there. But she refused to admit it. "Is there a point to this conversation?" she asked. "Or did you just stop back by to start another disagreement?"

Chad let out an annoyed breath and glanced into the hall, toward the studio door. Finding it still closed, he lifted a questioning eyebrow, but didn't say anything. Instead, he walked closer to where she stood, facing her. A determined look glittered from his huge, lash-fringed, pale-blue eyes. "Lift up your arms," he commanded.

"What?"

"I said, lift your arms. I didn't stop back here for something. I'm back for good, and ready to search you."

"You aren't serious," she argued, though in her gut, she knew he was. She glowered furiously. "You don't really intend to search me for stolen items."

"Guess again, stranger," he drawled, then motioned his hands, indicating she had yet to lift her arms as ordered.

Boiling inside, as angry with herself for having suggested something so foolish as she was with him for calling her on it, she did as told. Although she could not lift her arms high over her head because the dress was not cut to allow that freedom, she stretched them out level with her shoulders.

Locking his gaze with hers, he proceeded to move his hands over her clothing in search of unfamiliar objects.

Starting at her waist, he ran his palms over the pink material, curling his fingers to fit the changing shape of her body. Finding nothing tucked away there, he moved his hands higher, over her rib cage, then slid around to roam the gentle slope of her back. She glowered at him, a warning not to bring those exploring hands around to the front, and decided she had at least won that battle when he suddenly dropped them down to her hips. There, he felt through the skirts for items she might have stuffed inside those oversize underdrawers she was forced to wear.

Still finding nothing, he knelt and felt of her canvas shoes. "Lift your skirts."

"What?"

"You heard me." He arched an eyebrow when he glanced up at her. "It's not like I'm likely to catch sight of anything I haven't already seen."

Mortified by that none-too-subtle reminder of what had happened the night before, and not wanting to discuss how skillfully she had been manipulated, she snatched her skirts high enough to allow him a better feel of the baggy legs of her underdrawers. She gasped when his hands slid higher and felt along the material caressing her inner thighs.

Fighting a strong desire to offer a well-placed kick, aware

she had as much as given him permission for this thorough
search, she pressed her mouth together to keep from uttering
a sound while his fingers prowled one of the few areas he
had neglected the night before. She would not give him the
satisfaction of knowing just how strongly his actions affected her. She swallowed to ease the constriction in her
throat when suddenly he stood, facing her again.

"Are you finished yet?" she said through clenched teeth
as she dropped her skirts back into place. Why was he doing
this? He knew she wasn't a thief. He had only accused her
of that so he would have a logical reason not to leave her
alone in that house, knowing she would search for more
evidence.

Her eyes widened. Maybe *that* was what he thought he
would find on her. The evidence he so longed to unearth
himself. Did he really think she would be foolish enough
to hide that on her body? Did he take her for an idiot?

"Not quite."

She blinked at that response, not certain if it was in answer to her unspoken question, or the spoken one.

Gauging her uncertainty, his blue gaze probed hers a moment longer, then sank to her shoulders while he felt the
fabric there, but lifted again to watch her face when he next
explored the area between her breasts. His eyes remained
locked with hers while he then fanned his hands outward,
pausing with her breasts flattened against his palms, before
finally stepping back.

"Well, if you have anything on you, it's hidden in places
I didn't find."

She couldn't imagine where that would be. He had just
reacquainted himself with almost every part of her body—
and then some.

"Are you satisfied now? Or do you want me to take my
clothes off so you can shake them?" She shot him a ven-
omous look, letting him know it was not an offer he should
accept.

Chad's eyebrows lifted in thought while his gaze drifted downward again, causing her a moment of alarm. Surely he understood she had said that to be sarcastic. She had already discovered the effect he had on her and had no intention of taking off even one stitch of clothing.

"No, that won't be necessary," he finally answered. "But I'd like to check your belongings now."

Jenny's eyebrows quirked, surprised to note the husky tremor in his voice. Had he been physically affected by his own search?

As if suddenly he needed more breathing space, he stepped away from her. "Where are they?

Jenny pointed in the general direction of the bedroom, glad now she had thought to gather some of Janeen's clothes and stuff them into an empty valise. Her pulses still raced from his extremely thorough search of her as she followed him down the hall and into the bedroom they had shared the previous night.

It wasn't until inside that she realized she had forgotten to shove the dagger deep between the mattresses and to take the camera out from under the bed. She had planned to just set it aside as if it awaited being packed.

Remembering he planned to search any place she might have hidden something, her heart slammed with such force against the constricted walls of her chest, it made her gasp for her next breath. The dagger she could explain, and explain honestly. She wanted protection. But how would she explain having hidden a camera under a bed without looking like the thief he claimed her to be? Would he then use that to have her evicted from her great-grandfather's house?

Panic filled her. How would she return to her own time if she no longer had access to the camera?

"Where are your things?" Chad asked after looking first at Tyler's belongings scattered across the top of a small dresser, then at the valise she had set on the floor beside a chair.

"Right there." She pointed to the valise, open with clothes spilling out. How could he possibly miss something so obvious? "The bag still on the floor."

"That's yours?" He lifted an eyebrow. "That looks exactly like one of Tyler's bags."

Jenny sucked a quick breath. She hadn't expected Chad to recognize it. "Well, then *there's* proof I really am Tyler's sister. We have bags exactly alike. We bought them at the same store during on of his trips home."

His mouth flattened as he cast a doubtful gaze in her direction. "If anything, that's pure coincidence." He knelt, his trousers stretching taut over well-muscled legs while he stuck a hand into the bag and felt around. He didn't bother taking the clothing out, and looked only mildly satisfied when he stood again.

"Since I don't take you for a fool, I doubt seriously you would put anything you hoped to steal in the very room you'd be sleeping in. I'll wait until we've packed more things away, then search the remaining areas of the house. Just like I'll search *you* again before you leave here."

Jenny opened her mouth to protest, but decided against starting another argument, fearing it might delay him from leaving the room.

She glanced at the bottom of the bed. The way things were going, she halfway expected to see the camera slide out into the open and perform a little tap dance.

"You said you're back here to stay. Where are the packing crates you went after? Didn't you find any?" she asked, already headed for the door. With any luck he would follow her into the kitchen where she had nothing to hide. "How are we going to finish the work without more crates or boxes?"

"The mercantile only had a couple of empty crates, so I'll have to build some. The lumber, nails, saw, and hammer I'll need should arrive in a few hours, along with a large barrel of sawdust from the mill."

"Sawdust?"

"To pack around the breakable items. Pat, over at Hinze's Mercantile, had only one small stack of old newspapers in the back, so I had to think of something else. Pat did say he would have his boy, Stobie, carry what newspapers and crates he did have over to the lumberyard in time to be delivered with the rest of the materials I need. He also said he'd stop back by the telegraph office for me, and see if I had any messages waiting. I still haven't heard back from Janeen again, or from two of the liveries I wired."

Jenny tried not to let it bother her that he had thought to check for messages. If Janeen wired him the truth, she would deal with that then. For now, she had enough to concern her.

With that thought, she resumed filling the box. Within minutes it was ready to have the lid nailed in place.

"So, what do we do until the lumber arrives?" she asked, wishing he would leave again, perhaps to hurry his order along.

He shrugged. "The studio really needs to be straightened up before the packing gets underway. I guess we could start tidying all the mess you claim those two mystery men made."

Jenny bristled at yet another insinuation she had lied when, except for details directly related to her identity and those related to the photo she'd developed, she had tried to be as honest as possible. But rather than argue with him when she could offer no proof, she followed him willingly into the room. While he took time to open a few windows, she started right to work, alert to the continued possibility of evidence while she sorted and straightened.

With Jenny now the watchful one, making sure Chad didn't slip something into *his* pockets or perhaps out an open window, she worked at one desk while he worked at the other.

As soon as they finished bringing order to the two desks,

both inside and out, they started on the items scattered across the floor nearby, careful not to cut their hands on the tiny bits of splintered glass from a drinking set and photo frames that had been knocked to the floor and broken.

While stacking photographs in neat piles according to size and content, she came across one of Chad and a woman who looked to be just a little older, standing side by side in front of a large, wooden building with the words "Jordan Feed and Tack" painted across the top in fancy bold letters.

She studied it a moment, wondering about the woman, who was *pretty* but not beautiful, something Jenny easily related to.

She knew the woman in the photo could not be his wife because Beth Donner had indicated it had been a while since his marriage, and this photograph did not look all that old, maybe five to eight years. Beth had also indicated Chad had no desire to remarry, so it couldn't be a second wife. That also ruled out a fiancé. Was the woman perhaps his sister? She bent closer, squinting for detail. No, they looked nothing alike.

So what was their relationship?

Curious, she carried the photo over to where Chad sat on the floor, repairing a photograph frame. "Here's one with you in it." She held it down so he could see it, then knelt so she could see him.

Chad tilted his head to get a better look, then smiled. It was the first genuine smile Jenny had seen from him. She sucked in an astonished breath, for he had a stunning smile, the sort where dimples lengthened into groups of long, curved indentations down both cheeks. Not at all like the cold, sardonic smiles he had offered until now—though even those had an effect on her.

"That's from the day I opened my store. Hard to believe it was taken nearly eight years ago," he told her, setting aside the broken frame to give the photo his full attention.

"Tyler was so happy for me, he took at least a half-dozen photographs before I'd even opened the door."

Reaching out to take the photograph, his voice carried the fondness that came with cherished memories. "Marge didn't want to be in the photographs, but Janeen insisted. She told her that as my office clerk, she would be the one doing the most work, and therefore deserved to be in the first-day photographs, too. But Marge didn't like the dress she had on that morning, plus she's not one with an easy smile. It took some real finagling to get her to stand there and look pleasant long enough to get the pictures Tyler wanted."

"So Marge works for you?" Jenny asked, not certain if she was more pleased to find out the woman in the picture was just an employee, or to see the candid smile lifting Chad's handsome face—both then and now. "She's not your sweetheart?"

"Marge?" He chuckled at the thought. It was a deep, pleasant sound that came from well inside his throat. "Believe me, there's nothing sweet about Marge Manning. Especially if anyone proves foolish enough to misplace an invoice."

Still smiling, he studied the image a moment longer, then stretched to place the photograph on top of the nearby desk in an area where no other photographs lay.

Aware he had singled it out to keep, and not caring in the least, Jenny resumed gathering the tossed and torn photographs, keeping Chad in a light mood by commenting on some of them. With the tension fading, Chad told her stories about Tyler she hadn't heard; funny as well as sad.

Pleased to be learning so many new things about a man she had admired all her life, making him seem all the more real to her, Jenny encouraged Chad's tales. She laughed right along with him at some of her great-grandfather's antics, too enthralled to notice the growing heat in the house.

The things her great-grandfather did to get a photograph.

4 BESTSELLING HISTORICAL ROMANCES BY YOUR FAVORITE AUTHORS CAN BE YOURS, FREE!

Kensington Choice, our newest book club now brings you historical romances by your favorite bestselling authors including Janelle Taylor, Shannon Drake, Rosanne Bittner, Jo Beverley, and Georgina Gentry, just to name a few! Each book is filled with passion, adventure and the excitement of bygone times!

To introduce you to this great new club which is part of Zebra Home Subscription Service, we'd like to send you your first 4 bestselling historical romances, absolutely free! And once you get these 4 free books to savor at home, we'll rush you the next 4 brand-new books at the lowest prices available, as soon as they are published.

The way the club works is that after your initial FREE shipment, you will get our 4 newest bestselling historical romances delivered to your doorstep each month at the preferred subscriber's rate of only $4.20 per book, a savings of up to $7.16 per month (since these titles sell in bookstores for $4.99-$5.99)! All books are sent on a 10-day free examination basis and there is no minimum number of books to buy. (A postage and handling charge of $1.50 is added to each shipment.) Plus as a regular subscriber, you'll receive our FREE monthly newsletter, *Zebra/Pinnacle Romance News*, which features author profiles, contests, subscriber benefits, book previews and more!

So start today by returning the FREE BOOK CERTIFICATE provided. We'll send you 4 FREE BOOKS with no further obligation: A FREE gift offering you hours of reading pleasure with no obligation...how can you lose?

*We have 4 FREE BOOKS for you
as your introduction to
KENSINGTON CHOICE!
To get your FREE BOOKS, worth
up to $23.96, mail the card below.*

FREE BOOK CERTIFICATE

Yes! Please send me 4 Kensington Choice (the best of Zebra and Pinnacle Books) Historical Romances without cost or obligation (worth up to $23.96). As a Kensington Choice subscriber, I will then receive 4 brand-new romances to preview each month for 10 days FREE. I can return any books I decide not to keep and owe nothing. The publisher's prices for Kensington Choice romances range from $4.99-$5.99, but as a preferred subscriber I will get these books for only $4.20 per book or $16.80 for all four titles. There is no minimum number of books to buy and I may cancel my subscription at any time. A $1.50 postage and handling charge is added to each shipment. No matter what I decide to do, my first 4 books are mine to keep, absolutely FREE!

KC0796

Name _____

Address _____ Apt. _____

City _____ State _____ Zip _____

Telephone ( ) _____

Signature _____

(If under 18, parent or guardian must sign)

Subscription subject to acceptance. Terms and prices subject to change.

4 FREE
Historical Romances

*are waiting
for you to
claim them!*

(worth up to
$23.96)

*See details
inside....*

All too soon, the noon hour rolled around and the sheriff returned, determined thcy go with him to eat. But, again, neither Jenny nor Chad wanted to leave. Especially not Jenny, who had truly enjoyed the past couple of hours listening to Chad's tales about her great-grandfather.

"But you have to eat," the sheriff pointed out, scowling when he glanced around the room, noting the progress they had made. "Both of you. If you're worried about someone breakin' in here again while you're gone, I can have one of my deputies come over and watch the house for an hour or so."

"That's not the problem. I'm just not hungry yet," Jenny told him quite honestly, still full from the eggs and toast she had cooked that morning.

"Neither am I," Chad chimed in. "Besides, I have to be here when Jacky brings the lumber I ordered so I can show him where to stack it." He glanced at the clock, blue eyes narrowed while calculating. "He should be by here any time now."

The sheriff studied him a moment then turned again to Jenny. "What about you, Ruth, er, I mean, Miss Dykes? You don't need to be here when the lumber arrives. Are you sure you won't go have some of that meatloaf with me?"

"I'm sorry. I'm just not hungry," she repeated, not about to leave Chad there alone—not even if she were starving.

That response wasn't the one he wanted. "What about supper, then? You two will have to be hungry again by then. I'll stop back by to get you both."

Chad, who now sat in a chair facing an open file cabinet, looked at him curiously. "Why do you feel it necessary to escort us to dinner? If we get hungry, we're capable enough to walk down to the Stover House ourselves."

Annoyed, the sheriff shoved his hat back and glowered at him. "Yeah, well, you may be capable enough, but sometimes I wonder if you're smart enough." He jutted what there was of his receding chin, now shaved. "Look at you. You're still in the same clothes you had on yesterday."

Jenny jumped immediately into that fray, thinking to help shame Chad into leaving. She could get a lot more accomplished with him gone. Readying things to pack slowed her down, and the longer she spent taking care of such trivial matters, the longer before she found what she needed. She was ready to single out the murderer and go home. "The sheriff's right. If you're so determined to stay here, you really should take the time to go gather some clean clothes. You never did get around to that last night."

"I'll take care of that later," Chad said, his tone low and deliberate. "For now, these clothes will do."

Not wanting him in another black mood, Jenny let the argument pass, as did the sheriff. Thankfully.

"I see you two have started cleanin' up in here," he said, stating the obvious while, again, he shifted his attention to Jenny. "Find anything I'd be interested in knowin' about?"

"Not yet," she admitted, wishing she had a different answer for him. She had hoped by now to have come across whatever it was those men had wanted. "But we are keeping an eye out for anything that looks in any way suspicious."

The sheriff took a deep breath, then surveyed how much of the room still lacked attention. They barely had put a dent in the clutter. "Tell you what. If I get time, I'll come back this afternoon and help you finish up in here while Chad builds those boxes you'll need to ship everything. Maybe by then I'll have a response from Mrs. Tyler and you'll know more about what to do with everything. I'm not sure she'll want *everything* shipped."

Not about to argue against an extra set of hands, Jenny smiled and turned on the charm the sheriff seemed to like so well. She even went as far as to bat her eyes. "That would be nice."

Chad's expression hardened, but he didn't comment as he resumed his work, straightening what few files had been left in the drawers while also examining the contents of each.

Even after the sheriff left, Chad remained in a dark, reflective mood. It was as if the sheriff's short visit had reminded him of how easily she had gained the man's trust. That could have Chad wondering if she had just tried to work that same sort of magic on him by suddenly being so friendly.

By the time the wagon carrying the materials he had ordered arrived an hour later, he was back to barely talking. He had become so quiet in that time, it startled her when he turned from the window and finally spoke. "It's Jacky with my order. Come on outside."

"Why?"

"Because now that the lumber is here, I can get started on those crates."

"But what's that got to do with me? I don't know how to build crates." Her gut wrenched. She had hoped to use the time he spent building crates privately probing for evidence.

"I don't trust you, remember?"

She set aside the stack of receipts she had found and now sorted through. "So you expect me to go outside and do nothing while you build those boxes?"

"That's right." He pointed to the door. "You aren't staying in here where I can't see you. Not with me having no proof of who you are yet."

She tapped her foot, studying his determined expression, then quietly stood. For now, the wise choice was to go outside with him. Perhaps after he had built several boxes, she could convince him her energy was being wasted. Maybe then he would allow her back inside to fill those boxes.

"Fine. If you want me to sit and watch you work, then that's what I'll do. I'll sit and watch you work."

Which was exactly what she did do. While Chad retreated to the side yard to build crates of different sizes, Jenny sat in a large wicker chair near the front corner of the wide veranda with its white spindled banister, watching him work. Having moved outside in the open shaded area where a gentle breeze curled around her, she realized just how hot she had gotten inside the house.

Even though used to being outdoors without air-conditioning while off on extended nature shoots during the summer, she was not used to all the stooping, lifting, and bending. She had worked up quite a sweat beneath the heavy clothing, and was glad for the moment of cool respite.

Jenny also did not mind idly watching Chad work out under the trees, noting again how solidly he was built while he hammered away. Because of the heat, he had removed his shirt, allowing her a sun-dappled view of his rippling back muscles as he sank the fat nails with as few as two whacks.

This was not a man who shied away from hard work, a realization that didn't quite fit in with what she'd discovered about him thus far.

While allowing her thoughts to follow what was a natural course for a woman faced with a handsome, half-naked man, her heart pounded at a rate far faster than Chad's hammer.

Chad was indeed a very strong, very fit man—quite strong enough to have rammed a large knife through her great-grandfather's ribs. But what would drive him to do that? Earlier, he had shown a sincere fondness toward Tyler, a fondness that had surprised her.

What could possibly have driven a man who so obviously cared about her great-grandfather to murder him?

With fresh doubts nagging at her, she yearned to return inside and resume the search for clues. She had to find out just who killed her great-grandfather. Whether Chad proved guilty, or someone else. She had to know.

Perhaps if the sheriff was there to watch over her while

she worked, Chad would let her go back inside. She glanced east toward the jail, but saw no sign of Sheriff Mack along the busier end of town. Shifting, she looked in the opposite direction, to the west of Black Rock. There stood a dozen or so more houses, all with big, shaded yards that bore both flower and vegetable gardens, but no sheriff. Nor anyone else for that matter. The residential part of town was dead.

Her attention drawn next to the land beyond the houses, she caught glimpses of a wide, slow-moving creek that wound a shallow path down from the northwest. Ribboning across the valley floor, it curved around a tall, jutting hill that looked about a mile away. There it dipped permanently out of sight.

So this was what Oklahoma looked like, she thought, distracted by the stark, rugged hills that jutted along both sides of the wide, flat valley—mostly covered with sparse, gray vegetation.

Turning to view the town again, she still did not spot the sheriff among those moving about, but she did pay closer attention to the layout of her strange new surroundings. Black Rock was larger than she had pictured it being during her youth.

From where she sat, closer to the west end of a wide, graveled street, she counted three saloons, two restaurants, a domino hall, a town hall, a bank, a courthouse, a freight office that also had a sign that said "telegraph," a lumber yard, a post office, the jail, a church that looked like it might double as a school because of the playground equipment, and a couple of buildings that had signs with lettering too small to read from there.

Down the only side street within view, she saw yet more brightly painted signs, identifying such establishments as Beverley's Law Office, Goodman Hardware, The Alley Saloon and Eatery, Donner's Apothecary, Ann Harris Dress Shoppe, and Dr. Collinge's Medical Post.

On the next street over, rising above the shorter buildings

along Main Street, she spotted a three-story white building with "Stover Hotel & Rooming House" painted in bold green letters across the top: the place the sheriff so desperately wanted her to eat.

The town was so much like something right out of an old western movie, she halfway expected to see Jimmy Stewart come sauntering down the street—a dusty, beat-up hat plopped on his head.

"Ruth, come here!" Chad called out, effectively breaking her wandering reverie.

She looked out across the yard expectantly, having temporarily forgotten she was Ruth. It wasn't until he turned to look at her directly that she realized he was calling her.

"It won't hurt you to come over here and help me a minute. This board is badly warped. I need you to hold it in place for me."

Glad he had taken her lack of acknowledgment for inconsideration instead of proof she wasn't who she said she was, and eager to do something besides just sit there watching this gorgeous man work, Jenny hurried to do as told.

Big mistake. She became even *more* aware of Chad's overpowering masculinity after she had moved closer to the flexing muscles and the glistening skin she'd admired earlier from afar. Her heart fluttered with the unbidden thought of how firm and smooth that skin had felt beneath her fingertips the night before.

Flustered by the memory, she tried not to stare at him while she held the board exactly like he showed her and he quickly drove two nails in place. When finished, she did not immediately return to her chair. Instead, she stood off to one side, watching his movements from a closer vantage point, her skin tingling at the thought of being that near such obvious power. Again she was reminded how he certainly would have had the strength to drive that knife into her great-grandfather's chest, especially in a moment of rage.

She shuddered at the thought, but pushed it aside. She no longer liked thinking of him as a murderer.

"I wonder how many crates we're going to need," he commented, pausing to push unruly strands of damp hair away from his face, giving her a better view of those sexy, lash-fringed, pale eyes. Eyes so probing, they could look right through a person. Like they did her now.

She drew a sharp breath. "I don't think there's any way to know until we start packing and see how things progress."

He glanced at the half dozen wooden boxes he had completed, then at the planks still unused. "Well, I'll build as many as this lumber allows, and if it turns out that isn't enough, I'll send for more lumber."

With the silence between them effectively broken, Jenny asked how many he thought he would end up with, and for the next few minutes the conversation moved from the number of boxes to matters of even less consequence. Finding him quite likable when discussing matters unrelated to the murder, Jenny developed a fresh hope that she had been wrong about Chad from the beginning. It was possible. Besides his having been so quick to accuse her of crimes she couldn't possibly have committed, what did she have to go on really? Size, shape, and color of clothing.

There had to be other men in that town just as tall and just as thick across the shoulders with scuffed black boots and a dark-brown hat who also had been off somewhere where they couldn't account for. Chad couldn't be the only one.

A metallic creak caught her attention. She turned toward the unexpected noise. As if she had mentally summoned someone else who fit the same general description to prove her point, a man of Chad's equal height and breadth stood inside at the open gate, staring at them.

"What are you building?" Not waiting for an answer, he pushed the gate further open and headed toward them. He looked at Jenny curiously while awaiting Chad's response.

"Building crates to pack Tyler and Janeen's personal belongings in," he said, barely looking up. "Care to help?"

Jenny returned the man's questioning look, noting he was dressed far less casually than Chad, and had on boots with no scuffs. But that didn't mean he had never worn scuffed boots.

"No, I'm headed to work. Irene was later than usual coming back from her lunch, so I just now finished with mine and am on my way back to the mercantile to finish out my day." His mouth flattened as if he had really rather not return to work. "I heard all the noise and saw you out here working, so I thought I would stop by to see if Sheriff Mack has any idea yet who murdered Tyler."

Chad laid the hammer aside, then reached for his shirt, but rather than slip it on, he used the hem to wipe a patch of damp sawdust off his forehead. "As far as I know, Wade doesn't know anything other than the fact someone pretty strong was involved, and an expensive knife was used."

"But I heard there was a witness." Again he looked at Jenny. "Some folks are saying there's a woman who may have actually seen the murderer up close."

Chad cut Jenny a disgruntled gaze. "That would be Ruth, here. She claims to have entered the house in time to get a look at the man, but for some reason she can't describe much about him."

"Ruth?" He took off the bowler hat with one hand at the same time he straightened his black business coat with the other, as if just knowing her name gave him a reason to impress her. He waited expectantly a minute, but when Chad didn't bother to conclude the introductions, he finished them himself. "My name is Anthony Andrews. I'm a longtime resident of Black Rock and live right next door." He pointed toward a frame house a half block away that was similar in style but not quite as large as Tyler's, one painted a soft gray instead of brilliant white. "Did you really see the murderer?"

"Yes."

"What did he look like?"

His eyes narrowed slightly while awaiting her answer. Was that because of an insatiable curiosity, or out of worry?

"It was pretty dark in the room where he was and he wore a black cloth over his face, but I could tell he was a man about your size and shape, and he wore dark clothes that were clearly too large for him, probably hoping to hide his true bulk. He'd already murdered Tyler and was still inside the house when I first entered, but then he ran right past me when he realized someone else was inside."

"Did he say anything while you were there? Did you get to hear his voice?"

She thought a minute. She'd heard a grunt when they had collided, but nothing more. "Not *that* time."

His eyes rounded. "You've had contact with him more than once?"

When she informed him of the second incident, although not really sure which man she had heard speak, he looked truly alarmed. "You mean to say the murderer is still in town?"

"He was as of last night," she reiterated, not wanting him misled. She studied Chad's grim expression a moment. "As for today, I can't say for sure where he is."

Anthony swallowed so hard his Adam's apple bobbed, his eyes still wide when he turned again to Chad, "Do you think they'll catch him? Do you think they'll ever figure out who murdered Tyler and put him away? He was such a nice man. I'd hate for his murderer to go free."

Chad pursed his lips. "With our sheriff the one out trying to find him? Who knows what will happen? You didn't happen to see or hear anything, did you?"

"I couldn't have. I was at work when it happened," he said a bit too adamantly, making Jenny wonder if she feared Chad for some reason—or if he was perhaps guilty himself.

If only she could read the thoughts behind those big round green eyes.

Chad studied Anthony's alarmed expression a moment, then reached for his hammer again. "Well, if you hear any talk that might help the sheriff figure out who the killer is, let me know. I'll pass it along to him."

"I will," Anthony said with a firm nod, already stepping away, his gaze distant with whatever thoughts now plagued him. "But for now I need to get on back to work. I'm allowed only thirty minutes to eat my lunch. And with the mood Old Man Hinze was in, I'd hate for him to fire me just for being a few minutes late."

Chad watched him leave, then glanced briefly at Jenny before resuming work.

Reminded that she still knew so very little about whoever might have killed her great-grandfather, Jenny stood watching his progress a moment, antsy now because a full day had passed and she was no closer to solving the mystery than she had been shortly after she'd arrived.

Still eager to make headway, she longed to return to the house and resume her search, but didn't know how to approach the subject without triggering Chad's anger all over again. About the time she had decided to heck with him, she would simply go back into the house and start to work, a movement caught her eye. A young black woman stood on the veranda watching them.

How long she had been there, Jenny hadn't a clue.

"Who's that?" she asked in a voice just loud enough for Chad to hear.

Chad glanced up to see who she meant, then waved. "That's Nora Simmons. She was hired to come in and cook for Tyler while Janeen was away." He frowned, as if puzzled by her presence. "Surely she has heard about the death by now."

Snatching up his shirt, he slid his well-muscled arms back

into his still-rolled sleeves and started off toward the house.
Jenny followed.

The woman, frowning, hurried to meet them partway.

Nine

Nora Simmons was a tall, slender, attractive black woman who appeared to be only a few years younger than Jenny. She had on a simple-cut, dark-gray dress that fit her curves loosely, and wore her long black hair in a tight, braided twist. She moved down the steps toward Jenny and Chad with a natural grace that worked well with her long arms and legs.

"Are you Mr. Dykes's sister?" she asked as soon as they were close enough to hear her without having to raise her voice again. She studied Jenny's face with a sharp eye.

"I am," Jenny answered promptly, extending her hand before having considered that in the 1890s a woman might not extend her hand to another woman, even in greeting.

Nora accepted the handshake reluctantly, as if by doing so she committed a moral crime. "Then you are the one I come to talk to." Her voice was soft and filled with a southerner's inflection as she placed her hands quickly back to her sides. "The sheriff told me about you being here."

"You want to talk to me? About what?" Jenny couldn't imagine. She had never heard her Grandma Vic mention anyone named Nora.

"About my duties," she answered with a resolute lift of her dark chin. "I was hired to cook Mr. Dykes meals while his wife went back East to visit her folks, and since I'm paid a full week in advance, I come here to cook for you. Leastwise every day but Sunday and until Monday afternoon, at which time you can decide whether you want to keep me on by paying me for another week or let me go."

"You're here to cook?" That prospect was too good to be true. "But there's hardly any food in the house."

She frowned, perplexed. "What happened? Did somebody rob the root cellar, too?"

"Root cellar?" Jenny cut her gaze to Chad, annoyed he'd never mentioned this root cellar to her. What other secrets did he keep from her?

Chad appeared to be just as baffled. "Don't look at me like that." He held up his hands as if declaring no knowledge of the cellar. "I've been over to eat a time or two, but I was never around whenever Janeen cooked. I know nothing about where she keeps things."

Jenny glanced back at the house. *A root cellar.* Odd they hadn't noticed such a thing while packing up the kitchen things.

"Where exactly is this root cellar?" Jenny finally asked.

"Up under the house. Like most root cellars around these parts. You get to it from back here." She headed around to the far side of the house. There, near the back, between two large nanina bushes still more wintery-red than summer-green, lay a small, slanted door painted white like the house, which she threw back and then descended the narrow, planked steps inside. She reached for a small, dusty lamp, pulled matches from a drawer at the base, then lit and adjusted the flame.

Exchanging baffled looks, Jenny and Chad followed her into the cold, dank room carved directly into the ground. Both quickly scanned the area, clearly with the same thought. Whatever those men had searched the house for and had never found might have been hidden there inside the dirt cellar. But all that sat on the sagging planked shelves was an assortment of dusty jars, a small, wooden barrel labeled cheese, and two large, lidded tin canisters, one marked flour, the other sugar. Other than the various food items, and an open jar of camphor, the closet-size room was empty; and the dirt floor undisturbed.

Disappointed, Jenny followed Nora back out into the bright sunlight, squinting until her eyes readjusted to the difference.

"Since the food is still there, ma'am, if it is okay with you, I'll resume my duties by cooking supper." She held up a couple of jars she had taken off the shelves. "There's starter for bread on the counter in the kitchen, vegetables in the garden out back, and meat and apples in these jars. How about a fresh loaf of bread, a nice hot beef stew, and a cobbler for dessert?"

"Sounds wonderful," Jenny answered readily, her mouth watering at the thought. She walked with Nora toward the back door. "Need any help?"

Already she planned to help Nora get started as promised, then slip off to poke around the studio again. Her pulses raced with the hope that this time she would find whatever it was those men had wanted.

"No, you don't," Chad called after her, as if able to read her thoughts. "Look, stranger, I'm still the one in charge here. And you're staying out here with me."

Tired of being intimidated, and thinking she now had a logical excuse to be inside the house, she spun around and faced him squarely. "No, I'm not. It's pointless for me to sit out here being idle. I don't care who has been put in charge here, I'm going back in to help Nora. Someone needs to show her where the utensils are, since so many of them have already been packed away."

"Oh, but I won't need any help with that," Nora replied, dark eyes rounded. "I'll just search around until I find what I need. Besides, it wouldn't be right for you to come in and do any of my work. You're Mr. Tyler's sister. You shouldn't be doing any work at all. You stay out here in this nice cool breeze and continue enjoying Mr. Jordan's company like you were."

"But that's just the problem. I don't particularly 'enjoy' this man's company, and I don't intend to sit around out here doing absolutely nothing just to suit his whims a moment longer." Having said that, and hoping Nora's presence would force him to keep his temper in check, she again started toward the back door. Nora followed, unblinking. Clearly, she didn't know what to think of Jenny's outburst.

Jenny listened for Chad's angry retort, surprised when instead of demanding she come back there immediately, his next words weren't even addressed to her.

"Nora!" Chad called just as the two had stepped onto the back porch. "Make sure she helps you."

Nora glanced back at him, her forehead furrowed as if asking just how she was supposed to do that. She was the employee, and Jenny was supposed to be the sister of the man who had originally employed her. "Yes, sir, Mr. Jordan. I'll do what I can."

Having finally run out of both lumber and energy, Chad tossed the hammer, saw, and what few nails he had left onto the back porch to protect them from the elements, then wiped his brow with the back of his arm. An hour had passed since the two women had gone inside to cook, and in that time Chad had worked up such a heavy sweat, his long hair and the waistband of his trousers were soaked.

The time had come. He had to go home and get fresh clothes. He couldn't bear to stay in these a moment longer and had already tried to tug into some of Tyler's to see if he could get by without having to leave again at all. But Tyler's clothes had proved too small to wear even temporarily.

Still, he hated the thought of leaving Ruth Dykes, or whoever she was, inside Tyler's house even long enough to run home, toss a few days worth of clothes into a bag, grab his own razor and comb, and run back. *Even with Nora there to keep an eye on her.*

Again, he wiped his forehead with the back of his arm, then remembering the bandanna folded into his back pocket, he pulled it out and wiped his face dry with the black cloth while still wondering what he should do.

Thinking it better to have two people there to watch over such a crafty impostor, he refolded the bandanna, tucked it back into his pocket, and headed for the back pump to wash his upper body and rinse the sawdust out of his hair.

With his skin cooled, and feeling a lot less sticky, he slid his shirt back on and went inside, surprised to find Ruth actually helping.

He had expected to see her sitting in a corner sulking after finding out how dependable Nora could be when given an order. Instead, her concentration was on the contents of the large bowl in front of her.

Although still eager to change into clean clothes, he remained in the kitchen, watching Ruth work, trying not to remember how he had nearly lost control the night before. *Damn* but he had wanted her. Despite his suspicions, he'd wanted desperately to finish what she had so blatantly started. If she had not been the one to pull away, he wasn't so sure he would have.

His stomach tightened when he realized how easily she had manipulated him with that voluptuous body. She had exactly what a man wanted and in exactly the right proportions, and she knew it. Knew how to use it. And if he hadn't pulled his senses together long enough to let her know he understood exactly what was going on, and could play the game, too, she might have lured him all the way into her sensual little trap.

It was that one little question "Tell me what you know" that had brought an abrupt end to her play. It had let her know she had been just a little too obvious, that a scheme to seduce his loyalty wouldn't work.

But now while he watched her work, watched the movements of that same supple body, knowing exactly how she looked and felt without that dress, he almost wished she hadn't called the game short. He still ached with the need she had so skillfully awakened inside him. Damn her for having so easily found a weakness in him. And damn *him* for having that weakness.

He would have to be extremely careful around her from now on or chance falling prey to her again.

Disgruntled, but determined not to allow her to play him for a fool again, he continued his wary vigil until finally the sheriff appeared again. As Chad expected, Wade came, as determined as ever they accompany him to supper, unaware until he had fully entered the back door that Nora was there already preparing a meal.

"What she doin' here?" he asked Chad, scowling while he watched Nora squeeze and punch a large mound of bread dough with her floured fists.

"I'm here finishing my duties," she answered for herself, glancing up just long enough to make eye contact. "I know you think this ain't necessary, but I was paid to work through Monday afternoon, and that's just what I intend to do. I don't like having money I didn't earn."

The sheriff shoved his hat back and glowered at her. "Is that why you kept askin' all those questions about Tyler's sister? You were plannin' to come here and cook for her?"

She nodded, her forehead notching at the sheriff's anger. "I don't like feeling like I cheated nobody out of their money. This way, I can still earn what was given me and feel good about keeping it. Even my husband says this is the thing for me to do."

"But I was plannin' on them havin' supper with me this evenin'. I was lookin' forward to gettin' to know Tyler's sister a little better." He turned his mouth down like the sulking child Chad knew him to be. "Plus, I figured she'd like a chance to be alone with her brother for a while and we could go over after we ate. The undertaker has him ready for viewin' now."

How commendable, Chad thought, knowing full well what the sheriff really wanted. The same thing he now wanted. Ruth.

As if having been given a stage cue, Jenny cut her dark gaze to the window, looking impressively shaken as she moved away from the worktable. "I'm sorry. I'm not ready for that."

"But you do plan on goin' to pay your last respects at some point, don't you?" the sheriff asked, not giving up on an opportunity to be alone with her. "I could come by for you in the mornin', take you to breakfast if you like, then walk you on by Miss Deborah's Dress Shoppe so you can get yourself a proper black dress for the funeral Sunday, since I imagine you didn't pack anything appropriate for such as this. I could then see you on to the undertakers."

"Sunday?" Jenny's gaze dipped to the pale-pink dress she wore, as if seeing nothing wrong with the color, then lifted to peer at the sheriff again. "The funeral isn't until Sunday?"

"That's when most funerals are around here," he noted. "After the Sunday services directly followin' the death."

Looking oddly disconcerted by that, she took a deep breath and let it out slowly. "Then I have plenty of time to get a dress. I'll wait until I have more of the work behind me."

"But—"

"Thanks anyway."

Aware Wade had no hope of changing this stubborn female's mind, and not expecting her at the funeral anyway, Chad intervened, leading the conversation in the direction he wanted. "Sheriff, why are you so determined to get her out of this house?" Not that he disapproved, for he would like her out of that house himself.

"It's not just her. I'd planned for you to come, too."

"Then what you want is us *both* out of the house."

The sheriff stiffened. "No, of course not. I just figured you two would want to pay your last respects is all. Other folks are. Besides, in all the time Miss Dykes has been here, I haven't had much of a chance to talk to her. I was hopin' to get that chance during the walk over. I'd like to get to know her a little better."

That was exactly what Chad had wanted him to say. "Good. Then why don't you stay here and keep her company while I go home long enough to throw together some clean clothes?" He fought the urge to smile at how easy that had been as he plucked at the front of the dark-blue shirt he had worn the past two days to indicate the need. "That way we don't have to worry about those intruders returning while there's no man here to protect her."

The sheriff's expression lifted instantly, a perverse gleam brightening his green eyes. "I'd be glad to keep the pretty little lady company while you're gone."

If only our industrious sheriff could be as interested in solving Tyler's murder as he was in attracting this beautiful woman, Chad thought irritably, having realized early on it would be up to him to figure out who killed his best friend and bring him to trial. "Good. It's settled then."

As expected, Jenny's supple lips tightened into a tight, thin line. "Really, Sheriff, I am a little too busy for company right now."

"Doing what?" Wade asked, already removing his hat to stay. "I can help with whatever it is. Want me to bring some of those crates in from outside?"

Chad wanted to laugh at how every muscle in Jenny's body had tightened. He had outmaneuvered her and she knew it. "While the sheriff is helping you here and I'm off getting those clothes, maybe I'll take the time to stop by and see if there have been any 'telegrams' for me. Maybe from some of the liveries over near Perry."

At hearing that, the sheriff dragged his wandering gaze

off Jenny, frowning again. "Well, don't expect a wire from Janeen Dykes. She's in the hospital, and the family isn't passin' along any messages either to her or from her just now."

"In the hospital?" Chad's heart jumped to his throat. Her condition had to be extremely serious before they would take her to a hospital. "Anything to do with the baby?" Dear God, please don't let her have lost the child, too. Janeen could never survive two such losses.

"Partly. As I understand, she collapsed with the vapors and, because of the risk to the baby, they want to keep her calm and in bed for a while. At least until they are sure the fall didn't make matters worse than they already were. Afraid the signs she's about to lose that baby will only get worse, they don't want any more of our news disturbing her just now."

That was understandable. Damn inconvenient, but understandable. "Then we'll just have to wait until she's better to find out more about our Miss Dykes."

He reached into his back pocket and took out his bandanna again while meeting her startled gaze. He found perverse pleasure in the fact he had obviously struck a nerve with that last comment. But why? Didn't she know they would continue to pursue the question of her identity?

Already headed for the door, eager to pack those clothes and get back, he heard the sheriff asking if they had come across anything new that might indicate who the killer was.

Not likely she'd tell you," he thought has he started off in a trot.

Still stunned, Jenny watched while Chad jogged out of sight, the black bandanna still trailing from his hand—a piece of cloth that could easily cover his lower face. After hearing how fondly Chad had talked about her great-grandfather, she'd come very close to convincing herself he couldn't possibly have had anything to do with the murder. It was hard now to consider him suspect again. But he carried a bandanna exactly like the one the men searching the house had worn.

A chill skittered down her spine. *Everything* she knew about the murderer fit Chad to some degree. Even so, she knew the facts could still fit someone else. Yet common sense told her not to rule him out as a suspect simply because she had started to like him.

She had to get into that studio and resume her search. And she had to do so before Chad returned.

Turning to the sheriff, whose gaze was on the scooped neckline of her great-grandmother's dress, she smiled sweetly. "I do appreciate your offer to help, but I also know how busy you are, what with so many crimes to solve right now. That's why I won't hold you to your promise to stay and help."

"Oh, but I don't mind," he answered, finally pulling his gaze off her cleavage long enough to meet her gaze. "What is it you want me to do? Help straighten and pack up in the studio? Did you two finish up in there?" He swallowed hard and glanced toward the studio door, still shut.

"No, we haven't. But that's not the sort of help I need," she said, not about to let him go bumbling around in there. Judging the sheriff to be the extremely macho type, she'd already figured out what sort of request would send him running. "No, what I'd like for you to do is help me with the cobbler I just started. I'll need a nice soft crust."

"You want me to make a crust?" he asked, clearly offended.

Nora stared at them both, as if unable to believe half of what went on in that house, while she divided the bread dough and put it into two pans.

"Yes, Sheriff, since you don't mind helping, you can make the crust while I get the filling ready. That is, if you have time. I realize what a busy man you are."

He jumped at the opening just as quickly as she had expected. "That's true. I am. Very busy. Why, I got another three telegrams just today from people wantin' to know more about that bank robbery we had July Fourth, and what it was like to put together a posse and get right in after those Craig boys, knowing what a danger that posed. I really should be writing them back the information they need."

"Oh, then I'd be the first to understand if you decide not to stay and help us cook. An important man like you? I really don't think Chad realized what an inconvenience it would be for a man like you to stay and help us in the kitchen." She continued to ooze charm and sensitivity while she guided him toward the door. "Tell you what, since I have Nora here anyway, why don't I let you go on and get some of that work done. Maybe then you'll free up enough time to stop back by after supper to share some of my apple cobbler with us."

"That would be nice," he said, already reaching for his hat. Looking as confused as he was relieved. "About what time?"

"Anytime you want. We'll be here. Or at least Chad and I will. Nora will be on her way home soon, I'm sure. She has a husband to see to."

He hesitated just inside the door, glancing at Nora, who'd just slid the two pans into the oven. "When do you plan to get back to packing up the house?"

"After supper. Once it's cooled off again." She purposely fanned her neck, knowing that would distract him from whatever else he was about to say. She wanted him gone. "If you still want to help some, maybe you can do so then."

He nodded, considering that while she nudged him on out the door. Jenny held that sweet smile until the sheriff had rounded the house, headed back toward the street, then rolled her eyes skyward and blew out a relieved breath.

"Yes, I know," Nora said, grinning as she set the hot pads she'd used on the counter next to the stove. "He's one of the most annoying men I know. But the folks who vote around here obviously don't see that."

Jenny laughed, then reached for the glass of water she had left on the table. *One down, one to go.* "You're already finished with the bread?"

"Except for taking it out of the oven."

"And you're finished with the stew?"

"Except for stirring it now and again to make sure it doesn't burn."

"Well, then all I have to do is make the crust for the cobbler, pour the filling in, and we're done."

"Except for cleaning up the mess." Nora headed to the sink to pick up a damp rag.

Watching the clock, Jenny hurriedly threw together a quick crust, barely taking the time to press it out smooth, while Nora cleaned the counter where she'd worked. About the time she finished, Jenny put the cobbler into the same oven with the bread, and, seeing Nora through with the rag, again let out a relieved breath. Only five minutes had passed. There was still time. "All done. I guess you'll be going home now."

Nora blinked, then frowned. "Not until I've taken the bread and then cobbler out of the oven."

Jenny's stomach knotted. By the time they finished baking, Chad could be back. "Oh, but I can do that. You've already done enough. Besides, you have a husband to get home to. He'll be wanting supper, too."

"He understands. My work comes first."

"And your work is done," she reiterated, wagging a finger at her playfully while her heart raced at an unprecedented speed. What if Nora wouldn't leave? "Now, you go on home like I told you. I'll see to the bread and cobbler."

Nora glanced at the clock, then at the door. "Well, if you're sure."

"Of course I'm sure." How she sounded so calm was beyond her. "Now, go."

Minutes later, with the house again empty, Jenny hurried into the studio. Because of the afternoon shadows, she paused long enough to light one lamp, then started again where she had left off earlier.

Finding nothing of value, she hurried next to the one file cabinet they had not sorted through yet. Still fighting the contrary clothing of the time, which allowed for very little range of movement, she started with the bottom drawer, still open from the intruders having gone through it. Finding nothing of use there, she moved to the second drawer, then the third, until finally she stood to go through what had been left inside the top drawer. When she did, a stack of six books sitting on top of the cabinet caught her eye.

At first she had no idea why, for they looked ordinary enough at first glance, but a closer look revealed one little peculiarity. The fourth book down had a hole about the size of a postage stamp cut neatly into the black leather spine, dead center, just below the title.

A tight knot formed in her chest when she realized what she had found. Her great-grandfather's camouflage camera. The one he had used to get his famous picture of the Dalton brothers. The one her grandmother had cared for all these years and had eventually willed to her.

Jenny had forgotten all about it.

Oddly comforted to find something she had actually seen and touched before, in her own time, she gently took the top three books off the stack and set them aside. There was the circle cut into the side she expected to find. Plucking out the core, she was amazed to find the lens so sparkly clean and clear. By her time, the lens had turned a murky yellow and the leather had become a dull, dried-out gray.

Gingerly, she drew the camera into her hands. The leather looked new again, but then it should, since by her calculation, the camera was now only four years old.

Delighted with the find, she carried it over to the lamp for a closer inspection. "French, Latin . . ."

Her heart froze just as she started to read the third false title. There inside the hole was a number. *The camera had film in it.* Exposed film. Or at least part of it was exposed.

Could the evidence they had all looked for be inside that camera? Is that why her great-grandfather had gone to such trouble to make it blend in with the rest of his studio?

Hardly able to swallow, she glanced at the clock. Twenty minutes since Chad had gone. Did that leave her enough time to develop the film inside before his return?

Or would it be better to wait for another opportunity?

She pressed the camera against her thudding heart while trying to decide what to do.

What if there were no more opportunities? What if when Chad returned with his clothes, he never found another reason to leave? Or *worse.* What if he came back waving a stack of telegrams informing him no woman from back East had hired a buggy from Perry to Black Rock?

Whether he was guilty of Tyler's murder or not, he would have her out the door so fast her head would spin.

No, this could be her *only* opportunity. She had little choice but to take it.

Ten

Carrying the camera she had found in one hand and the burning lamp with the other, Jenny went first to the windows to make sure Chad was nowhere to be seen, then headed immediately to the darkroom. With hands trembling in anticipation, she pulled the door closed and started to work, praying she had enough chemicals left to do the job. She had cut it too darn close when she had developed that last print.

Checking labels, she discovered she still had enough developer, fixer, and acetic acid, but she needed more distilled water for the final rinse. She certainly didn't have time to boil, then cool the water. She'd have to make do with plain water.

Her insides churning harder with each minute that passed, she carried the water bottle to the kitchen, filled it, and returned to place it with the other materials she needed. She had just reached over to turn the lamp down to a faint glow before opening the camera when she heard the back door clatter shut.

Saints help her. She was about to be caught.

Not knowing why she suddenly felt so guilty when *he* was the potential suspect, she hurried to put the camera on a shelf so it again looked like a stack of plain books. Hoping to get out of there before Chad had a chance to realize where she had gone, she snatched up the lamp to turn it out, then headed for the door to the studio. With any luck, she would have just enough time to make it out a window before being noticed. Once outside, she would loop around back and pretend to be coming in from the privy.

Still holding the smoking lamp, she entered the general studio as fast as her long, burdensome skirts would allow. With her eye trained on the nearest window, she barely caught sight of the room around her.

Too late.

Chad stood in the dead center of the studio, arms folded across a granite chest, glowering at her.

She froze.

"Where's the sheriff?" He glanced past her into the darkroom, but clearly didn't expect to find anyone there.

She swallowed back the panic rising in her throat. She had to stay calm. She was not the suspect here. "He's a busy man. He had to leave."

"And where's Nora?" His words cut like shards of steel.

"She finished her work and went home."

His blue eyes narrowed with frightful intent when he unfolded his arms and moved toward her. He had changed clothes and now wore a light-blue shirt and black pants, both perfectly fitted to his strong frame. "Which, with me gone, left you conveniently alone. What were you doing in there?"

Jenny cut her gaze in the direction he indicated, her mind a tumultuous whirl. What excuse could she give for having gone into a room she had already straightened? Finally, she decided to forget caution and tell him the truth. *Let him be the one to squirm.*

"After everyone left, I returned to the studio, looking for evidence that might prove who committed the murder." She gestured to the room around them. "Because this is the area that attracted the two intruders, I figured this is the area in which I would find the proof I need." Not certain how he would react to the next part of what she had to say, she again cut her gaze to the nearest open window, a dozen yards away. Did it still offer a means of escape? Or was Chad too close?

If nothing else, it offered a way for a scream to be heard out on the street. "And I think I just may have found that one piece of evidence everyone's been hoping to find."

"You what?" His expression went from skeptical to stunned to angry as he again looked at the darkroom door, now open. "Where? Let me see it."

His attention diverted, she moved several inches toward the window, hoping he wouldn't notice. She had taken a big risk telling him the truth. A foolish risk. But what could she do? She had flat run out of lies. "No. Not without the sheriff here."

"The sheriff?" His forehead notched.

Suddenly, she couldn't tell if he was angry or confused. *Or both.*

"That's right. The sheriff. I demand that he be here before I reveal anything about what I may have found."

He continued to stare at her, dumbfounded, as if not quite accepting what she had said. "You really want the sheriff here?"

"You bet I do." She lifted her chin defiantly, not quite understanding the baffled expression on his face but glad it had diluted some of the anger he had shown.

It wasn't the smartest thing in the world to make a suspected murderer angry, though she doubted he would try to kill her without knowing where she had hidden the evidence. "Until he's here to help protect what evidence I may have found, I'm not telling you a thing."

"Are you willing to go *with* me to get him?" he asked, sounding skeptical again.

She flattened her mouth. Did he think her demand was some ploy to get him out of the house again?

"Yes, I am, if that's what it takes to get him here." Despite a racing heart and trembling legs on the verge of collapse, she met his gaze squarely.

He studied her a minute longer, then spoke in a quiet voice. "You really *aren't* a part of all this, are you?"

"Me?" she asked, startled. Chad had made it clear he thought her an impostor—rightfully so—and possibly even a thief, but she had no idea he truly suspected her of anything quite that heinous. "You really thought I had something to do with the actual murder?"

"Until now." He nodded, although still looking at her as if he had a hard time accepting this new insight. "I thought it too convenient that you showed up out of nowhere just seconds after the murder had taken place. You even claimed to have seen the man who did it yet could give no real description of him."

"So you believed that I'd participated in some way?"

Again, he nodded.

Stymied, Jenny took a moment to absorb the full effect of his revelation. If Chad really thought all that, then he couldn't be the murderer, either. He would have known she had told the truth, at least about what time she had arrived.

Was he as innocent as she had started to hope? Or was this some sort of trick to throw her off track again? "But now, suddenly you believe I'm innocent." Simply because she wanted the sheriff there when she revealed her evidence?

"Of murder, yes."

"Oh? So you still think I may be a thief."

He ran a hand through his hair, then admitted, "Right now I don't know what I think. I know you aren't Tyler's sister. And yet you seem as sincerely concerned with finding out who killed him as I am." He blinked several times, as if to clear his head, then glanced at the clock. "I want to see that evidence, whatever it is. I'll go get the sheriff. He should be in his office."

"Wait." She wanted more time to think. "Not yet."

"Why?"

"Because I need a moment to decide if you are innocent, too."

"You need a moment to do *what?* Do you honestly think *I* could have murdered Tyler? Even after getting to know me? Do you really think I could have driven a knife through my best friend's heart?"

The sincere offense in his voice made her feel suddenly foolish. "The thought occurred to me."

"Why?"

"I don't know. You're the right size. The right shape. You have the right kind of boots, the right kind of hat, and earlier today you wiped your face with the right color bandanna. Plus you've been very careful about keeping an eye on me, as if afraid of what I might find."

"I was afraid what you might steal. I told you that."

"But I thought that was just an excuse to stay here and watch me. To make sure I didn't cause any trouble for you."

"So, from that, you assumed it was me." He sounded more hurt than angry, though anger still clearly had a place in his voice.

"Just like *you* assumed it was me," she reminded him, starting to get annoyed herself. She wasn't the only one who'd jumped to such an unfounded conclusion.

Silent a moment, he considered that. "You're right. It looks like we were both wrong." He paused, again reflective, then frowned when a new realization struck. "I thought you just told me you had new evidence. If that's true, then you'd already know it wasn't me."

How quick the man was to suspect her. "No, I said I *think* I may have found something. I'm not sure yet."

That accusing eyebrow of his crept higher. "How can you not be sure?"

She chewed her lower lip a moment, then turned back toward the darkroom. "Come with me."

Lighting the lamp again, she placed it on the main worktable, allowing the yellow glow to reach all areas of the room. She went immediately to the camouflage camera and turned it so he could better see the tiny, square hole carved into the back with the tiny number deep inside. "This is what I found."

"Damaged books?" He tilted his head to also look at the circular indentation on the side. He showed no sign of knowing what she held.

"You've never seen this before?" Her stomach tightened with renewed suspicion. If Chad was a true friend of Tyler's, he would know his favorite camera when he saw it.

"No, should I have?" His eyebrows flattened again, as if not sure where this was about to lead.

"I'd think so. It belonged to Tyler."

His recognition was immediate. "Is that his book camera?"

"Then you *do* know about it?"

"I know about it, but I don't think I've ever actually seen it. He kept it put away so certain people wouldn't know he had it." He reached out to touch the leather binding with sad reverence. "Tyler bought it a couple of years ago so he could take pictures of people who otherwise wouldn't have let him anywhere near them. It was his pride. But I don't understand. What's the camera got to do with the evidence you found?"

"There's film inside. Exposed film."

"You mean there are pictures inside? Pictures Tyler took?"

"Evidently."

His expression lit with new understanding. "And you think maybe it's those same pictures the two men tried to find. Pictures that might somehow help us figure out who killed him."

"I'm hoping. I was just about to develop the film and find out." She gestured to the three trays she had laid side by side and the assortment of glass bottles.

His mouth went slack. "Are you saying *you* know how to turn the film inside that camera into real pictures?"

"Yes. I'm a photographer, too."

That amazed him more. "You're a lady photographer?"

She quirked a smile. "I don't know if I can lay much claim to the lady part, but I'm a darned good photographer."

He, too, had to smile. "Do you need any help?"

"Just close that door to keep out the light and listen for intruders. If I'm right, and the pictures from that camera turn out to be the evidence those men were looking for, I don't want anyone taking them away from us."

Obeying, Chad stood by the door and watched her while she worked in an extremely dim light. After having a heck of a time getting the camera open, she first made positives of the pictures by exposing treated paper in the enlarger box, then poured the proper liquids into the proper trays, dipping the exposed papers inside and pouring the liquids back into bottles. After she dipped the treated papers in water for the third and final time, she set them on a nearby mat to dry.

"As soon as I've coated them with sealant, we'll turn up the lamp and have a look at what we have here." She bent close to try to distinguish shapes, but couldn't tell what the pictures were in the darkness.

Chad moved closer while she finished brushing on the sealant. "I sure hope you're right. I hope those pictures hold the answers to Tyler's death." He rested a hand on her shoulder, a comforting gesture she hadn't expected. "How many are there?"

"Five." She smiled inwardly at the gentle warmth his touch generated, pleasant despite the sweltering heat gathering inside the closed room. Already perspiration beaded her forehead and neck.

"Are they pictures of people?"

"We'll know in a minute. Move the light over here."

Eagerly, he reached for the lamp. "Is it okay to turn it brighter?"

She bent over and blew on the photographs to hurry the drying process along, even though they did not have to be completely dry at this point. She was beyond jeopardizing the image. "Go ahead."

The room brightened, casting dim shadows across the curled photographs. "Move it closer."

Afraid to hope, she stepped aside to give him room to look at the photographs with her, and frowned when she discovered nothing incriminating in any of them. Disappointed, she brushed her damp hair off her face with her wrist and headed for the door to let fresh air into that oven of a room.

With that done, she turned to Chad, surprised to see his look of astonishment as he moved one of the photographs closer to the light.

"Do you realize what we have here?" he asked, holding the print gingerly by the corners, his gaze riveted on the image.

What was that all about?

Clearly having missed something, she returned to his side and peered over his shoulder. Still, she didn't understand the tremor of excitement in his voice. "I see that we have a photograph of three men and a dark-colored horse with a number on its saddle at a July Fourth celebration of some sort, probably taken just this month since it was still in the camera. I also know by the banner stretched across the street that as part of the celebration there's a horse race planned for four o'clock. People are already lining the street for that." *What was so amazing about that?* "Who are those men there in the forefront? The ones looking over the horse obviously slated to be in the race?"

"The Craig brothers," he answered, pointing to them one at a time. "Eric, Jeff, and Clifton."

"The same men who knocked out your town's bank president, then robbed the safe of all the money?" She looked again at the photograph and decided the men, though dressed in normal street garb, certainly looked ruffian enough to have done something like that. But why should the photograph please Chad as much as it obviously did? Nothing she saw indicated the men were about to do, or had just done, something wrong. None of the three wore weapons, nor was there a bank in the background to hint at their planned activities. "I don't understand. What's so important about this particular photograph?"

"What's important is the fact that this was obviously taken about mid- to late afternoon of this past July Fourth. Look at the shadows. Look at the people. They're all starting to get ready to watch the race that the banner claims starts at four o'clock."

She had already noticed all that. Still, she had no idea why it should please him. True, she remembered from the sheriff's account that July Fourth was the day the three brothers overpowered the local bank president and robbed the place of practically every penny there. But she saw no indication in the photograph that anything of that nature was about to happen. But, obviously, Chad did.

"And?"

"And this picture was not taken in our town." He looked up, his mind still working with that fact. "This picture was taken down in Guthrie. That means none of the three were anywhere near here the afternoon Lance Maze claims to have been robbed."

"But the sheriff said he saw them, too. He told me he saw their faces clear as day. He said that after having gone looking for Lance, he came eye to eye with one of them. Made a big deal out of having stared him down and survived."

"Evidently all that was as much a lie as what Lance Maze told us," he replied grimly, tapping the photograph as proof.

The sheriff's lie came as no real surprise to Jenny since

he seemed the type who would exaggerate stories to make himself look the hero. She would wager now he never even had a clue the bank had been robbed until Lance Maze told him.

"And obviously Tyler knew it was all lies, too," Chad continued, his blue eyes distant while he sorted it all out in his mind. "And, knowing Tyler, who was never intimidated by anyone, when he returned from Guthrie and heard about what was supposed to have happened here, he confronted Lance with that lie by telling about the photographs he'd taken."

"So photographs were indeed what those two men searched for?" She looked at the print again, seeing it now with a new perspective. Her heart swelled with anticipation. The man who had a reason to want this photograph was the man who killed her great-grandfather. Killed him while trying to get his hands on these, probably thinking they'd been developed already.

Jenny felt giddy with anticipation. They were very close to solving the murder. Soon, they would have the killer in jail and she would be free to go back to her own time. And with plenty of time to get ready for her next photo shoot. No one would ever know she'd been gone. Except for Stillshot—and perhaps some of the neighbors he had surely terrorized by now.

She pushed that annoying thought aside. "Is the banker a tall, broad-shouldered man like you?"

"No."

"Then is he a small, slightly hunched man?"

"No. Why?"

She frowned. Already, she had a problem with her theory. Who else but the banker who had lied about who'd committed the robbery would have reason to want this photograph? "One of the two men who searched this place a second time was tall and bulky," she answered. "The other was short, skinny, and had hunched shoulders."

"Sounds to me like Sheriff Mack and his half-brother deputy, Walter." He stroked his chin while processing this new information.

"But why would they be searching the place if it was the banker who made up the story about the Craig brothers?"

"They are probably all in whatever it is that they did together. Lance and Wade have always been close friends. Wade's brother is the type to dó whatever Wade tells him. And Wade is the type to do whatever serves his purpose."

"Are the sheriff and bank president close enough friends to rob a bank together, then try to make it look like someone else did it?"

"Obviously so, which explains why the sheriff has been so intent on getting us out of this house. I wondered about that." He shook his head, as if it all made sense now. "They need us out of here so they can search again without getting caught." His eyes narrowed. "I knew there was a reason I didn't trust that man."

Finding it hard to believe the sheriff had the intelligence to have helped pull off anything so elaborate, she looked at the other photographs to see if they were similar. Although all five were of the Craig brothers, and all five were taken inside that same town on a day where the townsfolk were clearly celebrating the July Fourth picnic advertised on the banner, the only photo displaying the street banner, proving the date, was the one Chad held.

"So what do we do with the photograph now that we have it? If there's a chance the sheriff was involved, we can't very well turn it over to him."

"We'll have to sidestep him. There's a circulating judge coming in from Guthrie the first of next week who's to be here long enough to settle a federal land dispute. We can show him the photograph, explain how we came to have it, and tell him what you know about the men who searched this place. Meanwhile, I'm going to try to see if I can come up with more evidence. Something other than just this one photograph. Lance Maze is not a stupid man. He'll say next that it must have been someone who looked like the brothers robbing the bank."

Jenny wondered if the other photograph she had would be of any help. Although it didn't reveal much else, it did indicate the size and shape of the murderer. She headed to the drawer where she had rehidden it before using the tray again.

"We need something else that would prove they deliberately lied about the robbery," Chad continued. "Maybe I could talk to them separately, and while doing so, get one of them to slip up and contradict the other's statements. I could then testify to that. Of course, in the end it would just be my word against theirs. But still, it might throw added doubt."

"Or, we could set a trap for them," she offered, already concocting a better plan. "A trap that would get us another piece of physical evidence just as strong as that one."

That clearly interested him. "What sort of trap?"

"We indicate to them what we've found, then catch them in the act of slipping back in here and trying to steal it again." She pointed to the book camera, now lying empty with its back open. "And to make it more than just our word against theirs, we catch them on film."

Her eyes lit with excitement as she pulled the earlier photo out and handed it to him. "If we can get them to try it in the daytime, while this room is still filled with enough daylight, they would never even have to know another photograph was taken. But if they don't show up until late afternoon or night, the photograph won't come out much clearer than this one."

Chad glanced at the dim figure she indicated while listening to the rest of her plan.

"If that's the case, I'd have to be ready with a flash pan. But I could be hiding behind something so they wouldn't know I was there until the flash, which should blind them long enough for me to escape with the camera out a window."

Chad stared at the photograph, dumbfounded. "You had the presence of mind to try to take a photograph of the murderer?"

Not wanting to try to explain a situation she didn't quite understand herself, she gave an indirect response, "But as you can see, the photograph is too dark to do anyone any good. The subject was in the only room with no windows and too far away to catch much of the flash. We would plan our trap so the subject would be much closer this time. Who knows? It might be, once we've proved even one of the two is involved in illegal activities, we can then trick them both into a full confession."

Chad looked at her, impressed. "You're sure you can work the book camera, too?"

"If I have film for it, yes."

"But where would we get the film? I'm no photographer, but I know enough about Tyler's cameras to know you can't reuse what's left of what we just took out."

She shrugged. She hadn't seen anything that looked like film while cleaning up thus far. "We go back through those business receipts we found." She pointed to the papers now stacked neatly on the larger of the two desks. "We find out where he buys his film, then tomorrow one of us goes there and buys some. Meanwhile, we continue to pack, and complain, making it look as if nothing out of the ordinary has happened here. We don't want them guessing what we've found until the time is right."

Chad needed no further prodding. He rushed to the desk, then lit the twin lamp, and started sorting through the many slips of paper. He read each carefully for any mention of film. Jenny stood behind him, double-checking over his shoulder.

"Here it is. He bought film from a place called Sobey's

Camera Emporium all the way over in Oklahoma City. Think that's it?"

She read the line where he jabbed a finger. The cost was for the installation of Eastman flexible film, and the only one of her great-grandfather's cameras that used film instead of treated glass was the Scovill and Adams. "There's one way to find out for sure. Call them and ask."

"Call them?" He looked up, confused.

Remembering she had never seen a telephone in Black Rock, although certain they existed by 1896 at least in the metropolitan areas, she amended, "Send them a telegraph asking if they are the company who provides the film for the Scovill and Adams specialty camera. If so, since they are so far away, we ask if they will send a special messenger to Black Rock with a package. That way we can both stay here and continue packing as if nothing unusual was about to happen."

Chad shook his head in amazement. "You sure do stay calm under fire."

"That's just the way I am. I wait until after everything is over and there is no more danger, then fall to pieces." Which she would surely do the moment she made it back into her own time. And deservedly so. "Write down the information you need off there and go send that telegram. The sooner we can get that film here the better." She was eager to reload, place the camera where she could hide nearby and quietly work it, then lure the sheriff or the banker into a return visit.

Chad jotted down the name of the company, the street location, and how much the film cost in case there was more than one kind and they needed to verify they had the right film in mind.

"I won't be gone long. I'll send the telegraph, then go back by my house to get another pistol in case something goes wrong with the plan and there's trouble."

"Another pistol? I wasn't aware we had even one pistol."

He looked at her sheepishly. "I have one hidden in with the clothes I just brought."

"In case those men returned to search the house again?"

"Well partly, but I was more worried I'd need a way to keep you from bolting in the night with half of what Tyler owns. But now that I know you are not the enemy, I think it'd be better if we were both armed." He picked up the two photographs again. "Do you know how to shoot?"

"To a certain degree."

"Then I'll leave you with the one hidden in my clothes. It's small, easy to conceal, and shoots straight for quite some distance despite the short barrel."

"No, take it with you," she insisted, aware he would be in more danger out on the shadowy streets than she would protected inside the house. "It'll soon be dark and there's a good chance your Lance Maze is out there worried sick about what we will find here. If he sees you headed into the telegraph office and thinks you may be trying to get out information he doesn't want out, he might try to stop you any way he can. I should be relatively safe here, but just in case, I'll go get the dagger out of the bedroom and keep it nearby while you're gone."

"You *do* have the dagger?" He cut her a quick, accusing gaze.

Annoyed he continued to jump to false conclusions where she was concerned, she planted her hands on her hips. "I have no plans to steal the thing. I only borrowed it for while I'm here. For protection. From *you*."

He studied her a moment longer, then relaxed his tense expression. "So, you were as worried about me as I was about you, and had I made one wrong move—" He paused as if to search for a genteel way to finish the statement.

"I'd be field dressing you about now," she supplied, thinking it silly to worry about her sensibilities. She was a grown woman, not a child.

He blinked, then laughed. "Not exactly how I'd have phrased it, but I get the idea of the danger I faced."

Noting the hour, and hoping to get the telegraph off before the businesses in Oklahoma City closed so they would have an answer as quickly as possible, Chad carried the photographs into the hall. There he hid them under a decorative cloth on a small table jammed against one wall, then rearranged the objects on top. With nothing to indicate the photographs' presence, he hurried on to the kitchen table, where he had left his valise. Quickly, he dug a large derringer out of his clothing and left, ordering Jenny to bolt the door behind him.

With no more reason to share a bedroom, their suspicions of each other now quelled, Jenny bolted the back door as told, then carried Chad's valise to another bedroom and set it on the bed to get it out of the way.

Tempted to learn more about the man who had so completely piqued her interest, she decided to unpack his clothing, curious to know what all he thought necessary to have with him while protecting Tyler's house from the evil impostor. Inside, in addition to clothing of all kinds, which she folded neatly and set on top of the dresser, she discovered a shaving mug with a whipping brush, as well as an old-fashioned straight-edge razor. She also came across a small wooden toothbrush, a stiff-bristled hairbrush, again with a wooden back, and a tall, skinny bottle of "genuine bay rum." Uncorking it, she took a whiff and found the fragrance to be quite pleasant. The smell already reminded her of him, aware now she had caught that same scent the night before when he had tried to seduce her.

Her heart fluttered at the memory of what had almost happened between them, although now she was not nearly as mortified by it—having learned he was *not* her great-grandfather's killer. Given that fact, she had not almost committed an act of family treason. As it turned out, Chad really was Tyler's best friend. And a man with whom she now shared a common goal.

She smiled, warmed by the knowledge they were not enemies after all. They both wanted the same thing, to find Tyler's killer, and yet they had each started out suspecting the other.

She laughed at the absurdity, then having finished unpacking his things, left the bedroom to return to the studio. To avoid stumbling in the growing darkness, she carried a lamp with her. Barely halfway down the hall, the acrid smell of smoke stopped her in her tracks.

Fire!

Eleven

Not knowing where exactly the fire was, Jenny's first thought was to save the two pictures. The murderer might succeed in burning down the house, what with no way for her to summon a fire department, but he would not destroy the evidence in the process.

Running to the table, she slid her hand under the cloth, pulled out the two photographs, then headed for the back door.

When she neared the kitchen, the smell of smoke grew stronger but there was no sign yet of flames. Thinking maybe the fire was still of a size she could fight it, and thus save her great-grandparents' belongings, she hurried to the door where smoke now curled under the upper doorframe. A rush of relief and stupidity washed over her when she saw the cause. The house was not on fire. She'd been so distracted, she had fully forgotten about the bread and the cobbler. Smoke curled out of every open seam of the huge, cast-iron stove.

Hiding the photographs again, this time deep inside one of the lidded crates, she hurried to take the three blackened pans outside, not venturing farther than the back porch, since it was now dark. Carefully, she dropped the pans on top of a small stack of firewood, then returned inside to see if the stew had met a similar fate. To give the smoke a better means of escape, she left the back door open.

Coughing, and bending low, she used the same hot pads to remove the pan with the stew, glad to find that although the food had scorched, it wasn't ruined. They would not have to starve. Nor would they have to go outside the house for their evening meal.

Now that she understood the danger of being out on the street, and most especially of being alone with the sheriff, she did not intend to leave the house for any reason. Nor did she want to give anyone the opportunity to search the house again until they were ready for them to.

Forgetting her promise to arm herself with her great-grandfather's dagger, Jenny set about preparing the kitchen table for their meal. She chose eating in the kitchen over the dining room because that room had fewer windows. Wanting to have everything ready upon Chad's return, she used the same glasses and utensils they'd used for breakfast, but had to dig out two dinner bowls to accommodate the stew.

By the time she had set the table, transferred the still-bubbling stew to a large tureen, and filled the scorched pan with water to soak, the smoke had cleared. Spotting a hazy residue near the top of the tall counters and along the wall nearest the stove, she decided to wipe the soot away while awaiting Chad's return. Her thoughts were so focused on the work and her stupid mistake, she did not hear an approach to the back door. Her heart jumped nearly out of her chest when an angry male voice boomed only a few dozen yards away.

"Just what kind of fool are you?"

She cringed. Chad must have spotted the burned pans on his way in. "The kind who is too easily distracted, I guess." Her eyes widened when he stepped from the dark porch into the lighted room. He looked absolutely livid. *Jeez, it was only bread and a cobbler.* The pans weren't even ruined beyond cleaning. "Chad, it's not as if I committed a crime. It was just an oversight."

"Just an oversight?" he repeated incredulously. The muscles in his jaw turned rock-hard as he curled his hands into mighty fists. "Don't you realize the danger in an oversight like that?"

She glanced at the stove she had just wiped with the rag still in her hand. "Well, actually, I think the danger was minimal. There's not much way for a fire to spread from inside that oven. It's built solid, thank goodness."

"Fire?" Suddenly Chad looked confused. "What fire?"

"The bread and cobbler. Didn't you see them on your way in? I burned all three to a black crisp."

"And *that's* why the door was left open?" He blew out a shaky breath and closed his eyes to regroup his emotions. "Do you know what it did to me to come back here and find the back door wide open after I'd clearly told you to close and bolt it?"

"That's what has you so upset? You thought I'd deliberately disobeyed an order?"

His jaw flexed. "No, what has me so upset is that I thought someone had come here so bent on finding that evidence, they had broken in even with you here and hurt you." He moved forward, placing a hand on her cheek, gentle despite his anger. "I was afraid you'd met the same fate as Tyler."

Finding more than just comfort in his touch, Jenny swallowed hard. Did he have any idea at all what the warmth from his hand did to her? "You were worried about me?"

Moving another step closer, he lifted his free hand to her other cheek, cupping her face gently in front of him. Electricity fanned out from where he held her, causing her entire body to feel light and tingly. It took great effort not to close her eyes and become lost to the wondrous feeling.

"Yes, I was worried." His voice was vibrant with concern. "Although I still have no idea who you are, nor do I know your original reason for being here, I've grown quite accustomed to you during these past two days." The fear reflected in his eyes transformed into something else just as dark, and just as vivid. "I want the chance to get to know you better."

Jenny tried to swallow again but couldn't, recognizing this new emotion for what it was. With far less reason to distrust her now, Chad had let down his barriers and in doing so had become physically attracted to her—as strongly as she was physically attracted to him.

A dangerous combination. Especially when there was no one around to stop them from reacting to that attraction.

Afraid the tender moment might turn into one of volatile passion like the night before, something she was not quite ready to face again, she tried to think of a way to quell his male desire. Besides, to continue would be unfair to Chad. It could mislead him into believing they would still be together when this all was finally over.

Her heart twisted. *What if she did allow him to continue and he fell in love with her?* She would be setting him up for a broken heart, and setting herself up for one as well. If she gave in to the deep longing inside her, she, too, just might fall in love, and that would be disastrous. It would make leaving here—thus leaving Chad—the most painful thing she'd ever done. She would live the rest of her life with an aching heart.

"I'm sorry I left the door open like that. I really should have closed it again as soon as the smoke cleared." Effectively having changed the subject, she tried to look away, but couldn't. "It was a foolish mistake. I'll be more careful from now on."

"See that you are," he replied in a deep, throaty whisper, already pulling her closer. Clearly, he intended to kiss her.

Although her conscience demanded she not allow it, her selfish heart refused to listen. What lasting harm could one kiss prove? Surely he wouldn't expect her to stay simply because they had shared one little kiss.

Charged with anticipation, she parted her mouth to receive his, eager again for the power he held there. Her eyes drifted shut as she briefly wondered if he would leave her the strength to pull away once they had shared that kiss. Had her heart foolishly plunged her into an uncontrollable situation? One that would eventually reap nothing but pain? Or would the moment of pleasure prove worth whatever the outcome? At least she would have a few tantalizing memories to take back with her. Memories to warm her during all the long, lonely nights to come.

Convinced the risk would indeed be well worth the pleasure, she lifted her arms, prepared to slide them around his strong shoulders the moment his body melded to hers. If it came to that, she would give of herself completely and worry about the painful consequences later.

Still cradling her face, Chad paused, his mouth so close she felt the warm vibrations when he continued with what he had to say, "Stay as far out of harm's way as you can. I want you still around when this is all over."

Jenny winced. Those were the very words needed to jolt her back to her senses. The risk of heartache wasn't just hers. Chad would be hurt, too. Already, he had false hopes.

Quickly, she pulled away. "To prove to you I mean it," she said, her voice barely pushing past the constriction in her throat, "I'll go shut and bolt the door right now."

Without looking at him again, knowing that might be her final undoing, she hurried to do just that. After securing the door, she turned to face the table, then drew in a long, needed breath before looking his direction again. Still, she refused to meet his gaze. "Supper, or what's left of it, is ready. I hope you are hungry."

"Oh, *that* I am," he responded as he studied her awkward movements, a deep undercurrent in his voice. With eyes still glittering, he moved toward her, causing her heart to take another flying leap into nowhere; but instead of drawing her face in his hands again like she feared, he brushed past her to the sink, where he quickly washed for supper.

As relieved as she was disappointed, Jenny hurried to the table. With trembling hands, she lifted the top off the soup tureen and ladled two generous portions into the waiting bowls.

For the next few minutes, little sound was heard other than the clattering of spoons against porcelain until Jenny finally thought to question him about the telegram. With her pulse rate finally settled, her thoughts returned to matters at hand. "Did you get the message sent?"

Having just taken a large bite, he paused to clear his mouth before answering. "Yes, I had it sent off within five minutes after I left here. If it turns out the business was closed by then, the telegram will be sent over first thing in the morning. I had Andy put 'urgent' on it. I figure we should have a response by noon."

"What reason did you give Andy for wanting new film?" She worried what would happen should Andy tell the wrong person about the message.

"I told him that I felt it my duty to ship the cameras to Tyler's wife in good working order, ready to use. I was prepared to give strong reasons why, but as it turned out, he was more interested in hearing about you."

He took another bite of stew, his attention still on her.

"About me?"

"Seems the whole town is curious about the beautiful woman who has twice made an emotional dash through town, but otherwise rarely comes out of her brother's house." A hint of a smile tugged at his mouth, luring her attention to the splendid shape of his lips. Lips perfect for kissing.

Now where had that thought come from? Her heart rippled while she quickly shoved the unbidden image to the back of her mind. She had to get better control over her emotions if she was to do her great-grandfather any good.

What was wrong with her anyway? "And what did you tell him?"

She reached to brighten the porcelain lamp she had placed nearby. Maybe a sharper light would help.

"Just that you were doing all you could to help, which he thought an odd thing for me to say, having heard I didn't much like you. So I told him I'd since changed my mind about you and we'd become friends. To that he chuckled, probably wondering just *how* friendly we'd become while living here under the same roof. Since talking about you kept him focused on something other than my request for film, I didn't say anything to modify those thoughts. I just let him go on believing what he wanted to believe. Just like I always do." He grinned. "Truth is, I may have encouraged him when I gave him that playful wink. I hope you don't mind, but it was for our own good."

"Why should I mind what some man I've never met thinks?" she asked, aware the night before they had come very close to giving some very real substance to that gossip. Her senses vaulted at the memory.

"The thing is, it won't be just the one man thinking that. I know Andy. He'll tell everyone he sees what I said—or rather what I *didn't* say after he had all but accused me of seducing you." Setting his spoon down, he leaned forward, carefully measuring her reaction. When he did, his light-blue shirt stretched taut across his broad shoulders, causing her to look down. "By tomorrow, the entire town will think I've taken you to my bed."

"Let them think what they want," she responded, her attention again involuntarily drawn to the silent invitation glittering in his blue eyes. He was asking if she'd care to give truth to the gossip. "I'm not the one who'll be here to face them afterward, and, as I recall, the sheriff said you don't care what's said about you."

His playful expression changed immediately. "So, after

this is over, you'll be heading back to wherever it is you came from?"

"Yes, just as soon as I know Tyler's murderer is in jail."

"That's all that's holding you here?" He glanced down at his food, but did not resume eating.

Aware of his disappointment, she reached across the small table and touched his hand. "I'm sorry. But I won't be staying. I can't. I don't belong here."

After a long, reflective pause, Chad lifted his gaze. "Who are you?"

Not having expected the questions, Jenny's heart drummed a frantic rhythm against her chest as she rested her spoon on the edge of her bowl. For lack of anything else to do with her hands, she placed them in her lap, knotting them in the deep folds of her skirt. "What kind of question is that?"

"An honest one. I know you aren't Tyler's sister, although you do look amazingly like my good friend. Tyler told me all about his family and you were never mentioned. I also know you've been wearing Janeen's clothes since the first time I saw you, which, as you of course know, was shortly after Tyler's murder. That means you had to have changed into her clothing almost immediately upon arrival. At first, I thought that probably was because your own clothes were splattered with Tyler's blood, evidence you didn't want the sheriff to see. But now that I know you had nothing to do with the murder, I have no idea *why* you are in Janeen's clothes. Why aren't you in your own clothes? And why have you tried so hard to convince the sheriff and everyone else that you are Tyler's sister. *Who are you?*"

Jenny looked away. What could she say? He had her dead to rights. Tired of lying, and unable to come up with anything better, she told the truth. "You're right. I'm not Tyler's sister. I said I was because I knew the truth would be too hard to believe, and I didn't want the sheriff to discount anything I had to tell him about the murder. My name is really Jenny Langford, and the reason I look so much like Tyler is not because he was my brother, but because he was my great-grandfather."

"Your *what?*" His blue eyes rounded.

"My great-grandfather. I know it's hard to believe, because at times I don't believe it myself, but I've come here from a hundred years into the future."

"You what?"

"I'm not from the year 1896. For reasons I can only guess, I've been sent one hundred years back in time. Until yesterday, I was still in the year 1996, living a very dull, but wonderfully safe life."

Chad's forehead notched while that new bit of information settled. "You said earlier you are a photographer. And having watched you develop those photographs, I have to believe that. Is that your connection to Tyler? You two met because you are both photographers?"

She fought the urge to smile. Clearly, he did not want to believe such a strange truth. And who could blame him? At times, she didn't want to believe, it either. "No, I never met Tyler, although I wish I had."

Her heart ached with an intense sadness, knowing how close she had come to just that. "I don't know why fate brought me back to the very minute he was murdered instead of a few minutes earlier so I might have done something to prevent the murder, but that's the way it happened. I suppose he was destined to die, but perhaps his murderer was not destined to go unpunished. Originally, he did. But this time, he won't. That has to be why I'm here. To change history to the way it was supposed to be. Before I was sent here, I'd vowed I would see justice done if given a chance."

She paused to allow him to comment about such a strange set of affairs, but he ignored the opportunity to speak. Instead, he continued to stare at her questioningly, clearly trying to make sense of her story.

"That's why I was so eager to move right into the house. I wanted to be able to search for clues, anything that might implicate the murderer."

Finally, Chad looked away, his eyes dark with disappointment. "So what you are really saying is that it is none of my business who you are, and that I should quit asking." He pushed back from the table. "That's fine. You don't have to tell me the truth if you don't want to. It's enough I know you're trying to help. For whatever reason."

Seeing his injured pride, Jenny's heart went out to him. He'd wanted the truth, but she'd delivered more of it than he could handle. "Chad, who I am isn't what's important here. What's important is that we both are struggling toward the same goal. We both want to see Tyler's killer brought to justice. We need to continue working together if we hope to reach that goal."

"You're right," he said, erasing the hurt from his voice as he stood. "About so many things. Including the fact we should continue our packing, as if nothing out of the ordinary has happened. We don't want to draw suspicion. I'll haul in a few more crates so we can do just that."

"Be careful," she warned, feeling incredibly sad while she watched him head for the door with long, determined strides. "Someone could be out there."

He patted a small bulge in his waistband, where the ivory handle of a pistol barely showed. "I'm prepared."

Still, Jenny worried until Chad returned with the promised crates. After quickly washing the few dishes they'd used, setting them aside to dry, she put what stew was left in the tiny ice box. She returned the two photographs to their hiding place out in the hall, then followed Chad to the master bedroom to resume packing, knowing that a still-cluttered studio would be to their advantage tomorrow.

While working, they talked about matters related to Tyler and his death, and even related to Chad, but nothing else was said that had to do with her other than Chad's testing out the new name Jenny a few times. After finding she responded to Jenny better than Ruth, that was the name he used when the conversation drifted to the wonders of photography and Chad asked her to show him how to work the book camera.

"Why?" She paused after she had lovingly placed Tyler's hat in a large, round box she found inside the wardrobe, working it in around two of Janeen's smaller hats.

"Because I've decided I should be the one to take the photograph of whoever ends up coming here to search for our evidence. Being here then will be too dangerous."

She frowned. She had thought this settled. "Not if you are around to protect me."

"That's just it, Jenny, I'd rather not have to protect you at all. I'd rather you be off somewhere safe, so I could then concentrate on taking the photograph and getting out before the person can do any harm."

"But what if they both come? And what if they both are armed? Without someone else here ready with a gun, whoever takes the photograph might not make it out of the room. What good would that do?" She put the lid on the hat box and set it aside. "No, we're both needed for this to work. Me to take the photograph, then escape with the camera. You to provide cover for me should they be armed, which I'm pretty sure they will be."

Chad let out a short, frustrated breath, but gave up the argument. "Just be sure you head for that window the very second after you've taken the photograph."

Her heart warm now with the knowledge he cared so much, she smiled. "I won't take any unnecessary chances. I promise."

Having decided to stack the crates and barrels they had already packed near the front door out of their way, Chad lifted the one he'd just filled. With muscles bulging, he carried it out of the bedroom while Jenny put an empty one in its place. Down to the bottom drawer of the main dresser, Jenny bent to pull out the nightgowns and undergarments stored there, and was taken by surprise when she came across a particularly lacy chemise. She held it up against her and realized not only was it frillier than the rest, the top was cut much lower and the leg openings cut much higher.

A twinge of sadness tugged at her heart when she realized the reason her great-grandmother would own such a garment. The garment would never be put to such use again.

Gingerly, she laid it on the bed, and wondered about what precious memories the garment held. Memories her great-grandmother would cherish for the rest of her remaining days. They and the child she carried were all she had left.

Blinking back tears, Jenny sat beside the chemise, folding it with utmost care, then placed it in the box with Tyler's hat where it could easily be found.

At least her great-grandmother had been bold enough to have such memories, she thought sadly while she carefully replaced the lid. Many women of that time would not have bought anything so daring as this, not even for her own husband's pleasure.

Jenny wished she had such happy memories. Something to warm her on those long nights when there was no one around to comfort her but her cat. But how could she possibly have such memories? She had never found anyone who'd stirred her passions to quite that degree. The men she dated were fun to be with, and for the most part made her feel important, but they didn't ignite the sort of passion a woman was supposed to feel for a man. The sort of passion Chad had aroused in her the night before.

Reminded of the incomparable desire he had so surprisingly brought to life inside her, her senses took an unexpected leap. Until Chad's kiss, she'd never known such an intense level of emotion existed in her.

How wrong she'd been. A pity she hadn't met anyone like Chad in her own time. What a difference a man like that could make in her life. Her body ached with longing at the mere thought of what she had been missing.

Indulging herself, she closed her eyes and relived the moments of passion she had shared with Chad the night before. Her body throbbed with each remembered kiss—with each remembered touch—and for a brief moment, she wished she had not stopped him. Then, she, too, would have memories to cherish forever. Like her great-grandmother.

Quivering inside, she wondered what it was like to reach that revered pinnacle of desire, to know the magic only a man like Chad could provide.

Twenty-eight years old, and except for one fumbling exploration in the backseat of a Chevy Nova when she was only seventeen and another in her own apartment when she was twenty-one, Jenny Langford's intimate encounters with a man had never been fulfilling ones. Why should that fact suddenly sadden her?

"Are you tired?"

Jenny's eyes flew open. She had been so involved in her titillating thoughts, she hadn't heard Chad return. "What?"

"I asked if you were tired. You had your eyes closed and looked as if you were about to drift off to sleep sitting straight up." He pointed to the remaining clothes and toiletry items scattered about Tyler and Janeen's bedroom. "If you are tired, we can put off packing the rest of this until tomorrow. As long as it's obvious we're still making progress in our endeavors, it should throw off any worry about us having found the evidence."

Disconcerted to have had Chad in the room with her while her thoughts had taken such a daring turn, she blinked, then looked to where the clock had once sat, forgetting they'd already packed it. "Since it's probably getting pretty late by now, and with everything we'll need to get done tomorrow, it would be a good idea to get plenty of sleep. We'll want to be alert and ready to act when the time comes to spring our trap."

Nodding that he understood, he scooped up the lamp just as he followed her out of the room.

Still disturbed by her tantalizing thoughts, she tried to keep a safe distance between them while headed toward her bedroom. Pausing outside the darkened door, she turned and smiled as sweetly as her churning insides allowed. "I'll see you in the morning."

"Are you sure you'll be safe sleeping in there alone?" His gaze dipped to the scooped neckline of the pink dress she wore but cut quickly back to her face.

"Yes, there are screens on my windows to keep out any pests—both insect and human." And they had already closed and latched the windows in the studio, kitchen, parlor, and dining room, hampering ventilation but allowing for a stronger feeling of security. She would have closed her bedroom windows, too, but needed some air stirring to be able to sleep.

"But screens can be torn," he noted, glancing beyond her into the unlit bedroom. "Maybe I'd better check and make sure someone hasn't already torn any of them." He went on inside to do just that.

Still trembling with a need she had not yet quelled, Jenny wanted to call him back. Get him out of her bedroom. Before she gave in to this illogical desire.

But she didn't. Instead, she followed him inside and watched while he tested the screens by giving them gentle shakes with his strong, masculine hands. *Magical hands.*

Wetting suddenly dry lips, she took a deep breath and moved to the bed. She sank down in its feathery softness to give her shaky legs a break. "See? I'm perfectly safe."

Staring at the light gleaming across the floor, she waited

for him to leave, but he made no move toward the door. Instead, he set the lamp he carried on her bedside table, then came to stand directly in front of her. Her heart pounded with such unprecedented power she feared it would burst right out of her chest when he placed a finger beneath her chin and forced her to look up at him.

"I hope you don't think I'm being too protective, but I don't want anything bad to happen to you."

"I know," she replied, her voice barely a croak. "Without me, you'd never be able to get the photograph we need. You have to keep me safe."

A tiny frown creased his forehead while he continued to search her eyes in the golden lamplight. "That isn't the only reason I want you protect you. It isn't even the main reason."

"Oh?"

His eyes were so dark with male need, her pulses pounded harder in response. He wanted her every bit as much as she wanted him. Why not allow it to happen? Just this once.

What harm could it do to harvest a few precious memories to take back with her? Before, her main concern had been how unfair it would be to Chad, building his hopes, then dashing them. But Chad now knew she had no intention of staying. She'd told him that earlier. He knew she planned to leave just as soon as they had unearthed the murderers. Yet he still wanted her. He willingly risked whatever piece of his heart he might lose to her in their time together. Why should she not risk the same?

Besides, she was already faced with some degree of heartache when she left, because in the two days she had been there, Chad had already found a permanent place in her heart. As illogical as it seemed, in but two days' time she'd fallen for him. Already he was a part of her. A part of her she'd hold dear forever.

Amazed by that, she slowly rose to her feet, her gaze locked with his, her skin prickling with this new awareness.

"And what other reason do you have to want to protect me?"

A tiny smile played at the corner of his mouth as he slowly moved closer.

Twelve

"I have *this* reason," Chad replied, his words but a throaty growl. His gaze dipped to the sensuous curve of her parted mouth before slowly returning to her lidded, dark-brown eyes as he leaned forward to claim her lips in a deeply seductive kiss. His strong arms drew her soft body into the tantalizing warmth of his eager embrace.

Knowing this was the woman he wanted, the woman he wanted to cherish the rest of his life, Chad drew a soft handful of her hair to his cheek and breathed deeply the feminine scent lightly mingled with woodsmoke, while he bent to enjoy the sweetness of her mouth. How wondrously intoxicating she was. How he longed to devour more of her. Devour her until she was finally a lasting part of him.

Jenny, too, yearned for more, aware now this was exactly what she wanted. Moaning appreciatively, she slid her arms around his sturdy neck, drawing him closer, eager to treasure their one moment together to its absolute fullest. Eager to have her memories.

Loving him as she did, and wanting to be loved by him, she planned to give of herself willingly and take from him ravenously, then suffer whatever consequences might befall them.

"I want you," Chad confessed huskily, finally pulling his mouth free of hers long enough to study her reaction. "I've wanted you since that first moment I set eyes on you. Even when I thought you had something to do with Tyler's murder, I wanted you. And now that I'm no longer suspicious of you, no longer worried about your intentions here, I find I want you even more."

"And I want you," she admitted, seeing no reason he shouldn't know, although she would keep secret the fact she also thought she loved him. There was no reason to generate false hope, and no reason to make him feel guilty because he didn't return emotions quite as strong as hers.

In truth, she was glad he didn't love her. It would make her leaving there a lot less painful for him.

Savoring the moment, Jenny closed her eyes as his mouth dipped for yet another deep, devouring kiss, causing her to tremble with a incredible need she had yet to explore. She pressed closer against him, absorbing the rising heat of his body. What a wondrous sensation *that* caused.

When she widened her mouth to moan aloud her ecstasy, Chad took advantage and darted the tip of his velvety tongue inside. Her entire being ached with anticipation as her heart soared higher with every tiny thrust of his tongue, aware each time that he darted deeper and deeper, as if craving more and more of her.

Overwhelmed by the intensity of need that swept over her, she sensed this would not be anything like her other two sexual encounters. She ran trembling palms over the powerful curves of his back and shoulders, timidly exploring the hard muscles through the thin fabric of his shirt— muscles that had grown solid and strong from years of hard, honest labor, not from an occasional workout at the local gym. The rippling movement of all that power beneath her sensitive fingers heightened her awareness even more.

Burying her hands deeper into the soft material of his shirt, she became so engulfed by the feel of his agile body pressed so intimately against hers, and by the magic his pliant mouth performed upon hers, she was barely aware his hands had begun an eager exploration of their own. It was not until he had undone several of the buttons along the back of her dress and the material slackened that she knew undoubtedly where his exploration was taking them.

With a heart overflowing with what had to be love, and a body aching with desire, she continued to push aside all thought of the heartache she would suffer when the time came to leave him. She refused to let anything get in the way of this one moment of happiness—possibly the only true happiness she might ever know, brief though it would be.

Chad continued to work with the many buttons down her back with one hand, while the other moved to the front of the dress to take in one aching breast. Even through the soft cottony fabric, his touch set her aflame. Within an amazingly short time, he had the dress completely undone and the fabric pushed down to her waist out of his way so he could work next on untying the satiny straps of her chemise. Once he had that undone and out of his way as well, he stepped back just far enough to work the two garments down over her slender hips, until finally they dropped to the floor in a mingled puddle of pink and white.

Jenny gasped when the cool air brushed her heated skin, causing her nipples to harden further while tiny bumps of exhilaration scattered across her body. She expected to feel awkward as he stood back to gaze longingly at her nude body, but felt nothing but pride, for what he saw clearly pleased him. Studying his hungry appraisal, she arched her shoulders to give him a proud view, and smiled when it caused his dark eyes to darken further.

Eagerly, she stepped forward and, with fumbling need, worked the tiny buttons that held his blue shirt together.

Unable to stand there and ignore what had been so eloquently presented him while she worked so desperately to liberate him of his clothing, Chad explored the rounded softness of her breasts, caressing their fullness with the curves of his hands while his thumbs gently stroked the hardened tips, causing them to grow even *more* rigid. The pointed tips beckoned him. As did every inch of her sumptuous body.

But despite his own need, Chad fought the urge to conquer quickly, determined to make this as pleasurable for her as it would be for him. He would not allow her first time to be one of hurt and confusion. He would claim her as gently and as gratifyingly as he could. By doing so, perhaps he would give her a reason to stay and become his wife.

When finally Jenny had every opening of Chad's clothing undone, she slowly pushed the garments back and off his body, her gaze watching her own movements, mesmerized, while gradually she exposed his hard muscles to the glistening lamplight.

With bodies now void of all clothing and pressed intimately together, the kiss deepened, and what had started out as tentative explorations of each other exploded into a maddening frenzy.

Willingly, Jenny succumbed to the swirling sea of sensations that had so quickly engulfed her, surrendering to a floodtide of need so staggering, it was all she could do not to cry out with frustration.

Enraptured by the pleasure he gave her, she closed her eyes again, aware when his head dropped to nip playfully at one breast they were well past the point of turning back. Nor did she want to. What she felt for Chad was far too intense to let her consider anything at that moment but finding some way to please him as much as he now pleased her.

Lost to passions she had never truly known existed, and to desires that flourished with each new place he touched and kissed, she ached with a longing so volatile, so intense, it had to be met. The sweet taste of his mouth whenever he returned to devour hers and the familiar scent that enveloped him only excited her further.

While Chad continued his dizzying wizardry, Jenny's blood raced hot trails beneath her skin, making her feel vibrantly alive. Never had she known such a blazing need, such burning excitement. Never had her pulses pounded with such incredible force, throbbing and swelling in every part of her body while her senses whirled endlessly through a fine state of delirium—heightening her arousal while she yielded instinctively to his touch.

Soon it felt as if Chad literally had set her ablaze. Her body writhed as her hands dug into his back with all the strength she possessed. She yearned, somehow, someway, to bring him closer. She yearned to make him a part of her, if only for the one night—so much a part of her that the heartbreaking fact they would never share a future together could be temporarily forgotten.

Chad was astounded by the force of their passion. Aroused to the point of madness, he groaned while he pulled her with him onto the waiting bed. Lying partially atop her, yet partially to one side, he continued to torment the woman who had awakened his body as easily as she'd stolen his heart. He continued his careful ministrations until he had her thrashing beneath his touch.

Then just when it seemed to Jenny that she could stand no more of his bittersweet torture, he proved her wrong. He released her mouth from his hungry imprisonment to trail tiny, searing kisses down her throat, across her collarbone, then down again until he reached her aching breast, causing her passions to soar higher still. Eager to feel his hungry mouth again on her tender flesh, she arched her back, giving him easy access to her breasts. Shafts of pure pleasure shot through her as his lips first nipped at a sensitive tip, then suckled the tightened bulb until she felt ready to explode. Frantically, she tugged at his shoulders, letting him know the time had come to quell her throbbing need.

But instead of moving to satisfy her, he turned his attentions to the neglected breast, bringing her yet more quivering shafts of white-hot pleasure. When he finally liberated her throbbing breasts from his gentle assault and moved to take her mouth in one last soul-shattering kiss, she arched her body against his to indicate her urgency while she buried frantic fingers into his back. Inside, she blazed with need, and wanted desperately to pull him into the flames.

Slowly, Chad rose and looked down at her beauty one last time. He gazed first at her flushed face, at the enticing way her eyes had closed and her mouth was parted, then at how her swelling breasts strained forward, a result of the inferno inside her, and knew the time was right. Eager to feel her warmth, he took only a moment longer to gaze at her beauty, then lowered himself onto her, gently.

Flames of sheer rapture seared every fiber of Jenny's being when he finally moved to claim her. At last, Chad, the man she loved and would continue to love long after she had left was a part of her. That brought her an exquisite, almost painful feeling of completeness. A euphoria beyond any she had ever believed possible. And, incredibly, the overpowering joy continued to build with each movement that followed.

Jenny's breath, shallow and gasping, grew stronger and more rapid as she reached higher and higher for the pinnacle—until finally, in a glorious burst of ecstasy, she cried aloud Chad's name. Chad responded to her outburst of pleasure with a deep, shuddering groan that wracked his entire body again and again.

Fulfilled at last, they both lay quietly on the rumpled bed for a long moment, their bodies still entwined, their energy spent, languorous in the aftermath of their lovemaking.

It was Chad who first broke the warm silence that filled the room. "I want you to know I love you. Even though I still don't know who you are, or why you originally came here, I have fallen in love with you, and in only two days time." He rose to one elbow to better study her reaction. "I never thought I'd love again. Not after Rebecca."

"Rebecca?" Jenny's stomach knotted with immediate jealousy. Although in the back of her mind she remembered

Beth Donner having alluded to the fact he had been married before, and logic told her a man as handsome as Chad had to have had many loves in his life, she had selfishly hoped that his past had held no important women. Although she had no plan to be a lasting part of his life, she had secretly hoped his marriage had failed because his ex-wife hadn't quite measured up. But obviously that was not the case. Obviously she had left him, and he still hurt because of that.

"My late wife," he answered, his voice deep with emotion. "I don't talk about her much because it still hurts to realize what I lost, even after ten years."

"How did she die?" A tiny part of Jenny didn't want to hear any of this, while a larger part had to know more about the one woman who had stolen Chad's heart.

"The doctor said it was heat stroke, made worse because she was seven months carrying what would have been our first child." He looked away, obviously not wanting her to glimpse his anguish. "It would have been my son."

"Oh, Chad, I'm so sorry." Never would she have guessed he carried such pain. "I didn't know."

"Of course you didn't." He forced the sadness from his voice. "Like I said, I don't talk about her much. But I did love her. Still do. Never having found anyone to match her caliber or her spirit, at least not until now, I've had little interest in a real relationship since. That's why I'm so glad I found you. You've made me realize I *can* love again. And having found you, I can't bear the thought of ever living without you. Don't leave when all this is through. Stay and marry me. I'll make you forever glad you did."

Jenny's eyes widened with instant regret. She had misjudged the situation completely. Chad had made love to her, thinking she would stay and fill the painful void in his life. A cold, sickly feeling snaked into her stomach, making her flinch with shame and self-loathing. "You can't possibly mean that. We've only known each other two days," she argued even though she, too, had just considered the possibility of love.

"Oh, but I can mean it. And I do." He lifted his free hand to stroke the curve of her cheek with his fingers. "I want what we just shared to be ours forever."

Tears filled her heart, then spilled over into her eyes. She had been so overwhelmed with what she felt toward him, she overlooked the true depth of his feelings. How selfish could one person be?

"But I can't marry you. As much as I might want to, I can never be your wife."

"Why?" He looked at her fearfully. "Are you already married?"

"No, but that has nothing to do with it." She wiped at her tears with fumbling hands. She had not wanted to hurt him—she had wanted only to share a moment of joy with him. How had this all gone so wrong? Was it because emotions stronger than she'd ever thought possible had taken over?

"Then what *does* have to do with it? Why can't you marry me?"

"I told you. I don't belong here." She sat up and clutched a bed pillow to her, suddenly offended by her own nudity, for it was a result of what she had just done to Chad.

That response obviously confused and frustrated him. He, too, sat up, his face contorted. "But you do belong. You belong right here. Beside me. For the rest of my life. For the rest of *our* lives. Can't you see that? You and I are meant for each other. I know that as well as I know my own name. You could at least stay here long enough to find out if I'm right."

The pain that tore through Jenny's heart was so intense she didn't think she could bear the onslaught. Tortured by the sincerity in his voice, aware he had confessed his true feelings, she fought a very real urge to bury her face in that pillow and cry huge, rasping sobs. "Chad, I explained to you earlier I'll have to leave here shortly after the murderer is apprehended. I meant that."

He studied her pleadingly. "Is it because of something in your past? Is it the same reason you won't tell me who you really are? Believe me when I say that whatever this terrible secret is, it won't make a difference in how I feel. Please believe that. Say you'll at least stay long enough to give me a real chance. I've waited too long to feel like this again. Please say you'll stay and find out just what it is you do feel toward me."

When all she could do was shake her head no, he bent to be able to look better into her eyes and tried again, "It's true, Jenny. As impossible as it may seem to you, I do love you enough to forgive anything from your past. Anything. Just please say you'll at least *consider* marrying me."

Unable to believe the generosity of his nature, and still very near bursting into tears, she tried again to explain. "You don't understand. Our lives are too different. We are from two different worlds." She had tried telling him just *how* different, but he had not believed her.

"Our lives may have been different until now, but even so, we are very much alike," he countered, and reached out to dab away another tear that collected at the corner of her eye. "We share more than the desire to see Tyler's murderer brought to justice and the willingness to put ourselves in danger to do that. Far more. Can't you see that? Why else would just talking about it have you crying like that?"

When her only response was to let her lower lip tremble while blinking back a fresh onslaught of tears, he hurried to add, "When two people love each other as much as I think we do, they can conquer any obstacle. No matter what it is you're afraid to tell me, whatever it is you're hiding from, it can be overcome. At least give it a try."

Jenny's heart wrenched nearly out of her chest when she saw the hope still glimmering in his pale-blue eyes. A very real desire to stay right there with him and indeed be his wife pitted itself against another need just as real and just as vital: the need to return to her own time. The mere notion of staying there in the nineteenth century where everything and everyone was so foreign to her terrified her, despite her love for Chad. If only she could find someone like him in her own time. But that would be asking the impossible, since she had a sneaking suspicion there weren't too many men like him even in *his* time.

The emotions warring inside Jenny continued to pull her in two directions at once, causing more havoc than she wanted to bear. "Oh, Chad, if only it were as simple as you think. But it isn't. I can't make my life here with you. It wouldn't work. I could never fit in."

"Why not?" His expression hardened when he pulled his hand away and fisted it against the rumpled bed.

"Because, like you just said, you don't know who I am. I am not at all the woman you think I am and I doubt I ever could be."

"You're dwelling on the past again."

Jenny looked away. It wasn't the past she considered. It was the *future*. She was a woman of the nineties, the *nineteen* nineties. She would be totally out of her element here. Even love could not compensate for that. If she stayed, he would find himself married to a woman ignorant of so much about his world.

"Chad, I have to consider both the past and the future."

"And your future should be right here with me. With a man who loves you enough to allow you to put whatever is in your past behind you."

Jenny could not believe the compassion that was so much a part of Chad Jordan. Briefly, she pushed all other thoughts aside and fantasized what it might be like to stay and be married to him, to have such a wonderful man doing what he could to please her for the rest of her life. But, within seconds, the reality of their situation returned. She could not allow him to be deluded by such false hope any longer. "Still, I can't stay."

"Why?" he asked again, so filled with frustration, his lips flattened against clenched teeth. Suddenly, he stood and started snatching clothing off the floor, throwing hers in her direction when he came to it. "You have yet to answer that one simple question. Why can't you stay and marry me?" He waved his shirt to emphasize his anger. "You've as much as admitted you care about me, if not in actual words, then surely in action. And I've already explained how much I love you. What's keeping us from being together? What is it I'm fighting against?"

Another tiny piece of Jenny's heart tore off and fell away. If only he hadn't fallen in love with her. It would have made her eventual leaving so much easier.

"Chad, don't do this," she said, forcing the words past the painful constriction that clamped her throat while hurrying to put Janeen's clothing back on. She was so filled with heartache by then, her blood ran cold beneath her skin. "Just accept the fact that I can't stay."

"Not without knowing why. Is it that you think I'd make a poor husband?"

Hardly. More visions of what it would be like to be married to a man as wonderful and as exciting as Chad drifted before her while she finished with her clothing. If only it were feasible for the two of them to be together. But it wasn't. "No, this has nothing to do with you. *I'm* the reason I can't stay."

Dressed again, Chad studied her a long moment. "There's a tiny part of you that wants to stay here with me. I can see that by the confusion in your eyes." He looked hopeful again. "I think I know the problem. My proposal came too suddenly. It caught you even more off guard than it caught me. You need more time to think about it." He smiled, relieved. "That's why I won't press you for a decision right now. Take time to give my proposal more thought before coming to the final decision. Can you at least do that? Can you at least give it more thought?"

Able to do little else *but* think about his generous proposal and what it might be like to accept such a thing, Jenny nodded. "All right, Chad. I'll give it more thought. But don't get your hopes up. It's not likely I'll change my mind. We really *are* too different for anything as lasting as marriage to work." Their worlds lay a *century* apart. A future together was unthinkable. Unless of course the camera didn't work when she tried it again. Her stomach knotted at the thought.

No, she refused to think her theory about the camera might be faulty. Fate couldn't have meant for her to be here forever.

Chad studied her a long moment, then headed toward the hall. "We have a long day ahead of us tomorrow. I'll see you first thing in the morning."

Jenny's heart twisted while she watched his retreat. She couldn't bear the thought of spending the night in that bed alone, not after what they had just shared. Although she should let him go, the desire to have him nearby was too great. "Chad?"

He turned instantly.

"Don't go. I've changed my mind. I want you to sleep in here with me."

He met her gaze questioningly. "Are you sure?"

She nodded. "I don't want to be alone."

"Do you realize that if I stay, I probably won't be able to keep my hands off you?" He took a tentative step in her direction. "What happened earlier could very well happen again."

"As long as you understand that it won't influence my decision in any way, I'm not against it happening again."

"Won't influence your decision? How can you say that?" Moving closer, he searched her face intently as he pulled her loosely into his arms, dipping to kiss her lightly below the ear. "How can our lovemaking not influence you at least to some degree?"

Jenny closed her eyes against the delicious shiver that caused. "I just don't want you to be more disappointed if I don't change my mind and agree to stay and marry you."

"But you've promised to think about it," he pointed out, dipping to place a second kiss below the other ear. "That's enough for me."

"As long as you understand how I feel," she continued, her voice scarcely a whisper, already falling prey to his mastery. Her heart clamoring again, she allowed him to pull her in the direction of the rumpled bed.

Jenny fell asleep that night pretending, for the sheer pleasure it gave her, that there was nothing to prevent her from becoming Chad's wife, nothing to keep her from enjoying such pleasure for the rest of her natural life.

It was not until the first blush of morning, when she awoke to the smell of fresh coffee that she allowed reality to take hold again. As much as she loved Chad, because of the odd circumstances, he would never be a permanent part of her life. She could enjoy what little time they had left together to its fullest, but eventually she would have to leave him. Possibly as early as that very afternoon, for today was the day they were to put their plan into action. Today, they would set out to get the other photograph they needed, and as soon as they had it, and had presented all their evidence to the judge Chad mentioned, she would be free to return to her own time.

Reminded of all that lay ahead, she slid out of the tall feather bed and knelt to make sure the camera she'd hidden was still under there.

Relief mixed with yet more sadness when she saw that it was. It meant she still had a way to return to her own time.

Dressing quickly in yet another of Janeen's dresses, this one lavender like the first, she brushed her hair, pulled it back into another ponytail high on her head but didn't bother trying to tuck it into a loose bun. No matter how many pins she used, it refused to stay long anyway.

Entering the kitchen moments later, her heart leaped at the sight of Chad sitting at the table, sipping his first cup of coffee. How handsome he looked in the stark white shirt, not yet fully buttoned, with light-brown trousers that molded to his legs so well.

"Good morning," she said, still aching with the thought that if they got the photograph they needed and Chad was able to get it and the other photos to the traveling judge from Guthrie by that night, she'd never behold this heart-warming sight again.

"Good morning." He smiled dimple deep as he gestured to the coffeepot on the stove, then to a tall jar sitting on the table. "Since we're out of eggs and the milk smells too sour to make skillet cakes, I'm afraid all I could find for our breakfast is coffee and canned peaches. Hope that will hold you until I can go to the store and buy some of the food stock Nora asked me to buy."

"Peaches will be fine," she said, knowing she could make the day on his wondrous smile alone, pleased he was willing to smile at her at all. Especially after last night. Clearly, he thought he'd yet change her mind.

"I'll stop in and buy the items she wanted and a little more ice for the box at the same time I check on that telegram. That way, while we're waiting for the camera emporium to deliver that film, Nora can be cooking a good, hardy lunch for us."

"What time should she be here?" Jenny asked as she unscrewed the lid and divided the sliced peaches between the two bowls Chad had put on the table, not certain what to expect that day.

"I don't know. I didn't get the chance to ask her since

she was already gone by the time I'd returned from getting my clothes." He gave her a playfully accusing look. "But I'd think about ten o'clock or maybe eleven," he replied, watching her scoot one of the bowls in front of him but not yet bothering to pick up his spoon. "I'll go check on the telegram and get the food she wanted well before then."

"How long do you think it will take a rider to bring the film here once they tell us they have it and we arrange to pay him when he delivers it here?"

Chad stroked his firm chin, smooth from the morning's shave. "If he rides straight on, stopping only to rest and feed himself, and feed and water his horse, I'd say about eleven or twelve hours."

"That long?" How big was this state?

"No, probably longer. I can't imagine anyone being willing to made a ride like that in one day. Not in the middle of July. I myself usually stop off in Guthrie for a night."

"So it'll be tomorrow before we have the film?" she asked, aware that meant she'd have another night with Chad. Her heart fluttered happily at the thought. To keep him from seeing the resulting glimmer in her eyes, she picked up her spoon and started eating her peaches.

"I'd think late tomorrow morning at the earliest. And that's *if* they have a rider they can send straight out. Otherwise, they'll have to ship it by train and freight wagon and it could be sometime Sunday afternoon since the freight line from Perry never runs on Sunday morning. But that might turn out to be to our advantage anyway. By waiting until Sunday afternoon to tell the sheriff we've finally found some evidence, we won't have to worry so much about someone slipping in here for a look around while we're both at Tyler's funeral. We also won't have to spend as long protecting whatever photograph we manage to take once they finally do come looking. Keep in mind, that judge probably won't arrive here until sometime Sunday night, and the sooner to that time we take the picture, the easier it'll be on us."

In which case, Jenny still had Friday *and* Saturday night with Chad. Not an upsetting possibility at all, she thought as she plopped another spoonful of the sugar-coated peaches into her mouth. "Then you don't plan to give the photographs to the judge until after he's arrived here?"

Chad, too, started to eat. "I think it would be a lot safer that way. If we end up having to use the flash while taking that photograph, they are going to know right away what we've done. We'll have no choice but to hide out somewhere until we know it's safe to come back here and develop it. By that time, the judge should have already arrived anyway. Besides, we wouldn't be safe out on any of the main roads after all that anyway."

Hide out? She paused with her spoon in mid-air. "You don't plan to stay here and protect Tyler's house while waiting for the judge?"

"Not if they're aware we took the photograph. My greatest concern is you. If we end up having to give ourselves away by using the flash pan or by making too much noise, we'll take that camera and head straight out of town. We'll do that to throw them off, then loop back after dark and stay in the feed loft of my store. There won't be much in the way of comfort, but from up there, we should be able to take a pot shot at anyone who tries to approach us."

He paused long enough to take another bite of the peaches. "Late that same night, if all goes well, we should be able to sneak back here, develop the picture, and sneak back to the feed store again without being seen. How much time will have passed by then will depend on how long it took them to make their move to find our reported evidence. But as long as we've waited until Sunday afternoon to tell them what we think we've found here, the judge should arrive by the time we've developed the photograph. Even if the film comes earlier than we expect, and we decide to go ahead with everything tomorrow, we won't have to wait for him too long."

Reminded of the danger they faced, Jenny stared absently at what little fruit remained in her bowl. "Either way, we're safe enough right here until tomorrow."

"Yes, as long as we continue to pretend nothing has changed. That's why we'll spend the daylight hours today packing as much as we can."

"The daylight hours?" Her eyebrows knitted questioningly. "What about tonight? Won't we still be packing then?"

Chad's dimpled smile was immediate. "Not if I can help it. I have *other* plans for us tonight."

Thirteen

"Bad news," Chad said as soon as Jenny had followed him out of the kitchen where Nora busily put away the ice and the food items he had brought back with him. He watched Jenny's expression turn instantly grim.

"What sort of bad news?"

"We can't just buy the film and have it shipped here. The telegraph they sent says they have to install the film directly into the camera themselves. It has to do with the way the camera is designed to run a special film indicator alongside the film, and how the whole thing needs to be mechanically sealed. It's the only way they'll sell us any."

Jenny continued to frown, though she didn't look nearly as upset as he had expected. How could he have forgotten her claim not to fall to pieces until all danger was over? It was that strength backed by a certain vulnerability that had attracted her to him in the first place. Well, that and those fascinating brown eyes.

"Then I guess one of us will have to carry the camera to Oklahoma City. And since you already know the way, you're the better choice. When can you leave?"

"Right after Tyler's funeral. If I leave before then, people might think it strange. Besides, Sobey's Camera Emporium won't install the film until Monday morning anyway. They made that clear in the telegraph."

"So there's nothing we can do until then?"

Again, she did not look as upset as he'd expected.

"Not that I can see. I'm willing to leave right after the funeral and ride through the night so I can be there waiting first thing Monday morning. I'm not sure how long it will take them to install the film, but if I can be on my way back by noon Monday, I should return early Tuesday. The judge will still be here, so that shouldn't be a problem. We can still follow through with our plan, we'll just have to put it off longer than we'd planned is all."

Seeing her frown deepen instead of smooth away, he reached into his pocket to pull out the folded piece of paper. "If you think that maybe I'm delaying the process on purpose just to keep you here a few days longer, then here's the telegram."

"No, that's not what's bothering me." She didn't reach for the paper. "I'm just wondering if we'll still have things to pack by Tuesday. If we finish the job too quickly, then there won't be a logical excuse for me to stay on. But if we work too slowly, that'll be noticed, too. And how will I explain your sudden absence? The sheriff will want to know where you've gone and why."

"I've got that all figured out. I've already sent myself a letter telling me my uncle in Dawes is in jail again, needing me to come bail him out. That's happened often enough, it should go without question. I stopped by the post office on my way back here and tossed the letter in the regular mail slot."

"But what about the postmark? Won't the sheriff wonder why such a letter was mailed from right here in Black Rock?"

"Postmark?" Did she mean that little x they wrote across the stamp to keep a person from using it again? "I don't know about where you are from, but around here every town's X is just alike. There's no way anyone can tell by that where a letter's been mailed from. Once it's been sorted from the rest and filed in my slot, no one will have any idea where exactly it was mailed from. Marge will pick it up early tomorrow morning and either leave it on my desk or bring it over here for me to see. And, with me gone to help my uncle, it just stands to reason it'll take longer to finish the packing here."

Finally, she smiled. Such a beautiful smile. "Is Dawes far enough away to support your absence two entire days?"

He nodded, then pulled her into his arms, unable to resist holding her. "The only really bad thing about all this is the fact that the sheriff will know you're here alone. That worries me."

"Don't let it. I'll be careful. Besides, you do plan to leave me with one of those pistols, don't you?"

"Of course."

"Then I'll just let it be known I'm armed and nervous about suddenly being alone here. That should keep just about anyone away from my door."

He chuckled, despite his lingering fear. "You know, I had a dream about us last night. I dreamed we were already married and had a child. A little girl who looked just like you."

"Chad, don't," she cautioned, and pulled away. No semblance of a smile remained on her beautiful face. Unwilling to hear him out, she turned and left the room, leaving him with an ache in his heart that he had no intention of living with for very long. He had to find some way to make Jenny want to marry him.

With little they could do before Monday, Jenny and Chad continued to pack Tyler and Janeen's things at a leisurely pace, stopping in the heat of the afternoon to go outside and enjoy the cold lemonade Nora had made at Jenny's request. Both Nora and Chad found it quite odd when Jenny insisted Nora sit with them, too.

By the time Nora left early that Friday night, Jenny and Chad had finished packing two more rooms, but still had the studio, the dining room, the parlor, the attic, and what items they continued to use in the kitchen left to go.

Chad reiterated he had no plans of continuing to work into the night. He pulled the curtains in the parlor so they couldn't be seen from outdoors, and they played cards for a couple of hours until each had won equal hands, allowing them to leave the game equally victorious. Then, at Jenny's suggestion, Chad brought in the large metal tub and helped her get ready for a much wanted bath, which in the end they shared, as they also later shared her bed.

Saturday proved to be a repeat of Friday, except Jenny went into town and purchased, using money Chad supplied, a black dress to wear to the funeral. The sheriff caught up with her there and pressed his company on her. Not wanting to alert him to the fact she and Chad were now on to him, she allowed him to escort her from the dress shop, home, where a very cool, very reserved Chad greeted them just inside the kitchen. It was the same cautious Chad who had greeted the sheriff ever since Wade had shown Jenny such obvious attention, so it went largely unnoticed.

While the sheriff was still there, questioning them about what progress they had made, Chad's office clerk, Marge Manning, appeared at the back door with the letter. Great timing.

"This came for you," she said to Chad, cutting her green gaze first to the sheriff, then to Jenny after she entered. Marge was a short, thin woman with dark blond hair twisted into a tight knot. Her wooden expression never changed, whether talking to Chad or sizing up Jenny. "It says it's important, so I brought it on over."

"Thank you," he replied in a louder voice than usual, reaching for the envelope. "I wonder who it's from?"

All eyes turned to Chad while he made a big production out of opening the envelope, then unfolding the paper inside. His grimace looked so authentic, Jenny wondered if he had gotten a different letter from the one expected.

"It's from my uncle Archibald over in Dawes."

"What's he done now?" Marge asked, her deadpan expression unaffected by that news. She dropped her gaze to the paper in Chad's hands. "And how much is it going to cost you?"

Chad let out an exasperated sigh, then set the letter aside, so anyone who wanted to could glimpse the message. "It doesn't say what he's done. Just that he's in jail again and wants me to come get him out. He doesn't even say how much it'll cost me this time." He cut an annoyed gaze to Jenny. "What great timing for you. Looks like you'll be getting rid of me for a couple of days after all."

"Good." She answered with just the right touch of animosity, since the sheriff still believed bad blood flowed between them. "All you've done is get in the way here anyway."

Nora's eyes widened, though she pretended to be too busy peeling potatoes to hear anything said, while Marge proved far less discreet. Marge stared directly at Jenny, her expression still frozen in such a way Jenny couldn't help but stare back at her.

Did the woman never show any emotion?

Chad pretended to ignore Jenny's comment. "Sheriff, do me a favor. Make sure this woman doesn't leave town before I get back. I still don't trust her. She's after something here. I just haven't figured out what yet."

The sheriff's eyes lit at the prospect, but before he could comment, Jenny came back with her planned remark. "Don't worry about me. I'm not going anywhere. And I don't need the sheriff watching over me while you're gone."

"Oh? And what if those men you claim broke in here and searched the place come back?" Chad asked, his voice dripping with so much hateful sarcasm, he had everyone's attention again. "Won't you need the sheriff keeping his eye out for their return?"

"I'll keep my own eye out for their return, thank you. I do keep that loaded pistol, you know."

Marge finally blinked.

The sheriff's gaze cut to Jenny immediately, his expression far less pleased than before. "You have a pistol?"

Nora stopped peeling potatoes, the knife poised in her brown hand, but she still didn't look up.

"Yes, Sheriff, I always travel with a pistol. A lady never knows what sort of riffraff she's apt to run into while out on the road."

"Oh, yes, Wade, she has a pistol all right, and is just a little too quick to want to use it. The dang woman nearly shot my ear off yesterday. Didn't you hear the gunfire over here late yesterday?"

"Well, no, but I was away from town for about two hours yesterday afternoon. Why'd she try to shoot you?"

"Because he went outside without telling me," Jenny answered for herself. "I heard him out in the yard and thought he was one of those two men come to cause trouble."

"All I wanted was to go use the privy," Chad explained, sounding incensed. "Who knew I needed to announce something like that?"

"And she took a shot at you?" The sheriff clearly wanted to know exactly what happened.

"Missed my ear by mere inches."

Marge stretched a grin. Finally, something had struck a response from her. "I'll bet *that* startled the need to go right out of you."

"And then some," Chad admitted, then pressed his mouth into a tight, flat line, undoubtedly to keep from grinning himself. He pointed an accusing finger at Jenny. "The woman is unbalanced. She's a danger. She's a menace. She's a . . . a—"

"A poor shot," Marge supplied when it was clear Chad had run out of things to call her.

Chad lifted a cautioning eyebrow but let the comment

go. "People should be warned to stay away from here. Especially while I'm gone."

"When will you leave?" Marge asked.

"Not soon enough," Jenny supplied, causing yet another grin to flicker across Marge's face. For some reason, the woman liked to see people stand up to her boss.

"I'll leave tomorrow. After the funeral," Chad put in, then glowered at Jenny. "But I should be back late Monday night or early Tuesday. Long before the packing is finished here."

"Don't hurry on my account," Jenny supplied, then snatched the box that carried her new dress up off the counter where she had left it, and stalked angrily out of the kitchen. She didn't return until everyone but Nora had left the house.

"Mind telling me what that was all about?" Nora asked, now busy peeling carrots. "You never took no pot shot at Mr. Jordan. Leastwise, not while I was here and I was here right on up to nearly dark."

Jenny smiled. She hadn't expected Nora to believe any of what they had said. Not when she had been there to see how well they worked together, and how much they enjoyed each other's company. "That was my way of keeping the sheriff from pestering me while Chad's gone. Having just spent the past hour and a half in Sheriff Mack's annoying company, I was afraid he'd see Chad's having to be gone two days as a good opportunity to come calling or some such."

"So you hoped to frighten him into keeping his distance?" Nora asked, then chuckled. "Good performance. You should have been an actress."

"What about me?" Chad inserted, coming in from outside. He had walked Marge back to the feed store to collect the rest of his mail and make sure the window he planned for them to use was left unlocked. "I thought I did a pretty good job, too."

"I'm just glad you understood what I was trying to do,"

Jenny said, still for Nora's benefit. It was important Nora not be suspicious of what they had done. There was no sense drawing her into all this. "I was worried you might not catch on, and that you or Nora would say something to contradict me."

"Not me," Nora put in quickly. "It's not my place to be telling no one about no one else's business."

Which was exactly what they had counted on. "Thanks. And for that you should be rewarded. You can leave early today. Just as soon as you have added all those vegetables there to the pot roast, and have the rolls ready to put in the oven, you can go ahead home."

Now that they had accomplished what they had set out to do, which was alert the sheriff to the fact she would have a loaded gun during the time Chad was away, she was eager to be alone with Chad and celebrate their victory. Besides, with Chad leaving that next day right after the funeral and not returning until early Tuesday morning, at which time they would set their dangerous plan into motion, tonight could very well be their last night together.

She wanted to stretch the bittersweet moment and make it last as long as she could because soon she would be returning to her world, a world that had air-conditioning, computers, television, makeup, blow dryers, and microwaves—but no Chad.

Why did all thoughts these past few days always lead back to Chad?

"And have you burning the bread again?" Nora asked with a raised eyebrow. "I think maybe I'd better stay and see the meal through to the serving like I did yesterday."

"What if I promise to be the one to watch the bread?" Chad put in, clearly just as eager to be alone with Jenny as Jenny was to be alone with him.

Nora looked surprised at that until she glanced up to see the adoring way Chad looked at Jenny. Then it was as if she suddenly understood. "I guess if that was the case, I'd be a little more willing to leave here a little early. Just as long as I know my hard work isn't going to end up in some black heap out on the woodpile again."

Jenny grimaced at the reminder. "Okay, Chad will be responsible for the bread, I'll be responsible for the roast, and you yourself have already taken the pie out of the oven to cool. That should keep anything from ending out on the woodpile."

To Jenny's relief, Nora proved receptive to that and was quick about finishing the vegetables. Within an hour, she had cleaned the kitchen, and by late afternoon was on her way home.

"At last, all alone," Chad said just minutes after Nora had left, coming up behind Jenny while she stood at the stove. He slid his strong arms around her and pulled her gently back against him.

"Chad!" she admonished, although playfully, her heart battling a powerful combination of sadness and joy. "The back door is still open and the curtains on the windows beside it are not pulled. What if someone were to come to the back porch looking for us? What would they think?"

"That I was one lucky man to be standing here in this kitchen holding such a beautiful woman," he answered in earnest, his warm, vibrant voice tickling her just behind the ear.

Her body shivered with how good that felt. "But what if it was the sheriff—?"

"I see your point," Chad said, already pulling away to go close the back door and pull the curtains together. "Seeing me holding you like that would sure give him a reason to question our performance earlier."

"And we certainly don't want that," she added, glad he had decided to provide the privacy needed to continue. Reaching first for a quilted hot pad, she ducked back as she lifted the iron lid off the pot roast to make sure there was still enough liquid inside. A spicy pillow of steam curled from the large pot as she poked at the vegetables with a fork. "Almost done. Are you hungry?"

"Am I *ever*," he growled, returning to place a kiss on the back of her neck.

She chuckled, aware of his meaning. "Then check to see if the rolls are done."

"The rolls?" he asked, clearly disappointed. He leaned around her so she could see his sulky expression. "You want me to check the rolls?"

"Yes, remember? I'm responsible for the roast. You are responsible for the rolls. And we don't dare let either of them burn."

"Why not?"

"Because Nora would have my hide come Monday if she returned to find more burned pans to deal with. Besides, as hard as we've worked today, we need the sustenance."

"Sustenance," he repeated thoughtfully. "Yes, sustenance to give us the strength for what lies ahead." A slow, delightfully sexy smile stretched across his seductive mouth, shifting his dimples into long, deep curved lines.

"Oh? And just what does lie ahead?" she asked, hoping for a sample.

He did not disappoint her. Before the question had fully passed her lips, he had spun her around to face him and had kissed her so soundly and so thoroughly, it left her head spinning and her pulses pounding.

"That is what I have in mind for us." His voice was deep and rich with desire.

"Ah, a far better dessert than the pie Nora left behind," she murmured, then playfully pushed him away, knowing if she didn't put needed distance between them, their supper would indeed be ruined.

He laughed as he took the hot pads out of her hand and bent to check the bread. Seconds later, he pulled the pan out, and set the golden-topped rolls on one of the cooler areas of the huge stove. Rather than transfer everything to serving bowls for the table, at Jenny's suggestion they filled their plates directly from the stove.

Supper proved to be just as light-hearted while they ate the delicious food and washed it down with more of the lemonade Nora had made. By the time they had finished and Jenny had put the dishes in the sink to soak, they were too full to consider even one piece of Nora's thick-crusted apple pie.

Instead, they retired to the parlor, where Chad quickly pulled the curtains across the night-darkened windows, then lit one frosted oil lamp on a table nearby.

"Care for a game of cards?" he asked, though not with any real enthusiasm. The deck they had used the day before still lay exactly where they'd left it.

"No. I'd rather just sit and enjoy your company," she answered honestly, sadly reminded this could very well be their last night together. She patted the sofa cushion beside her.

"Then enjoy it you shall," he said with aplomb as he sank upon the very spot she had touched, his pale eyes glittering in the dim light.

Lifting her hand to touch his thick soft brown hair with the tips of her fingers, she smiled. Already her body felt vibrant in anticipation of what she knew would eventually happen. "Are you ready for your long trip tomorrow?"

He frowned, obviously not having expected conversation to be a part of her enjoyment. "As I'll ever be. Since I'm supposed to be headed to see my uncle, I'll leave out riding southeast, but will turn back toward the main road to Oklahoma City as soon as it's safe enough."

"Just be sure it *is* safe. I don't want any harm coming to you." The mere thought made her ache inside.

"Nor I you," he said, as he, too, looked suddenly very serious. "I don't think I could bear it if I came back here and found out you had been hurt." He studied her a long moment, as if memorizing every tiny detail of her face. "Who are you?"

Jenny's heart wrenched at the unexpected question. She had hoped he would let that question go unanswered. But he clearly waited a response.

"My name is Jennifer Langford. Jenny for short. Like I told you." Obviously that wasn't enough. His forehead still notched questioningly.

Having already tried what she thought a believable lie, as well as the not-so-believable truth—and having been shot down both times—she quickly concocted a new story, a combination of truth and lie. "And I really am Tyler's sister, but—" she paused for effect, "—an illegitimate sister Tyler probably never even knew existed. I didn't know myself who my father was until I was nearly grown, much less that I had two half siblings out there somewhere. Only recently did I find out where Tyler lived, and came here to confront him with the fact his father had had a brief love affair with my mother. When I told you I had planned to surprise my brother with my coming here, I'd been careful to omit just how *much* I planned to surprise him."

Silently, she apologized to her great-great-grandfather, a man of faultless reputation. "That pretty much explains why the sheriff thinks I look so much like Tyler. I saw the resemblance myself when viewing the pictures of him in the studio. My mother always did say I looked a lot more like my father than I did her, and I guess that must be true. Tyler and I both must have taken our looks from that same man." She bent her head as much to look downhearted as to hide her eyes from Chad's probing gaze. She feared one good look, and he would know the truth. "I do so wish I'd have gotten here in time to know my half-brother. And to learn something more about my father."

Although the story was elaborately contrived, oddly enough it was the one Chad finally accepted. "I'm sorry. I wish I could help, but I never knew Tyler's father. I do remember he was an important lawyer back East. But I guess you already know that much."

She nodded that she did. Victor Dykes not only was an important lawyer, he had been a hero in the War Between the States, as the people of the time preferred to call it, and would be just over sixty years old had he not been shot to death in the streets of Philadelphia trying to save a woman from an attack a year earlier. He's who her grandma Vic was named after. Of course, Jenny couldn't very well tell Chad any of that.

"But there has to be more to him than that. Just like there was more to Tyler than I ever imagined." Which was true enough. Since having come there, she had found out so much more about the man her grandmother had idolized all these years. If only her Grandma Vic could have shared in all this.

Tears stung Jenny's eyes at the memory of the dear old woman, one who had never known her father but had always adored him. "I'm grateful you had so many stories to share with me about my brother. He was truly a fascinating man."

Even though Chad looked sad for her, Jenny did not feel too guilty about his believing a lie, not when she had tried convincing him of the truth first. The only thing that caused any pang of guilt was the fact he still believed they were meant to be together. For that, and for the pain it would eventually cause him, she was deeply sorry.

As a compensation of sorts, she reminded herself how deeply it would hurt her, too. She still marveled at how quickly and how deeply she had fallen for Chad, and how amazingly what she felt for him continued to build.

When the time finally came to leave, she would be every bit as devastated as Chad. But, if all went according to plan, at least she would return having accomplished what she had come there to do. With Chad's help, her great-grandfather's murderer would not go unpunished. Not this time. This time, he would be publicly exposed and eventually arrested.

With such sound evidence as they would have to show him, that visiting judge would have little choice but to find the men guilty.

That alone made this whole, heart-breaking trip worthwhile. It gave her one more reason to treasure her last days with Chad.

Fourteen

Chad left for Oklahoma City shortly after he had walked Jenny back home from Tyler's funeral, a short graveside service attended by an amazingly large crowd.

Because Jenny had tearfully requested no company, she was able to spend the rest of the afternoon alone, reflecting over all she had learned about her famous ancestor in her five days back in time, and over all she had learned about herself as well.

She had discovered she not only had the capability to love a man in every true sense of the word, but to love him with a all-enveloping passion.

Having never known such an experience, she had always believed herself to have some sort of emotional shortcoming, at least where intimacy was concerned. But the truth was, she had just never before met a man like Chad Jordan, a man who could reach the depths he had reached. How she hoped to find someone like him back in her own time. And now knowing it wasn't some failing of hers, she would make a concerted effort to find such a man.

If only that man could be Chad.

Delving in a sad fantasy, she considered what it might be like if it was possible to take someone back into the future with her. What if Chad ducked under the cape with her, and held on to the camera along with her when taking that next photograph? Would he, too, be transported through time? Could she then take him into the future with her?

But could she really do that to him?

Her heart sank. In his own time, Chad was a man of importance. An intelligent man. A confident man. A man people respected. In her time, he would be a man suddenly dealing with a world he couldn't fully comprehend. Confused by all he wouldn't understand, he would feel awkward and would seem uneducated to those around him. He would no longer be that special man.

No, as dearly as she would love to have Chad with her forever, she could not do that to him. She could not ruin the man he *was*—just to have the man she *wanted* by her side.

That meant, in two days time, if everything went according to plan, they would go their separate ways.

Trying not to dwell on such unhappy thoughts, concentrating instead on what would happen after Chad's return, Jenny made it through the first long, lonely night without him.

Monday, Nora returned for her final day of work, hinting she could easily continue cooking for her another day or so, but Jenny saw no reason to put her at risk. Besides, she and Chad would need her gone when the time came to set up the studio. So late Monday afternoon, after preparing Jenny a light meal of chicken and rice and while Jenny still packed away Tyler's belongings, Nora said good-bye to her new friend, unaware it was to be their final good-bye.

That night, after eating all she cared to eat, for her appetite was wan, Jenny felt even lonelier than the night before, and was relieved to tears when Chad returned with the book camera just after sunup.

Although he had not shaved in the two days he had been gone and his hair was wind-tousled, he had never looked better to her than the moment he stepped through that back door, the camera in one hand and a loaded gunbelt in the other.

"Was there any trouble while I was gone?" he asked, smiling despite how tired he must be.

"None. The sheriff stopped by Monday morning to see how I was, and I greeted him at the door with my pistol." She grinned. "For some reason he didn't stay long. You should have seen his mustache twitch."

He laughed as he set the items down and opened his arms to her. She went into them eagerly. How good it felt to be in his embrace again.

"I'm glad the man knows how and when to practice caution," he commented, clearly amused.

She laughed with him, tilting her head back so he would kiss her. Which he did. Long and hard.

Afraid where the moment would lead them, and too emotional at the moment to make love to him without crying, Jenny eventually pulled away and picked up the camera. There in the tiny hole that served as the film indicator, was the number one.

"I see you got the film."

"Enough to take forty pictures, if needed," he answered proudly, finally coming out of the dusty, lightweight jacket he wore. Beneath it, he had on a pale-blue shirt, open at the collar, that matched his eyes perfectly.

"We only need enough for one," she pointed out unnecessarily, mainly to keep the conversation focused on what lay ahead. "That's all we'll have time for."

"I know, but that's evidently what that camera takes. A rolled-up strip of film that allows for forty pictures." As if aware he wasn't his most presentable, he quickly raked his hands through his tousled hair, then rubbed his roughened jaw with his palm.

"You look exhausted. Have you slept at all?" she asked, worried he wouldn't be his sharpest when the time came to spring their trap. Or maybe she hoped to find a reason for delay. She couldn't be sure. Now that the danger was upon them, she had grave misgivings. If any part of their plan went wrong, their very lives would be at risk.

"I caught a few hours sleep early this morning, just before the emporium opened," he told her, then smiled. "And I caught myself napping during the ride back." He smiled that sweet, reassuring smile of his. "I'll be fine. All I need is a bath and a shave. But I can't take the cold water like you can. Start some to boil for me."

Jenny's pulses accelerated at the thought of Chad taking a bath to revive himself. Considering their past, he would have no qualms about undressing and bathing right there in front of her. Could she bear seeing that exquisite body again, knowing she'd soon be denied its pleasure?

Tears filled her eyes, making her turn away.

"What's wrong?" He had headed for the back door, but upon seeing Jenny's sudden mood fall, he rushed back to take her into his arms again.

"Nothing," she lied, but because it was such an obvious lie, she quickly added, "Except maybe that I missed you. And worried you might have come to some violent end while off trying to help. I realize no one knows yet about the photographs we have, or about the one we intend to get; but still I feared those men might suspect something amiss and in an attempt to find out what, they would do you serious harm."

"And I worried the same thing," he said, dabbing her tears with a gentle hand. "Only about you. I was pretty sure the sheriff wouldn't head out after me, knowing that would leave you and whatever evidence there might be behind. But I worried he'd catch on that something was wrong and try to force the information out of you. But we worried for nothing. We're both here, and we're both unhurt."

"So far," she put in glumly.

"And we still will be when this is all over and done. Not only will we have the element of surprise on our side, we will have each other. We'll each make sure no harm comes to the other. Besides, I think it's pretty much a bungle-proof plan."

Knowing it wasn't, and needing more of his comfort, she

pressed her cheek against his shirt-clad chest and breathed deeply the male scent that was Chad. "I love you. I want you to know that." She couldn't return to her own time without having admitted what she'd come to know while he was gone.

He kissed the top of her head. "Good. Because I love you, too. And always will."

Feeling suddenly awkward and fearing the direction of their conversation, Jenny finally pulled way. "Go get the tub so you can take your bath and be ready when the time comes to set our plan in motion. We certainly can't have you looking like that when the town learns you're a hero."

"Yes, ma'am," Chad said with a chuckle, saluting as he again headed for the back door.

While Chad sat in the large, round metal tub and first shaved, then bathed with the tiny sliver of soap they had left, Jenny made breakfast. Cooking kept her thoughts directed to matters unrelated to the exhilarating fact Chad was in the same room with her, gloriously naked.

After eating voraciously what she cooked, they carried the camera into the still-cluttered studio and placed it with other books on top of a tall filing cabinet they had pulled a couple of feet from the wall. Because of the general disarray of the room, relocating the filing cabinet was hardly noticeable. Nor was it noticeable when they then moved a second filing cabinet from out of the darkroom and placed it beside the other so Jenny could not be seen from the center of the room. Not as long as she stayed seated on the short three-legged stool Chad placed in a small gap formed between the wall and the cabinets.

With the camera aimed directly at Tyler's desk, they pulled back all the curtains and opened all the many windows to provide both the light needed for a clear photograph and easy access to the room.

Although uncertain which man would respond, until now the studio windows had proved a favorite means of entering Tyler's house uninvited. Still, they left the side door unbolted in case they suddenly chose to try an easier route.

Shortly after eleven o'clock, with everything ready, Chad headed off for the jail to set everything in motion. While pacing about waiting for his return, Jenny picked up a photo of her great-grandfather and studied it. Proudly, she noted his dark, shimmering eyes, his well-defined cheekbones, his long dark hair and his thick, drooping mustache. Such a handsome man. A man who had deserved to enjoy a long and happy life. A man her family would mourn for a century to come.

Reminded of her mission, she smiled sadly while she set the photograph back down and stepped away from the table. "We're going to get them, Grandma Vic. And we're going to do so by catching them on film using Tyler's own camera." Her smile widened. How appropriate that seemed.

Chad entered the jail with long, determined strides, not surprised to find the sheriff tilted back at his desk sipping coffee and reading his mail at that hour. "Wade, I'm glad I caught you in. I need to talk to you."

"About what?" His chair came forward with a clunk. He looked immediately on edge.

"Are we alone?" He cut a fearful gaze to an open door he knew led to the cells.

"Yeah. I got no prisoners right now, and my brother's off getting a new pair of boots." He stood, his face twisted with worry. "What this about?"

Chad stood directly across the desk from him and spoke in a low, urgent voice to effect the result he wanted. "About something we just found hidden inside Tyler's house."

"What is it?" he asked, swallowing so hard his Adam's apple bobbed twice. "What did you find?"

"I'm not completely sure yet, but I think we may have found some evidence that points to a man who very well might have been involved in Tyler Dyke's murder. If nothing else, what we found proves the Craig boys were not involved in that bank robbery here, which means Lance Maze has some serious explaining to do." Chad was careful not to insinuate the sheriff had any explaining to do, too—for having said he also saw the Craig boys. "Knowing that, I think we're going to find out that Lance Maze robbed his own bank."

"Why? What sort of proof is it?"

"It's a photograph that clearly places the Craig brothers way down in Guthrie within about an hour of the bank robbery here."

Wade swallowed again, then stuck out his hand. "Let me see it."

Chad held up his hands so show they were empty. "I didn't bring it with me. I was afraid to be seen with it, so I hid it again in Tyler's desk."

"In his studio?"

"Yes, in the big desk, where he did most of his paperwork. I put it in the top drawer, under the ledger book where it can't be easily found. So it's safe enough for now, I guess. But I'm still worried."

"About what?"

"I have to make a quick trip over to Perry, something very important I promised my uncle I'd do for him, and I won't be back until late. That's why I came by here first. Will you keep a close eye on the house while I'm gone? I don't really like leaving that beautiful woman over there alone. Not with such a dangerous piece of evidence in the house."

"Does she know it's there?"

"Yes, but I don't think you have to worry about her stealing it," he said, pretending to misunderstand. "She doesn't know the true significance of what we found, and I thought it best not to alarm her by explaining it to her. All I did was tell her not to let anyone know about the thing because I might be able to use it later for something personal I was doing, and she bought that."

Careful to use the name the sheriff knew Jenny by, he finished, "Last I saw, Ruth was in the dining room packing away Janeen's whatnots, without a care in the world."

The sheriff stroked his receding chin, clearly piecing the information together as quickly as Chad gave it to him. "So she doesn't know she's in any danger?"

"No more than before."

"Good. It's probably better that way. I'd hate to have her takin' pot shots at the wrong person just because she was feelin' a mite fidgety."

"That's exactly why I've kept her in the dark." Chad felt his ear, as if reminded of an earlier incident while headed for the door, then paused. "Just keep a close eye on the house until I can get back, then I'll bring the picture over here for you to keep until we can notify a judge. Say, isn't there a federal judge already in town this week?"

Wade's eyes rounded into two big pitiful pools of green. "Yes. Judge Livengood's here settlin' a land dispute."

"Good. We can turn the photograph over to him. But it'll have to wait until I get back."

Having laid out the information exactly as planned, Chad left, headed in a different direction from Tyler's house. But as soon as he had passed the high fence around the lumber yard, he circled around and headed for the back of Tyler's house in dead run.

Jenny waited near the window where Chad planned to reenter the house unnoticed from the street. Having already cut the screen on three sides, all he'd have to do was pull himself through and tug the screen back down to be less obvious from outside. After that, they'd immediately take positions in the studio.

Aware their plan could take a nasty turn at any point, her

heart hammered with ravaging force while watching the back hedge for sight of him. Finally, he appeared through the tall bushes, his expression intent while he hurriedly climbed through the window.

"He'll be here soon," he said through rapid breaths from having run most of the way. "I suspect he's in Lance Maze's office at this same moment, asking him what to do."

"Then we'd better get into place." Jenny turned to leave only to find Chad's hand on her arm, holding her in place.

Without a word, he pulled her into a quick, hard kiss, then released her as suddenly as he'd captured her, giving her heart yet more reason to pound ferociously.

"Don't forget your pistol," he said, as he followed her through the house.

"It's already on top of the file cabinets," she assured him. "It's hidden among all that clutter that includes the flash pan and the matches. And yours?"

"Already inside the darkroom."

"Then we're set."

Within minutes, Jenny had climbed over a hip-high stack of boxes blocking one side of her cubby hole and sank down out of sight. Perched on the small wooden stool behind the two tall file cabinets, she waited while Chad hurried into the darkroom and closed the door, ready for Jenny's call in case something should go wrong and she needed sudden protection.

Hours passed. Long, *hot* hours, especially for Chad who stood inside the windowless darkroom, sweat pouring from him in a steady stream until he developed such a thirst, he had to leave his post long enough to get a drink of water. While away from his hiding place, he offered to light a lamp in the dining room to make anyone outside think that was where Jenny still worked.

By the time he returned to the studio with a tall glass of

water for Jenny, too, afternoon shadows had filled the room. That meant she'd have little choice. She would have to use the flash pan after all. *If* anyone ever came.

"What's keeping him?" Jenny asked, her voice barely above a whisper while Chad carefully picked his way around the still-cluttered room. "I don't know how much more of this waiting I can take."

"I don't know what could be keeping him." He peered over the cabinets while handing her the glass. "Unless for some reason Lance Maze wasn't in his office today. I guess I should have checked on that, knowing Wade wouldn't have the courage, much less the common sense, to come up with his own plan of action. Not on something this serious."

"What if they don't come at all?" She stood as much to stretch her hot, achy legs as to see Chad's face better in the growing darkness. Her heart went out to him when she noted his drenched clothing and hair. It was hot enough seated behind those filing cabinets, even while wearing just a thin chemise under her great-grandmother's dress. It must be like an oven inside that darkroom with the door closed. "What if they've realized—"

A neighbor's yelping dog cut her words short. The first indication something was amiss.

Placing a finger to his lips, Chad pointed for her to sit back down, then immediately returned to the darkroom, where he closed the door with a quiet click.

Jenny's heart raced with such force she feared it would burst right through her chest while she sank back onto the stool and waited for whatever would happen next.

The next sound came from just outside the side window farthest from the street. A twig snapped. Which wasn't much of a surprise since Chad had thought to scatter twigs and sticks in front of all the studio windows, those being the only windows not protected by screens—except for the one Chad used earlier. But the sheriff or banker had no way of knowing about the severed screen on the window around back.

Another twig snapped by a different window, this one not too far from the side door. Either two people lurked just outside, or one person moved about very quickly, trying to decide which window to enter. She listened more carefully.

The second snap was followed by a quick, sharp breath that probably would have gone unnoticed had Jenny not been so attuned to any and all noises. It was a gasp barely heard, followed by one tiny thud and a scrape.

Glad she had the stool, for her legs would surely have buckled by now had she been standing, Jenny shifted forward to peer through the narrow space between the two file cabinets, a three-inch gap that allowed her to see exactly when their intruder opened the intended drawer.

Even in the growing darkness, she spotted shadows moving as she heard a crate being lightly pushed out of the way. At least two people had entered the room. Possibly more.

Wanting to be ready for whoever had the honor of opening the desk drawer, she lifted her left hand and rested it against the top of the cabinet just out of sight, but within inches of the camera itself. Singling out a single match, she held it in her trembling hand and waited, that hand poised near the whet rock Chad had given her light the match.

Minutes later, two men stumbled into her line of vision, but in the coming darkness they were little more than faceless silhouettes dressed in shaggy shades of gray and black. The larger of the two wore a hat in addition to oversize dark clothes, and had positioned himself so he could aim at either the darkroom door or the door that opened to the rest of the house. He stood there, stout legs parted, pistol drawn, while the smaller one moved farther into the room, and again out of her sight.

Clearly, the larger one, who she assumed was the sheriff,

remembered having been told she had been inside the dark-room with the door closed the last time they had searched the house and worried she might be there again.

That was not something she and Chad had considered.

No longer able to see the smaller man, she heard objects being moved. Heavy objects. But no one bothered to approach the desk.

Trusting Chad to have been clear when telling them the evidence was inside that top drawer, she grew impatient. Were these men idiots?

Fear bounced inside her stomach. The larger man continued to face the darkroom, pistol ready while the other continued to make noises farther away. Jenny prayed Chad wouldn't decide to come out of hiding for any reason. Even a man as capable as Chad had no chance against a gun already aimed.

The thought of his beautiful life being ended so brutally terrified her. Even though she wouldn't be there to share much more of that life with him, she agonized with the fear of his death.

But what could she do? There was no way to let Chad know what happened on this side of that closed door. Not without giving her own position away. And that meant not only giving up a chance at that picture but also putting them *both* at risk.

All she could do was sit and wait.

And pray that Chad didn't decide to investigate the activity neither of them had predicted.

An eternity later the sliding, bumping sounds stopped and the smaller man moved back into her sight. He paused beside the desk, as if to listen, then circled around and sat in the chair.

Before turning his attention to the desk drawer, he lit a nearby lamp and turned it down to a faint glow. He provided just enough light to spill over the desk and inside the drawer.

With both men now concentrating on the desk, and the room still relatively dark, Jenny shifted to a crouched position to peek at her quarry over the bulky cabinets. Cautiously, she moved her left hand higher until it rested just above the shutter release. With the flash pan still carefully positioned on top of the opposite file cabinet, the small pistol right beside it should she need it, she took a deep breath, then struck her match against the whet rock.

The faint sound split the room, the first real indication the men weren't alone. They both looked up just as she touched her match to the tiny mound of black powder with the one hand, then pressed down on the shutter release with the other.

"It's a trap!"

Instantly the sheriff leaped toward her, his pistol no longer aimed at the darkroom door.

"Chad. Now!" she shouted as she grabbed the camera with one hand and the pistol and her long skirt with the other, then vaulted over the short stack of boxes they had used to block in one side of her hiding spot.

Seconds after her foot cleared the boxes, the sheriff's free hand closed around her arm. He jerked her around to face him with such violence, it sent the camera and pistol both clattering to the floor.

Frustrated that he had not been more blinded than that, she tried to break loose and make another grab for the camera, but his grip held tight.

Her heart drummed a frantic rhythm while she waited for Chad to command him to let go.

But Chad had yet to come out of the darkroom.

A throbbing ache weighted her heart, sinking it into a now-familiar abyss of despair when she saw that as a precaution, the smaller man had scooted several pieces of furniture in the way. By the time Chad forced the door open, the sheriff had Jenny in a choke hold, the barrel of his revolver pressed against her temple.

The deputy still hadn't moved. Or even blinked. His eyes were frozen on Chad.

"Drop the gun!" The sheriff's voice was a panicked growl as he tightened his arm around Jenny's throat, causing her to cough.

Chad stared in horrified disbelief, his face pale in the dim lamplight from the distant desk.

"I said, drop your gun. Over there toward Walter."

Slowly, Chad did as told. Having come out prepared to get off the quickest shot possible, he eased the hammer back into place and gently tossed the revolver across the room, in the deputy's general direction. "Don't hurt her."

"I won't as long as you do exactly what I tell you."

Fifteen

"I'll do whatever you say, just don't hurt Jenny." Chad held his hands away from his body to prove no threat.

"Jenny?" The sheriff's hold loosened, but not enough for Jenny to break free. "Why'd you call her Jenny?"

"Because that's her real name. Jenny Langford. I told you she wasn't Ruby—or even Ruth, which is what she evidently had been told Ruby's name was. You should have listened to me, Wade. You might have been long rid of her by now."

"So, if she really isn't Tyler's sister, what did she come here for?" His pistol dropped away from her temple several inches as his grip loosened more, giving Jenny her first real hope. A little more distraction and she might be able to break free without getting her head blown off during the attempt.

Since the sheriff couldn't see her face from directly behind her and the deputy's stunned focus was on Chad, she stared intently first at the derringer, still on the floor by the filing cabinets only a few yards away, then at Chad across the room, hoping he would understand what she hoped to do—so he'd keep talking.

Chad's gaze met hers briefly. "Oh, she's Tyler's sister, all right. Just not *that* sister. Turns out she's an illegitimate sister he may never have even known about. She came here to confront him with their mutual parentage. And maybe try to con him out of a little inheritance money, having no idea Tyler had let his mother and his sister have everything."

Jenny blinked. Did he really believe that? Or was he just giving the sheriff something else to think about? Something else to distract his thoughts from what could happen?

"So she was after money after all? Good for her." He chuckled, then unexpectedly his grip tightened again, cutting Jenny's breath into short, painful gasps. "But I'm far more interested in other matters right now. Walter, grab that photograph and let's get on with it."

The first plan having failed so miserably, Jenny's heart sank as her fear shot higher. With no prompting, the sheriff was back on track, her chance to break free gone. Neither she nor Chad would have a chance to make a safe dive for that gun. And now they were about to find out Chad had lied about the photograph they so desperately wanted being in that top desk drawer.

"Walter, I said get me that photograph."

As if the sheriff's second mention had physically jolted him, the deputy finally blinked and resumed his search of the drawer. He lifted the ledger book out, then shuffled through the prints he found underneath it. "These can't be them. There's nothing here with the Craig brothers in them." He reached over and turned up the lamp to be sure then lifted his frightened, baffled gaze to the sheriff. "These here are all photographs of Mrs. Gaddy and that damn cat of hers. Every one."

"I should have knowed," the sheriff muttered. Jabbing the gun against Jenny's temple again, he turned his attention back to Chad. "Where's that photograph you told me about?" He twisted the cold tip of the pistol to indicate what he would do if not given the right answer. "The one of the Craig brothers you said was taken the same day as that robbery."

"Why do *you* want it?"

Jenny grimaced when Sheriff Mack's arm tightened more. She had to crane her head to one side to breathe.

The muscles in Chad's body tensed, but he made no attempt to rush either the sheriff or the deputy.

"That's doesn't happen to be any of your business. Just tell me where that picture is."

Jenny's struggle to breathe took all her concentration.

"It's out there in the hall," Chad answered. With his hands still extended, palms open, he started to back out of the room as if intending to get it for him.

"Hold it. You ain't goin' nowhere." He cocked the hammer on his revolver to let Chad know what would happen if he continued toward the door.

The action caused a deafening click in Jenny's ear.

"Walter will go get the photograph. You just stand right there with your hands in front of you where I can see them. Now, where exactly is that photograph?"

Chad pressed his mouth flat, hesitating, then sagged his shoulders. "It's in my shirt."

Jenny was too busy trying not to pass out from shortage of oxygen to remember if that was really where they had finally put the condemning photograph.

"Oh?" the sheriff responded, clearly insulted. "And now I suppose you expect me to let you just reach inside there and pull yourself out another pistol." He turned the gun away from Jenny all together to wave the deputy in Chad's direction. "Walter, we can't afford to take no more chances." Finally, he lessened his choke hold enough that Jenny didn't have to struggle for each short breath. "Get over there and see if he maybe really does have that photograph in his shirt."

Walter's watery green eyes stretched to fill half his narrow face as he pushed out of the chair and, with Chad's revolver clutched so tightly it turned his knuckles white, he started cautiously toward Chad. "Where exactly is it?"

A muscle worked back and forth in Chad's taut jaw. But nothing else moved. "It's in the front, on the left side."

Clearly the more frightened of their intruders, Walter's entire body trembled beneath the dark, oversize outer clothing he wore to disguise his small stature as he tucked the pistol into his belt, then leaned ever so slowly forward and poked Chad in the chest with the tips of his fingers. Once. Twice. Then took two steps back and let out a sharp breath. "It's there all right."

"Then reach in and pull the blame thing out," the sheriff told him, his grip around Jenny's neck slackening more, clearly exasperated with his half-brother. "But first, feel around and make sure he's not hidin' another weapon. Don't want to take no chance of him gettin' the upper hand here. Don't worry, I've got him covered." He pointed his revolver at Chad's head, the gleaming metal reflecting the lamplight. "One move and he'll have a hole in his forehead the size of a black walnut."

Walter looked at Chad, then the sheriff, then again at Chad. He swallowed hard as he leaned forward again and, with one arm stretched out until he was nearly off-balance, patted around on Chad's clothing. After finishing by bending and feeling through the leather of Chad's boots, he let out another shaky breath and smiled. "He's got nothing hid but the photograph."

"Good. Now get it and see if it really is what he said it was."

Wetting his pale lips, the deputy shoved his oversize sleeve high onto his arm, revealing another sleeve beneath, as he arched his elbow high so he could go into Chad's shirt at the neck opening, but then frowned when he realized it wouldn't fit as was. "I'll have to unbutton the shirt first."

"Then unbutton it."

The sheriff let out a hot, annoyed breath that made Jenny's skin crawl.

"Okay." Shifting his slight weight to the balls of his feet,

Walter stretched both arms forward again to carefully unbutton three of Chad's buttons, jumping slightly as each one popped through. As soon as the opening looked large enough, he used two fingers to pluck the damp shirt away from Chad's hard body, then slipped the other hand inside, quickly snatched the photograph out of its hiding place, and took two steps back.

"I got it!" Walter looked thoroughly pleased with himself as he waved the photograph for all to see.

"And is the Craig brothers on it?"

Walter turned the image toward the light, squinted, then grinned, clearly happy with what he saw. "Yeah, mister. It's them all right. And they are indeed in Guthrie, down by Hogan's livery." He squinted again. "It looks like they're getting ready for a horse race of some sort. Yeah, that's what they're doing all right."

"The Fourth of July horse race," Sheriff Mack muttered. "Damn. So Tyler really did take a picture of that."

"And you really did kill him for it," Chad commented, a cold blue gaze riveted with his, despite the gun still pointed directly at his head.

"I did what I had to do" came the sheriff's defensive reply. "Just like you'll now do what you have to do."

"Which is?"

"Which is accompany us out of town with no trouble."

"Out of town? Why?"

The sheriff let out a disgusted snort. "I happen to be at least smart enough to know I can't trust you to keep this all a secret, and I'm also smart enough to know that if two more people turn up dead in this very same house, I can't as easily declare robbery was the motive behind Tyler's death. That's why you two are goin' to have to just up and disappear. Permanently."

Jenny's heart plunged, but Chad remained calm.

"And what will you say when people start to wonder

where we are? I happen to be a regular fixture around here. People are going to notice we're gone."

The sheriff paused only a moment. "I'll tell them that you and the girl decided to go off and get married. Everyone in town is talkin' about how you two have been stayin' here all alone together all this time. It'll sound logical enough."

"You really think they'll believe we just up and quit packing Tyler's belongings to get married? You don't see any flaws in that reasoning? People know we're more conscientious than that. Or at least they know *I* am. I was Tyler's best friend for nearly a decade."

"Oh, but I'll make sure everything else is packed and ready to send before anyone realizes you're gone. I'll pack the rest of it myself if I have to. Then I'll tell everyone how as soon as you two finished your duties here, you came by my office to ask me to send it all on to Janeen, and to tell me you'd decided to get married and go live wherever it is she's from. That will work. It'll have to."

"But how are you planning to get us out of here without somebody seeing all four of us together? Won't that point fingers in the wrong direction? I think the smart thing for you to do now is admit your part in all this, and explain how Lance Maze made you do it."

"Oh, but we won't be leavin' here all together." Abruptly, the sheriff released Jenny, shoving her onto a nearby crate. When she automatically glanced to see how far away the pistol was now, he caught where her attention had gone, walked over, and snatched the tiny gun off the floor. Because they had thought Chad would be the one to need more shots, he had taken the revolver, leaving her with the derringer.

Now they had neither.

Holding his own revolver between his body and his arm, Sheriff Wade broke the small handgun open, pulled the two bullets out, then tossed the empty weapon into a box half filled with trash and broken glass.

"You won't be needing these," he commented with a cocky twitch of his mustached smile as he slid the two bullets into the pocket of his inside shirt. He then snatched up the hat that had fallen when he had made a wild leap to capture her and jammed it back on his head. Smiling now, clearly pleased to hold the advantage, he sat down in the chair behind Tyler's desk, facing them, and held his empty hand out to Walter. "Let me see the photograph."

Walter nearly broke his neck lunging toward him, the photograph jutting out of his hand. "Here."

Clearly, the deputy feared his half brother boss as much as he had feared Chad.

"Thanks." Dividing his attention between Chad who stood protectively beside Jenny and the photograph, he frowned. "There's nothin' here to indicate this thing was taken July Fourth. This could be any of several horse races they have over there in Guthrie durin' the year."

Chad rested a hand on Jenny's shoulder to draw her attention away from making a comment. Clearly, he had foreseen the possibility of being captured and not risked the most incriminating photograph.

"You're wrong. If you look over in the right corner there, you'll see part of a white banner with most of the word 'picnic' showing. There are only two times the people in Guthrie have a horse race at the same time they have a picnic. Founder's Day and the Fourth of July. And one quick look at the people's clothing lets you know it's not Founder's Day. That's in the winter. Those people do not have on winter clothes."

Sheriff Mack frowned, as if not certain whether to believe that or not, but evidently decided not to take any chances. He set the revolver down and tore the photograph into small pieces, then stuffed them into the same pocket with the two bullets.

"Now to take care of the photograph you two just took.

Walter, go look behind those file cabinets and bring me the camera she just used."

Walter lit a second lamp, then hurried to do as told, frowning when he leaned over the boxes and peered into the pocket behind the file cabinets. "There's nothing back here but a stool, a knife rock, and an empty glass. No camera at all."

"What do you mean there's no camera?" The sheriff scowled. Snatching up his pistol, he headed over to look for himself. When he saw the deputy had told the truth, he pushed his hat back and scratched his thinning scalp with the tip of his gun. "But they had to have taken a picture. Why else would she have given herself away with that big flash of light if not to get a picture of us breaking in here?"

The deputy looked frightened not to have an answer for that. "I don't know." He set the lamp down on top of one of the filing cabinets and looked again.

Wade glanced toward one of the two outer walls. "Maybe she had time to pitch it out the window," he muttered, his frown so deep his entire chin disappeared into the shadow of his wiry mustache.

He stepped over to the closest window, peered out into the shadowy yard, then shook his head. "It's not out here either." Tapping his fingers against the windowframe, finally he jerked the curtain closed then spun around to glare at Jenny. "Where's the camera?"

"What camera?" Jenny asked, amazed at how strong and perplexed her voice sounded, those being the first words she had spoken since having had her throat crushed. She curled the hands hidden in the folds of her skirt into tight fists, an attempt to fight her apprehension. "What are you talking about?"

Chad's hand squeezed her shoulder gently to give her support now that the sheriff's attention had suddenly swung to her.

"The one you took that picture with. Where is it?"

"You really think because I set off that flash I took a picture?" she asked, trying to sound as baffled as she wanted him to believe she was. "You caught us off guard in here. I knew we were trapped. I was just trying to blind you long enough to get out of here safely." Her mouth flattened. "Obviously it didn't quite work the way I'd planned."

"I don't believe that." He continued to look around, then blinked when his gaze fell on the book camera, still on the floor about halfway between the file cabinets and the desk.

Jenny's heart jammed into her throat.

"Hand me those three books," he told Walter, frowning as he pointed to the items with his pistol. "I want to have a look at them. For some reason she seemed right partial to them after the flash."

Chad's grip tightened, as if now taking needed support from her. "Sheriff, I thought you said you wanted to get us out of here."

Walter paused, half bent, arms stretched, to see what Wade's response would be to that.

"In time. In time. It'll have to get a little darker outside first. I've decided you're right. It might point a few unwanted fingers for any of us to be seen with either of you right now. That's why I'd rather us not be seen at all if I can help it."

"Any of you?" Chad repeated. "How many of you are there?"

The sheriff rolled his eyes, clearly thinking that a stupid question. "Enough to outnumber you two." He cut his gaze at Walter again. "I said, hand me those books. Then go pull the rest of those curtains together. I don't want to take the chance of someone lookin' in here from down the street and seein' what's going on. Not now that it is finally gettin' dark out and we've still got these lamps burnin'."

Walter bent further and tried to pick up the top book, jerking his head back in surprise when all three lifted off the floor. "Look what they have done. They've pasted these books together for some reason." He straightened and held the cube of books in front of him, looking at them curiously.

Having reached the end of his patience, the sheriff stomped forward and snatched the camera out of his brother's hands.

"What's this?" His face screwed up as he touched the lens Jenny had not had time to recover. "This book has something made out of glass stuck in it." His tight frown slowly relaxed into a slanted smile. "Looks to me like there's a camera built right into these books." He fumbled with it, trying to figure out where and how to open it. "Go get me something to pry this open with."

"What?" Walter glanced around, looking for a possibility.

"I don't know. Go look in there." He pointed toward the darkroom door Chad had left open. "There are probably tools of some sort in there."

Walter turned in the direction indicated and scowled while the sheriff tucked his revolver up under one arm to free his hands and continued to poke, prod, and pull at the camera, as if hoping to find a trick latch.

With both men's attentions elsewhere, Chad released Jenny's shoulder, every muscle in him instantly taut.

Jenny held her breath, guessing that as soon as the deputy disappeared inside the darkroom where he couldn't try to shoot Chad with his own gun, Chad would make a lunge for the revolver tucked up under the sheriff's arm.

"I'm not going in there," the deputy stated emphatically, his eyes as round as his face was pale. "Tyler Dykes was murdered in there. I'll go close all the curtains for you like you want," he said, already heading to do just that. "But I'm not going in there for no reason."

The sheriff looked up from the camera, perplexed by his deputy's sudden rebellion. "Why not? You went in there the other day with the others to get the body."

"But that was right after he'd been killed. Before his

ghost had had time to get back here and haunt the place. *And* it was daytime then."

"What are you talkin' about? There's no ghost here. If there was, you think he'd have let me get the drop on these two?"

"Oh, but he might not be able to come out here. Sometimes ghosts can't be anywhere except the exact place where they died."

"That's ridiculous. There's no such things as ghosts."

Walter stiffened his scrawny shoulders. "I don't care what you say. I'm not going in there."

"Okay, then don't. I'll open this thing my way," he growled through clenched teeth, then threw the camera against the wall with a hard, splintering crack. Pieces fell away as it bounced and hit the floor behind the file cabinets.

Tears poured from Jenny's heart at the thought of having surely lost not only the photograph they needed, but the treasured camera itself. She wondered if the damage just caused would appear on the camera waiting for her back in her apartment. Would their actions end up drastically altering the future? Or would everything be exactly the same, including her cameras? One thing was for sure. Unless something radical happened, they would not have changed the fact her great-grandfather's murderer went free.

"There," he spouted with grim satisfaction. "That takes care of that."

Just as Jenny sensed Chad about ready to spring forward despite the deputy never having left, Sheriff Mack jerked the revolver out from under his arm and pointed it at him. "Why are you suddenly so tense? You're not thinkin' to try and jump one of us, are you? Not when it could get you both shot."

Chad took an immediate step back. "No. Of course not. just couldn't stand seeing you smash Tyler's camera like that. I know how proud he was of it. It would break his heart to know what you just did."

Narrowing his dark green eyes, the sheriff studied him a long moment. "The man is dead. He can't care one whit what I do to his things. Don't you go tryin' to say different, encouraging Walter to believe in his ghosts. Now, I want you to sit down on that crate beside your lady friend there so I can keep an eye on both of you until I can find out what we should do next."

He waited until Chad had complied, then glanced at Walter who had finished closing the curtains and now stood in the middle of the room, looking very much like a frightened rabbit caught in an open field. "Walter, go over to Lance's house and let him know what's happened. Ask him what he thinks we should to do with these two now that we've got them."

Walter looked relieved to have a mission that took him out of that house. "Anything else?" he asked, already on his way to the side door.

"Just remember to get that gunbelt you had to leave outside by the window so it wouldn't get in the way of you climbin' in," the sheriff snapped. "And get back here just as soon as you've talked to him. I'm ready to get this over and done."

During the fifteen minutes the nervous little deputy was gone, Wade took off the bulky outer clothing he wore and stuffed it into the same trash box where he had tossed the pistol. Still in dark clothing, but now with a better fit, and sporting his well-worn tin badge, he stood leaning against the desk across the room with his gun pointed at Chad, lost in thought. When Chad tried to strike up a conversation to distract him, his efforts were met with a cold, silent glare. Wade clearly had no intention of speaking to either of them.

Eventually the deputy returned, also still dressed in dark-colored clothing, but now in a more normal size. Still, carrying Chad's revolver, he looked a lot less frightened than before.

"So what did he tell you?" the sheriff asked when Walter

didn't immediately say anything. "Did he come up with a plan?"

"He sure did. He come up with a real good plan. Wait'll you hear it."

"Come tell it to me." Looking relieved, the sheriff signaled him closer, but kept his weapon pointed in Chad's direction.

Jenny tried to hear what was said, but the deputy had an amazingly soft voice when he whispered. All she heard were the sheriff's resulting questions. After several minutes of both nodding and smiling intermittently, Walter stepped back and Wade turned his attention back to them.

"Well, Miss Dykes, or whoever the hell you are. I want you to go pack your clothes and get ready to leave. It won't be long before most of the folks in this neighborhood will be inside gettin' ready for bed. We'll be leavin' here then."

"But why do I have to bother with my bag?" Jenny questioned. She hadn't expected them to let her live long enough to make use of extra clothes. "Where are we going?"

"For now, to a farmhouse the bank recently repossessed. From there, I can't be sure yet. All I know is that we all are supposed to end up out there, and that you and I will leave first." He glanced at the clock. "As late as it is, we should be leavin' out of here in about half an hour. Walter and Lance will bring Chad along exactly one hour later."

Walter also looked at the clock, then frowned to see what time it was. "Only a half hour? But what if Mr. Maze hasn't gotten here by then?"

"Then you'll just have to stand guard over Chad alone until he does get here. Lance was clear about the times. Said he wanted to be back home by midnight or his new wife would ask too many questions. You said that yourself."

Shifting nervously, he looked again at Chad. "But what

if he tries to overpower me and take his gun back before Mr. Maze arrives? Maybe we had better tie him up."

"No need to," the sheriff said, quite sure of himself. "He won't try anything."

"But what if he does?"

"He won't. I've seen the way he looks at her. He wants more than simply to know what's up under her skirts." He then glanced at Chad, gave a disgusted snort, and spoke in a much louder voice so they would be certain to overhear. "Chad Jordan will do whatever you tell him to do for as long as he knows I have Ru—Jenny with me. He's the hero type. Always has been. He won't want to take the chance of me gettin' angry or nervous and killin' her on the spot. He'll do whatever it takes to keep her alive for as long as he can."

He chuckled when he then added, "And at the same time, she is goin' to do whatever I tell her to do because it's clear now that she loves him, too, and doesn't want to see him hurt, either."

Jenny couldn't argue that. And obviously neither could Chad, who sat beside her stewing.

"Now, little lady, you go get those clothes of yours packed. *All* of them." He then turned to the deputy. "And you go get those four horses Lance said he'd have ready by now. Bring them around back like he wants. Then go get my horse, too. Rebel is out front of the jail."

Walter nodded and hurried back out of the house with determined strides. A man with a mission. But Jenny didn't budge.

"Woman, didn't you hear me?"

"I don't see why I should bother packing my clothes," she told him. "I'm not really going to need them, am I?"

"You might not ever need them, but Lance says I have to make it look like you two left here of your own accord. That's why I don't want you leavin' nothing behind. Pack

Chad's things, too. Might as well save him from havin' to do his own."

Minutes later, Jenny was alone in the bedroom while the sheriff continued to hold a gun on a darkly scowling Chad. Quickly, she tossed Janeen's clothing back into the borrowed valise then refolded Chad's and stuffed it into his valise, stopping to handle his shaving mug with trembling fingers.

Anguish tore through her, knowing in a very short while that if the sheriff and the banker had their way, she and her beloved Chad would be dead.

This would be a case of "no witnesses left."

Tears burned her eyes, blurring her vision, as she realized just how badly she had failed in her mission. Now, not only would her great-grandfather's murderer go unpunished, he will have also gotten away with killing her and the only man she ever loved.

She glanced toward the bed they had shared and caught a glimpse of the very camera that had brought her there. *To meet her own death.*

Taking a deep, steadying breath, for tears could solve nothing, she used a corner of her skirt to dry her face. There had to be a way out of this.

Suddenly, it dawned on her.

That camera could be her salvation. All she would have to do was set it up, bracing that broken tripod leg with something, then duck up under the cape and take a picture. Having hidden away everything she needed in that room her first night there, she could be safely back in her own time before the sheriff even realized she had taken too long.

But that meant leaving Chad behind to face their wrath alone. A wrath made worse by her disappearance.

She couldn't do that. He had to be safe first. But what could she possibly do to save him? She didn't even have a gun anymore.

Her eyes widened at that last thought.
No, she didn't have a gun.
But she *did* have a dagger.

Sixteen

Afraid the sheriff would become suspicious if she took much longer, and knowing from his first trip out that the deputy could arrive back at any moment, Jenny hurried to the dresser. Kneeling, she stuck her hand behind it to where she had hidden the fancy dagger days earlier to protect herself from Chad.

Quickly freeing it, she wrapped it flat against her leg with one of her great-grandmother's long stockings.

After testing to make sure her skirt did not catch on the handle when she walked, she snatched up the two valises and hurried back into the studio.

"I did what you told me. Here's everything." She dropped the valises by the door and hurried toward Chad, eager to find some way to tell him she had thought to get the dagger.

"Not so fast. I got to be real careful. Bring those things over here. I want to go through them and make sure you didn't stuff another gun or a knife or something in there. Then, when Walter gets back here, I'm going to have him go into the kitchen and round up anything left in there that could be used as a weapon against us. I'm also going to have him check the rest of the house to make sure you didn't try leaving a note or something about what all has happened."

Glad now she had decided against doing just that, and that he was focused on the bags instead of her, she did as ordered, dropping the valises at his feet.

"No, put them up on the desk and open them."

Frustrated by the delay, she picked them up again and deposited them on the desk, taking only seconds to unbuckle the straps. "There."

Again, she headed toward Chad but was ordered to stop after only a couple of steps.

"Wait right there. I also haven't checked you for a weapon yet."

Jenny froze, her heart cringing. "A weapon?"

"I'm no fool. You've been out of my sight several minutes. You could have easily armed yourself in that time. Stand right there."

Jenny tried to look more annoyed than frightened when she drew in a deep, steadying breath, then turned to face him. Already the sheriff had one hand inside Chad's valise feeling around for hard objects. Seconds later, he did the same with hers. Satisfied, nothing of danger had been packed in either one, he signaled her to move closer.

"Now let's check you."

A gleam of something Jenny didn't care to identify glittered in his green eyes as he used his free hand to feel of her skirt pockets, then all areas of her upper torso, pausing to fondle her breasts.

She stiffened but said nothing while he caused the nipples to harden despite her determination not to respond at all. "Now let's see if you have anything up that skirt that might be of interest to me," he said in a throaty voice, clearly aroused by what he had done thus far. "Climb up on that chair."

Because his gun remained pointed at Chad, his finger flat against the trigger, Jenny did exactly as told, knowing in a very few moments, he would discover the dagger and take away her last hope.

He wet his lips in anticipation and bent to reach up under her skirts. But before he could do more than feel of her ankles, the deputy burst back into the room from outside.

Startled, the sheriff dropped the skirt and jumped back like a small boy who had been caught with his hand in the cookie jar.

"I got the horses tied up to the back porch," Walter told him, winded from having rushed. He still had Chad's revolver. "Yours, too. I even thought to go inside and swapped my pistol for your rifle and stuck that into your scabbard. Thought you might need it."

The sheriff leaned close to Jenny's ear. "We'll finish this later, when we get out to that house," he muttered, then in a stronger voice told the deputy, "Good, then we're ready to leave."

"But you still have about ten minutes before you have to go," the deputy said, cutting a concerned gaze to Chad who sat boiling from what he had just watched the sheriff do.

Clearly every inch of him was poised, eager to attack, but reasoning told him he would accomplish very little with a bullet hole in his chest.

"Ten minutes isn't all that much extra time for you to have to sit here," Wade replied. "Besides, I want to get her on out of here." He cut his gaze to Jenny's breasts, swallowed hard, then signaled for her to climb down from the chair.

Relieved to still have the dagger, yet terrified to know what the sheriff planned to do once they arrived at their destination, Jenny obeyed. With shaky legs and an aching heart, she met Chad's black gaze and waited to be told to grab the valises and head out the door.

"Since she isn't going to know anything much about riding a horse, we'll probably have to go very slow. Especially down the route I plan to take," the sheriff continued his reasoning. "That means we'll need the extra time. And like Lance said, we don't want to take the chance of us all being seen off in the same area within minutes of each other. That's why he wanted to wait so long in the first place."

"But Lance isn't here yet, and I really don't think it's a good idea to have only one man watching Chad Jordan. He might not be nearly as partial to the lady as you think."

The faint sound of the back door clattering shut caught everyone off guard. The sheriff grabbed Jenny again and pulled her body up against his, only this time instead of putting his arm around her throat, he snugged it around her breasts. By the time the hall door opened, he had swung her at an angle to face both the door and Chad, the pistol again at her temple.

Heart bursting, Jenny's prayed whoever it was wouldn't do anything foolish enough to cause this man to shoot.

Light footsteps sounded in the kitchen, then in the hall, but ceased a moment before the door slowly swung open. To her relief, the sheriff's gun fell away again the moment a tall, well-dressed man entered the room—although his arm stayed right where it was, pressing into her rounded flesh with sickening intimacy.

"Thank God, it's you," the sheriff breathed.

Walter, too, sighed with audible relief. "They were just about to leave."

"Good," the well-groomed man, obviously Lance Maze, said, his gaze going immediately to the bulge the sheriff's grasp caused above Jenny's curved neckline. It was a moment before he eventually lifted his attention to her face. His eyes rounded instantly. "She *does* look a lot like Tyler, doesn't she?"

He pointed to her face with the expensive-looking pistol he carried.

"I told you," the sheriff responded, his arm now rubbing up and down, enjoying the movement of her breasts beneath his forearm. By now, every man's eyes were on her.

From the corner of her vision, Jenny saw Chad slowly lean forward on the crate, as if testing their attention. No one seemed to notice the gradual movement. To keep it that way, Jenny pretended to respond to the sheriff's crude manipulations. She closed her eyes and moaned softly, tilting her head back against his shoulder as if suddenly weak with desire.

The sheriff sucked in a sharp breath, and shifted his arm enough to allow his hand to continue what his forearm had started. Having on nothing more than a cotton chemise underneath her great-grandmother's dress, and with the garments still damp from her having sat so long in the hot, un-air-conditioned room, her hardened nipples stood prominent against the soft fabric.

Lance moved forward to have a better look at what the sheriff had thus far accomplished, then as if suddenly aware of what she tried to do, spun around and pointed his fancy pistol at Chad.

Jenny gasped. Afraid he intended to shoot Chad right there, she had to return them to their original plan. "Come on, Sheriff. Let's go. *Now.*"

Clearly thinking she wanted to hurry away for the same urgent reason he did, he released her immediately and grabbed one of the valises with his free hand. Giving a brief flick of his revolver, he indicated she needed to grab the other one.

"Be careful out there," Lance told them, his gaze now fixed on Chad, who still sat forward on the crate. "We don't want anything going wrong."

"Nothing's goin' to go wrong. Tonight will end it."

"It had better, because I sure don't want to have give back any of the money I've stolen, not after I've promised Carole the house of her dreams. And I sure don't intend to spend even one day inside a jail cell."

"And you won't have to. Not after we get rid of these two." He tapped his pocket with the butt of his pistol. "I have the pieces to that picture Tyler told you about right here in my pocket."

Lance smiled, pleased by that. "Good job. Now get on out to that house and wait for us. We'll try to be exactly one hour behind you." Still staring at Chad, he narrowed his hazel eyes, as if to issue a warning. "If we're not there within that hour, shoot her. It'll mean this one caused us some trouble."

"Will do," he replied, then started Jenny toward the hall instead of the side door. She had gone halfway when she heard the deputy complain.

"I still don't see why we can't wait somewhere else. I get the willies knowing Tyler Dykes was murdered in that very next room. Why, if you look real hard, you can still see where the blood was in there. No amount of scrubbing will ever get all that up."

"Don't be so foolish!" came Lance's angry response. "It makes no difference where the man was murdered. It's not like he can come back here to haunt you. The man is dead. Just like these two will soon be dead. And dead is just that. *Dead.*"

Anguished, Jenny stole a quick glance over her shoulder, not surprised to find Chad watching her. They exchanged one last long look before she was shoved on out of the room.

Tears spilled from her heart. That one look spoke volumes. Certain now she loved Chad more than life itself, she would make whatever sacrifice necessary to keep him alive—even risk death.

Listening to Lance and Walter's continued argument as she made her way through a darkened kitchen, she prayed Chad wouldn't do anything foolish before she could find a way to get back there and help.

The three-quarter moon gave off enough glow to see without the aid of a travel lantern.

"Like this?" Jenny asked as she purposely stuck the wrong foot into the stirrup. The sheriff had no way of knowing she had had plenty of experience riding horses—and she planned to keep it that way. Having ridden horseback into the mountains and through thick forests many times to take nature photographs, she had long since become proficient in riding. But it was clearly to her advantage to let the sheriff believe her lacking.

"No," the other foot. That's the leg you're goin' to have to swing over to the other side."

Using the back porch as a platform, she followed his instructions and swung clumsily into the saddle. To keep the dagger concealed, she kept her skirts shifted to the far side of the horse, leaving the far leg completely covered but exposing the other to full view in the silvery moonlight.

Stepping down off the porch, the sheriff rested a hand on her bare leg, while he continued with his instructions. "Now grab up the reins and grip them in one hand while holdin' on to the saddle straps with the other so you don't fall off."

She did as told, pulling the reins too tight on purpose, making the horse shift nervously. "Like this?"

The sheriff took a half-step back. "No, not so tight. Leave a little slack."

"Like this?"

"Yes. That's better. Except when you're trying to stop the animal, always leave that much slack."

She kept a pensive yet attentive frown while he continued his limited instructions, telling how to make the horse move in the direction she wanted.

"Let's go," he finally said, after finally holstering his pistol, then climbing up onto his own horse. He pointed away from the main part of town. "That direction."

Because he had forgotten to mention how to get the horse to move, Jenny pretended to have a hard time doing just that. She tried rocking back and forth in her saddle, then leaned forward and thumped the horse on its ear.

"No, like this," the sheriff said, giving his own horse a

gentle nudge with an inward flick his heels. The horse started into an immediate walk.

Doing likewise, she headed in the direction indicated, the sheriff following far behind. Once out of town, though, he moved closer in and directed her to follow what was barely a wagon trail alongside the shallow river, then ordered her to cut north through a sparsely wooded area.

Determined not to get too far from the safety of town, for fear she might not be able to find her way back in time to save Chad, she tried to figure out how to get the sheriff to let his guard down. She needed enough distance between them to make a clean getaway, and needed to make that getaway while still close enough to town for him to not want risk using his gun for fear of alerting someone to his problem. That meant convincing him to take the lead, then slowly falling back.

"Wade?" she called back to him, knowing he had always longed for her to use his first name.

"What?"

"Wouldn't we be able to get there a lot sooner if you took the lead? Not only do I not know the condition of roads around here, I'm not even sure where we're going."

"You in some sort of hurry to get there?" he asked, clearly pleased by the prospect.

"Of course I am. I want to have time to show you that you have every reason to let me live." Holding on to the saddle as if afraid she would fall off, she glanced back at him and smiled despite her own vile words. "After all, Tyler was just a half-brother to me. I never even knew him. What do I care if his killer goes free? The truth is, I find the thought of me being with such a strong, fearless man very exciting. That's why I was so fond of Chad for a while. I thought *he* was the killer."

The sheriff clearly fell for that. He pushed his hat back, allowing the dappled light of the three-quarter moon to dance across his eager face while following a little closer behind. "You really thought Chad did him in?"

"All the clues I had pointed toward him. And when he realized I wanted to go to bed with him because of it, he then encouraged me to believe he was the murderer. He took full credit for what *you* obviously did."

"You and Chad?" he asked, swallowing hard. "Because you thought he murdered Tyler?"

"Yes. Me and Chad. Several times. But remember, that's when I thought he was the dangerous one. Now I know it was you." Seeing the way he shifted in his saddle, she considered changing tactics, talking him into stopping somewhere beside the road. As eager as he was, she could wait until she had every stitch of clothes off him before making an attempt to escape, but that might take too long. Every minute was precious. All she needed was a good head start, and someplace to hide. "Will this farm we're going to have a bed?"

His eyes stretched to their limits. "If it doesn't have one, I can sure make one real quick out of somethin'." He urged his horse into the lead, picking up the pace quite a bit.

Raising her voice little by little while allowing more and more distance to fall between them, Jenny continued to distract him by asking him questions men like Wade loved to answer.

"As handsome and daring as you are, I'll bet you've had lots of opportunities to please women. But then, that was pretty obvious by what all you did to me back there at Tyler's house." She swallowed back the disgust. "You had me wanting you right there. How many women have you had?"

"Oh, I've had my share," he bragged, talking over his shoulder while keeping his gaze on the road. Moving at a quicker pace in the dark took more concentration. "In fact, just last week, Mrs. Appletree lured me into her bed for a nice little romp. She pretended to do it to help convince me to let her husband out of jail for drinkin' and shootin' up that fancy new mirror at the Alley Saloon, but I knew that was just her excuse. She's half squaw, and, needing savage treatment, was more than ready for someone in her bed besides that sodden husband of hers. In fact, she did such a good job of convincin' me, I'm thinkin' of arrestin' her husband on a regular basis from now on." He chuckled at the thought, unaware of the distance stretching between them. "Yes-sir-ee, me and Mrs. Appletree. We're goin' to become real good friends."

Jenny's heart hammered with such force by then, she could hardly hear the clopping of the horses' hooves on the hard earth when finally she cut her horse around and kicked it into a dead run.

Immediately aware of what she had done, the sheriff uttered a strangled oath, then moments later, instead of a second set of horse hooves, she heard gunshots.

Being no more than a mile or two from town, and only a half mile from the last house they had passed, Jenny had not expected him to shoot. With her heart firmly lodged in her throat, she ducked low to make less of a target. That also allowed her horse to pick up speed.

Leaving the trail at her first opportunity, she cut through the trees, low branches swiping at her, until she arrived at a clump of underbrush large enough to hide behind. In the same area were several other such clumps. Glancing back and seeing he had fallen far enough behind to have lost sight of her after that last sharp turn she made, she forced her horse into the thicket, then pulled him to an immediate halt.

To keep the animal from whinnying, she rubbed his neck with hard, brisk strokes.

The sheriff approached the area close behind her, his horse still in a dead run, but he pulled the animal to a slow trot when he rounded that last turn she had made and realized he had lost her.

"So that was all an act, was it?" he shouted, slowing the horse more. "You think you were pretty clever, don't you?"

Watching his slow approach through the branches, Jenny held her breath and prayed he would go on past. She would wait several minutes and take off south, in the general direction of the winding river. She would then follow its banks back into town.

"If you really care about Chad Jordan, you'll come out from wherever it is you're hidin'. If we aren't exactly where we are supposed to be when Lance and Walter bring Chad there, he's a dead man. They'll shoot your handsome lover right between those blue eyes of his and it'll all be your fault. It'll be the same as if you killed him yourself."

Jenny pressed her eyes closed and tried not to' listen. If they had their way, Chad was a dead man anyway. Her only hope was to get back to town in time to help Chad escape, although she still wasn't sure how she would go about it.

"There aren't that many places you can be hidin' on a horse that big," he continued. "And if you'd ridden on, I'd still hear the horse trampin' through the brush. That means, if you don't want me to kill you right here and now, you'd better come on out." He waited a few seconds, then fired two shots into a clump of bushes, not the one she was inside, then cursed his empty rifle.

Doing all she could to keep her horse calm after the sudden gunfire, she could barely make out the sheriff's actions as he slammed the rifle back into its scabbard, then drew his revolver. He shot twice more into that same clump, then turned his attention to a second thicket. This one closer to where Jenny hid.

He fired three times into it. "I'll find you yet."

With the new danger of being shot even if he could not actually see her, Jenny reached for an overhead limb. Adrenaline pumping, she pulled herself up and into the tree. Her long skirts wrapped around her legs and kept catching on branches, slowing her progress as she worked her way to the opposite side. Just as she tried to reach for one of the larger limbs of another tree, her horse whinnied and stomped a hoof. Her heart bounced hard against her chest while she waited to see if the sheriff had heard it, too.

He had. He headed straight for her, his pistol aimed about the level he expected to find her. "Come on out or I'll shoot."

Jenny's blood ran cold. Within seconds, he would find the horse riderless and would then search the surrounding area for her, including up in the trees. Eventually, he would spot her.

Slowly, he nudged his horse closer, the handgun still aimed and ready.

Pulses surging at a painful speed, Jenny took the only action left to her.

With no time to pull her tangled skirts high enough to free the dagger, she made a wild dive for his arm.

Having taken him by surprise, she landed on the ground with a hard, painful jolt, the pistol in her hands. Surprised it had worked, and that she had not broken or crushed an important part of her body in the process, she rolled to a sitting position and pointed the gun directly at the sheriff's head.

With no intention of getting shot, the startled sheriff immediately threw up his arms. "Don't shoot."

"Don't give me a reason to." Shaken, but with no time to think about what all could have gone wrong had she not snapped the pistol out of his hand so easily, she pushed to her feet and straightened her ragged skirts so she could walk. When she did, she realized she had lost the dagger during the fall.

That made the gun in her hands all the more important. "Where are your handcuffs?"

"What handcuffs?"

"Oh, come on. Every sheriff has handcuffs. Where are yours?"

When he didn't immediately respond, she pulled the hammer back in much the same way he had earlier to show she meant business. "I still have Chad to worry about. That means I have to either handcuff you or kill you."

"They're in my saddlebags."

"Good. Now get down and pull them out for me."

"If I cooperate are you goin' to let me live?"

"For now," she said, though knowing she could never kill an unarmed man, no matter who he was or what he had done. "Now get down and hand me the handcuffs."

Swinging a leg over, the sheriff dropped to the ground, facing her. He then reached toward one of several pouches tied onto the saddle and started unbuckling it.

Remembering his earlier caution, Jenny commanded him to stop the second he had freed the flap. "Step back."

Doing as told, he stumbled on his fourth step back, falling backward onto the ground. His face went white when that caused her to wrap a second hand around the gun while it remained pointed at him.

"Don't shoot."

"Get up."

She waited until he stood again, now hatless, then while keeping the revolver pointed at him with one hand, she fished around inside the pouch with the other. Although finding no extra pistol inside as she had feared, she did locate the handcuffs, a small pocket knife, and a few other items she didn't recognize. But no key to unlock the closed cuffs.

"Where's the key?"

He slipped two fingers into his shirt pocket and came out first with pieces of the torn photograph, which he tossed aside, then with a small skeleton key. He tried handing it to her, but she decided not to let him get that close.

"No, here." She tossed him the cuffs, and he caught them in a reflex action. "You handcuff yourself to that tree. To that limb there." She gestured to one about chin high with several forks to prevent the cuffs from sliding off, the base about the size of a man's wrist.

Glowering, but still wisely cooperative, the sheriff did as told, but then tried to repocket the key unnoticed.

"No, toss that over here."

With her heart still hammering hard and fast, she waited for him to obey. But he stood there, facing his own gun, with the key trapped between two fingers.

Did he really think he was in a position to defy her now?

Jenny had no time for this. Five minutes had passed since she had taken the revolver away from him, and probably twenty-five minutes since they had left the house. She had to get back on the road. "I said, toss me that key. Or would you rather I shoot you to get it? Is that it? You've suddenly decided to die looking like a hero?"

A second later, he tossed her the key, but she made no attempt to catch it. As long as it was well out of his range, she was happy.

"Good boy."

He bristled at being called a boy, but there was little he could do to defend his manhood at the moment. "Are you plannin' to send someone back for me?"

"No."

His voice rose an octave. "You're plannin' to leave me here to starve to death?"

She sighed at how melodramatic that sounded. "We aren't that far from the road. Someone will come along eventually and will hear you call out for help."

By then her horse had moved out of the thicket and stood in a small clearing nearby. The sheriff no longer a worry, she hurried in that direction.

Unable to remember how many shots she had heard, and not all that sure how many bullets the sheriff's revolver held anyway, she stopped in a patch of moonlight and popped open the large gun. Her heart sank to discover only one bullet left.

Turning back, she snapped the weapon shut again and pointed it at the sheriff. "I need to reload. Where are your extra bullets?"

"I don't have any."

She cocked the hammer back again, knowing how that had panicked him before. "I asked you where the extra bullets are."

"And I told you I don't have any. Go ahead. Check my saddlebags. Come check my gunbelt. You'll see I'm telling you the truth. I never expected to be confronted. I didn't bring extra bullets."

"What about the two in your pocket? The ones you took out of the derringer?"

"They won't fit. Too small."

Frustrated, but not about to take his word for anything, Jenny checked the other pouches attached to his saddle, but decided to forgo searching him personally. That missing dagger could have fallen anywhere within his reach. He could have found it and retrieved it when he fell.

With yet more of that precious hour having ticked by, Jenny gave a quick search of the grass and bushes, hoping to find the missing dagger. It could come in handy while trying to rescue Chad.

But she didn't find it. Finally, she gave up, and after shooing the sheriff's horse away, climbed onto her own mount and rode off, armed now with the sheriff's own pistol and a determination of steel.

Finding the river quickly, she followed it as far as the edge of town. There, she left the horse tied to a bush and went the rest of the way on foot.

Approaching the back of the house from the opposite side, slowly so as not to disturb the horses, she considered again how there were *two* men guarding Chad, and yet she had only the *one* pistol in which there was only *one* bullet.

She needed something else to put the odds in her favor. But what?

As she neared the darkened window Chad had used earlier to reenter the house through Tyler's own bedroom, an idea struck her.

Although extremely risky, it was her only hope.

Seventeen

As angry as he was frustrated and frightened, Chad watched Lance and Walter alternately pace the floor directly in front of him, their shadows lengthening the farther they moved away from the only two lamps burning.

A time or two, he had considered trying to take Walter when the smaller man came within arm's length, his pistol usually dangling toward the floor. But Chad resisted the urge, each time remembering what the sheriff had said about killing Jenny outright if they didn't show up on time.

He grimaced. If he knew exactly which repossessed farmhouse they had taken her to, that would be one thing. He would rush these men and take their weapons right now. But the bank was notorious for repossessing property, and Jenny could be inside one of several neighboring houses.

A knot of helplessness tightened in his craw as he glanced at Lance, who spent most of his time shifting his pistol from one hand to the other while pacing, or standing and staring at the clock.

Chad understood what he was up against with Lance. Even with a gun pointed right to Lance's head, he would never give him the information Chad needed. Lance was smart enough to know Chad would never kill them without first knowing where Jenny was. That could be part of the reason they had separated them. It gave each of them an element of unknown, a feeling of vulnerability.

No, Chad took the sheriff's threat too seriously to cause

any trouble here. Until he knew exactly where Jenny was, he would continue to do anything they told him to do. And knowing he couldn't trick that sort of information out of a man like Lance, he didn't even try. Lance was far too sharp for that sort of thing.

But Walter wasn't. Which was why he doubted Walter even knew their eventual destination. That was probably one of the main reasons Lance was there. To keep Walter from making any serious blunders.

"How much longer do we have?" he asked them, unable to see the clock from where he sat.

"About fifteen minutes." Lance walked over to the clock and turned it enabling Chad to see it better so he wouldn't have to be bothered with the question again. When he did, he spotted a small stack of photographs and turned his attention to those. Clearly, he saw no threat to Chad's presence.

Fifteen minutes. Fifteen minutes to figure out what would happen after they arrived at the farmhouse, and come up with an effective plan of action.

Chad's stomach coiled tighter as he thought about what might already be happening at that farmhouse.

Simmering inside, he stared grimly at the clock while the minutes slowly ticked away—until a creak in the back of the house caught his attention. The noise sounded louder than the usual pops and squeaks a house makes at night.

Walter had heard it, too. He froze in mid-step, his hand falling immediately on Chad's pistol, now neatly tucked in his belt. "What was that?"

Yanking the weapon free, he swung around to aim it at the door closed to the hall. His eyes bulged with fear.

"What was what?" Lance set the photographs back down. He, lifted his shiny, pearl-handled revolver, and as a precaution pointed it in the same direction.

"I heard something in the back of the house."

The room went silent for several minutes, but no other sounds were heard. Still, Lance and Walter remained alert.

Chad, too, listened intently. He feared someone had somehow realized what was going on inside there and had foolish plans to try to rescue him. If Lance and Walter ended up being killed as a result, his chances of finding Jenny in time to save her life were slim. Or none.

"You must be hearing things," Lance finally decided, then returned to the photographs to show he was not so easily spooked. "You are way too high strung."

Walter, too, relaxed a bit, but still did not take his gaze off that door. Until suddenly there came a crashing thud just outside the window closest to the kitchen. Startled, he looked at Lance with wide, rounded eyes, then at the curtains, fluttering softly on a night breeze.

"I heard that," Lance admitted, already headed toward the filing cabinets. Quickly, he extinguished the lamp there, then moved toward the other lamp on Tyler's desk, carrying his pistol with him.

Chad listened for another sound, but heard nothing. Were there two people getting ready to save him?

"Who's out there?" Walter called, trembling uncontrollably while edging his way closer to the window closest to where that last sound had come. Just as he got near enough to part the curtains with the tip of his gun barrel, Lance turned the other lamp down to a faint glow.

Burning with frustration, Chad watched while Lance moved toward the window, too, his attention on whatever might be outside. He could easily take these two now that they both had their backs to him, but still he would have no way of knowing where Jenny was.

With just enough light coming from the desk lamp and from the street lantern across the way, he watched while Walter eased first a hand, then his head and the other hand holding the revolver out the window. Lance watched from only a few feet away, his pistol braced with both hands, ready to defend himself from whoever or whatever had made that noise.

"See anything?" Lance asked, tiptoeing so he could get a better look at the ground.

"Nothing." Protected by near-darkness, Walter leaned further out. "Nothing at all." He let out a sharp breath, then backed away from the window. "Must have been a dog or a chicken or something."

Chad felt a moment of relief, but his heart slammed hard against his chest again when, seconds later, he heard the faint turning of a doorknob. Someone else *was* in the house. Right inside that hall.

Every muscle in his body tensed while he tried to decide whether to be prepared to help take action or call out and warn Lance and Walter, who he could not let die just yet.

But Lance needed no warning. He jerked his head around to face the hall door just as it burst open, and into the dimly lit room walked Tyler Dykes, dressed in his usual dark colors with his hat pulled to its usual cocky angle.

And if that weren't enough to make the hair on the back of Chad's neck stand on end, across the front of the shirt was a bright red stain. Exactly where the knife blade had cut through Tyler's heart. In his hand was a polished revolver, and jutting beneath his thick, drooping mustache was a determined jaw.

Chad went numb, his mouth dropping open at the sight of his good friend walking upright. For a moment, he could not catch his next breath. Nor could he respond verbally. All he could do was stare while Tyler came to a halt in the middle of the room.

But Walter had no problem with a verbal response.

"Cripes! It's Tyler's ghost!" he cried at the very top of his strained voice. "And he's got a gun!"

"Shoot him!" Lance ordered, though he had a pistol of his own already pointed in that direction.

"And have him shoot back?" Walter trembled. "Besides, you can't kill something that's already dead." He immediately tossed Chad's revolver on the floor and started backing toward the window he had just poked his head through, his hands raised to show he was now unarmed. "Don't shoot, Tyler. I had nothing to do with it. I swear. I didn't even know what happened until after it was done and Wade told me about it."

Chad still sat in stunned silence while he watched the apparition stand, legs braced, and wave the pistol toward Lance, as if ordering him to drop his pistol, too.

Eyes wide, Lance glanced down at his pistol, then looked at the apparition again. He clearly had no idea *what* to do.

The specter took another step toward him and again waved the gun.

"Don't come any closer," Lance said, cutting his gaze to the same window Walter now blocked, as if checking for the quickest way out of the room.

Chad's stomach knotted at the thought of what would happen should these two men bolt. He would never find Jenny in time to save her.

Gun still held steady, the apparition took yet another step.

Lance's voice rose a level. "I said, don't come any closer. Or I'll shoot."

That brought the apparition to a sudden halt, as if somehow threatened by that last remark. It was during the silence that followed that Chad noticed a long strand of hair coming down out of the back of the hat. A strand much longer than Tyler's hair ever was.

Alert now to what was really happening, he scanned the floor to find out where his revolver had landed. Finally, he spotted it across the room. Over near the darkroom door.

"Ah, but Walter's right," Chad quickly intervened as he eased off of the crate. His heart fluttered with such rapid force against his chest, it felt as if it had suddenly grown wings. "You can't kill something that is already dead. Isn't that right, Tyler?"

When Jenny briskly nodded her agreement, the makeshift

mustache attached to her upper lip with flour paste broke loose and fell to the floor.

Her dark eyes rounded with instant alarm.

"You aren't Tyler Dykes," Lance said, voicing the obvious. "You're that fool of a sister." His gaze then cut back to the door she had left open. "Where the hell is Wade? What have you done with him?"

Aware now they were not facing Tyler's ghost, Walter realized immediately what he had done and made a dive for Chad's revolver at the same time Chad did.

Both got to the gun at the same moment, Walter grabbing it by the handle and Chad grabbing it by the barrel. Wrestling for possession, Chad was amazed at how strong Walter proved to be when driven by pure fear. He was like a starving dog hanging on to a bone.

With Jenny and Lance at a stand-off, Chad tried jerking the revolver loose, and twisting it. Still, he could not gain the possession he needed. Together, he and Walter rolled around the floor, bumping against furniture and open doors, each trying to pull the pistol in close to his body where he would obtain better leverage.

Struggling with all his might, and twice almost having it, Chad heard Lance shout, "Don't you move another inch!"

He listened for Jenny's response to that, his blood turning to pure ice when seconds later he heard two gunshots fired at almost the same instant.

Prodded by a whole new fear, Chad made one final jerk, freed the pistol, and rolled in time to see both Lance and Jenny crumple to the floor.

Eighteen

Unable to move, Jenny sat on the cold floor, her chest folded over her knees, trying to recover from the fact she had just shot a man. She hadn't meant to, but when she saw Lance take aim at Chad, something inside her snapped and she couldn't help herself. She had fired her one shot.

The noises across the room reminded her of the struggle between Chad and Walter, causing her to look that direction, though she could not yet sit up to do so. Relief washed over her, mixing with the shock she already felt, when she saw Chad standing, his revolver again in his hand, no blood on his clothing.

Walter now sat on the floor, his arms board stiff and stretched high, his gaze riveted on the pistol now in Chad's hand.

Glancing in her direction briefly, Chad wasted little time taking the twine they had used while packing and wrapping it again and again around Walter's wrists, then securing those bound wrists to the desk with yet more loops of twine.

As soon as he had done that, and checked to make sure Walter had no slack, he set his gun aside and rushed to her side. His face filled with concern when he knelt beside her still-crumpled form.

She was so relieved to have him there, about to touch her, tears filled her eyes. Still, she remained too weak to raise up.

"How bad did he get you? How bad did Lance get you?"

He tried to help her sit up, but she couldn't cooperate. She had never shot a man before. She was still doubled over from the shock of having watched her own bullet rip a hole in Lance's chest.

It had happened so quickly, in a way it felt unreal. Yet it *was* real. Very real.

She'd just shot a man. Probably killed him.

Finding just enough strength, she turned her head to look in Lance's direction. He lay perfectly still, blood pooling on the floor around him. She shook uncontrollably. She tried to close her eyes against the sight, but couldn't.

"Jenny. You have to let me have a look at the wound." He tried again to get her to sit up, and this time managed to do so, using his own brute strength to pry her chest away from her knees. "Where's the injury? Where'd he get you?"

She blinked at him, confused by his questions, then shook her head. "He wasn't shooting at me. He was shooting at you."

"You're not shot?" He looked afraid to believe that.

She shook her head, too emotional by then to say anything else.

Chad's blue eyes pooled with tears as he pulled her to her feet to have a better look, just to be sure. When she proved able to stand on her own legs, wobbly as they were, he hugged her close, squishing tomato sauce all over his shirt. The tomato sauce she had splashed across her chest, wanting it to look like blood.

For several long seconds, they stood there like that, holding each other close, neither aware of anything or anyone else in their world, until seconds later they heard footsteps on the porch.

Fear returned immediately.

"The sheriff," she cried, quickly pulling away. "He got loose."

Chad made a stumbling dive for his revolver just as there came a tentative knock on the door.

"Jordan? You all right in there?"

Not recognizing the voice, Jenny turned to Chad and noted his look of relief.

"Yes, Andrews, come on in."

Slowly the door opened, and the man from next door she had talked to days earlier entered, his gaze going immediately to Lance's body.

"What happened?"

Before Chad could explain, another person appeared on the porch, then another. All familiar to Chad. None to Jenny.

The gunfire had been heard blocks away, causing the neighbors to rush over and check out the noise. Some came still in their night clothes, others wore street clothes. All looked shocked to learn their own sheriff and banker had been involved in anything so shady.

Having recovered enough to stand alone on her own two feet, Jenny watched while Chad and Anthony checked Lance for a pulse, and found none.

By that time, Walter sat sobbing hysterically, wanting everyone there to understand he hadn't wanted anything to do with any of it. In his hysteria, he agreed, Jenny had had no choice but to shoot, and that if Wade was out there dead somewhere, he, too, had come to a just end.

Reminded of the sheriff, Chad asked Jenny what had happened. How had she gotten away from an armed man?

He listened with fear and pride as she explained what she had done and admitted how frightened she was.

"All I could think of at the time was what they would do to you if one of us didn't do something."

"It's what they would have done to us both," Chad agreed, taking her into his arms for another loving embrace. "What made you think of dressing up in Tyler's clothes?"

"I remembered how terrified Walter was of Tyler's ghost.

I decided to use that terror to our advantage. After all, all
I had was one bullet."

"One bullet? You came in here like that with only one
bullet?" He sounded like an adult reprimanding a small
child. "Knowing both those men were armed with guns?"

"But hoping Walter would be too afraid to use his."

He drew in a trembling breath, suddenly shaken. It was
a full minute before he had the strength to ask, "Where did
you leave the sheriff? We need to find him."

After giving Chad general directions, too shaken to remember specifics, he and several men left to go get their
final prisoner and bring him in.

"We'll have him back here in his own jail in just a few
hours," he had promised, pausing to kiss Jenny first lightly,
then long and hard. "You stay right here and let Marge take
care of you until I get back."

Jenny hadn't even noticed the small, expressionless
woman at Chad's side until then. Grateful not to have to be
alone after what she had just gone through, she nodded.

"Hurry."

"I will. We'll take lanterns to help us find and follow
your tracks. There can't be too many places along that road
where people have recently taken off through the woods
like that. We'll find him in no time."

As soon as the townsfolk had Lance's body removed and
Walter carted off to jail, Jenny and Marge retired to the
kitchen, where Marge proceeded to make a tin pot of hot
cocoa without bothering to ask if Jenny wanted any.

Too keyed up to sit, Jenny paced about the room, waiting
for Chad's return, hoping they would have no trouble out
of Wade.

Having come to realize just how very much she loved
Chad, she couldn't bear the thought of him being faced

with any more danger. She loved him enough she didn't want to spend even one more day of her life without him.

It was then Jenny knew she would never return to her own time. She would stay right there in Black Rock, and if Chad still wanted her, she would marry him and do her level best to fit into his life.

She smiled at the thought. She could see herself years from now, playing with his children and warming his bed.

Her body ached at the mere thought.

"That's much better," Marge said, having noticed the sudden smile. "You had me worried for a minute. I thought you were going to be one of those people who doesn't ever get over the shock of having killed someone. Even if that someone deserved it." Although she didn't actually join her in that smile, Marge's eyes twinkled with relief.

She gestured to the table. "Now you just sit yourself down over there and have a cup of hot chocolate. It's better for you this time of night than coffee or tea. It'll help settle your nerves and let you sleep later."

"Thank you," Jenny said, then, feeling better now, sat down and picked up the cup Marge filled for her while Marge walked over to make sure the back door was bolted.

Taking her first sip, she glanced at the clock. Already a half hour had passed. How long until Chad finally returned? How long until she was able to tell him about her decision to stay and be his wife?

"Over here!" John Vick shouted to the others, raising his lantern high to guide them in his direction. "I've found three sets of tracks. Two going in, and only one set coming out."

"That must be them!" Chad shouted back, and quickly prodded his horse in that direction. As soon as they had pooled into a group of six again, he held his own lantern high and coaxed his horse into the surrounding trees.

Because of the unnatural density of the woods there, the others had to follow single file.

Squinting, and gazing ahead into the darkness, he found a spot where the single lines of hoofprints ended into a small sea of prints.

Glancing around, he tried to figure out which tree the sheriff hid behind. He studied the different branches, looking for a glimpse of the handcuffs, but saw nothing.

"Wade. We've come for your sorry hide," he shouted, hoping for an angry response to guide them. A chill skittered down his spine when the only responding noises came from the men behind him. All five had caught up with him by then.

"Did you find him?"

"Not yet."

Frowning, he swung down off his horse and started making a large circle of the area, his lantern held high over his head. Anger struck him like a board shoved into his stomach when he finally spotted a pair of handcuffs dangling from a limb, open on one end. On the ground were pieces of a torn photograph.

"Looks like he got away," he told the others, so furious, the words had to be forced through clenched teeth. He studied the hoofprints again, noticing one set veered off to the west. Knowing exactly where he would have headed had he been left out there like that, and thinking his friends still had the advantage back at Tyler's house, Chad's legs felt suddenly weak.

"Looks like he rode off in that direction. You men try to trail him," he said, already handing his lantern to another man to help them watch the tracks. "I'm going back to warn Jenny and Marge that he's loose. Keep in mind, he could be armed. Jenny still had his revolver, but he also had a rifle."

Swinging back up into the saddle, he prayed he would not be too late.

* * *

"You've been through so much in your short time here," Marge said, clearly keeping the conversation going for Jenny's sake. She now sat across the table from her, but didn't drink any of the cocoa. "I can't imagine having gone through all that."

"Neither can I," Jenny admitted, looking down at herself, still dressed in her great-grandfather's clothing. She touched the damp area where she had used the soapy, wet rag Marge had given her to wipe away most of the tomato sauce.

It had bothered Marge to see all that red in the same general spot where Tyler had been stabbed.

"And *I'm* the one who went through it."

"Sort of like a dream, was it?"

"Exactly." Jenny nodded, taking another long sip from her cup. Marge was right, the cocoa was soothing her frayed nerves. "It was like one big long bad dream. Especially the part where I killed that horrible man. I still can't believe I did that."

"Nor can I." Marge stood, stretched her back, then headed back to the stove to get the metal pot that held more cocoa.

"Nor can *I.*"

The deep male voice rent the room with such anger, and such rage, it caused both women to scream in response.

"Sheriff Mack!" Jenny cried. Her gaze went immediately to the dagger gripped firmly in his right hand.

"In the flesh," he said, absently rubbing his wrist where the handcuffs had cut into his skin. His eyes were black with rage as he moved further into the room, having entered from the hall. "What happened here? Who'd you kill?"

His gaze darted around the room as if expecting to find someone else. Probably Lance or Walter.

Marge was first to recover, turning away from the stove to refill Jenny's cup as if nothing out of the ordinary had just occurred. "She killed Lance Maze," she answered in her usual monotone, without glancing up. "She had to. It was either kill him or let him kill Chad."

Her calm behavior clearly baffled the sheriff. He raised his voice to suggest more of a threat. "And what about my brother? What happened to Walter? Is he dead, too?"

"No. He's in jail. Seems he was part of some big scheme to cheat this town out of all its money." Marge bent her small frame over the cup, as if to check whether she had poured enough cocoa, then with the sheriff watching her hands cautiously, returned the pot to the stove. "They hauled him over there just a little while ago. Babbling like a small child, he was. Said something about you being involved."

"Where's Chad?"

"Gone to find you. He and several of his friends left just a little while ago." Turning away from the stove a second time, Marge met Jenny's frightened gaze, then stared pointedly at the cup she had just filled. A cup steaming again with hot cocoa.

Jenny understood the plan immediately, and tried to decide just how to go about it so they would end up with the dagger. She would wait until he clearly had his attention elsewhere. Or until he showed some sign of renewed violence. Whichever came first.

Joining Marge in an attempt to confuse him with casual conversation, she rested her hands on either side of the cup. "I don't understand something. I had you securely handcuffed to that tree. How'd you get away?"

"There was another key in my saddlebags," Wade answered with a curved sneer, letting her know how pleased he was to be able to tell her that. He shifted the dagger to his left hand, gripping it in his fist like a small child might his fork, then moved closer to the table.

Jenny kept a close eye on that dagger, aware he could

make a lunge at her at any time. "But I checked all the pouches. Besides, I ran your horse off."

"Oh, but you never checked that little pocket up front." His sneer widened at the frown that produced. "Seems you didn't quite take everything into consideration when you left me there. My horse is trained to come at the sound of my whistle."

Standing over her now, he threw his head back and laughed out loud. "Because usually he just comes close enough for me to go to him and slip a bridle over his head, it took me quite a few minutes to get him to move in close enough for me to get that key out. But eventually he did, and I had that other key and had my wrist free again. Having already seen where this thing landed," he held the dagger up like a prize, "I grabbed it up and headed straight here."

Rankled by the defiant tone in his voice, she thrust her chin forward and met his angry sneer. "But you didn't quite get here in time, did you? Lance is now dead, and Walter is in jail. And the whole town already knows all about you."

Marge nodded, drawing his attention to her.

"Doesn't matter what this town knows." Wade's grip tightened around the gold dagger. "I'm headed over to Lance's to get some of that money he stole, then I'm leavin'. But not until I've settled the score here."

Returning the dagger to his right hand, he turned to glare at Jenny just as she tossed the hot cocoa into his face.

Bending against the pain, Wade screamed at a blood-curdling level, but refused to let go of the dagger when Jenny tried to wrestle it out of his hand.

Reacting instantly, Marge reached again for the metal pot on the stove and used it to whack him soundly on the back of the head.

The sheriff stiffened, turned toward Marge with a most

indignant look, then crumpled to the ground, releasing the dagger to Jenny as he fell.

Thinking they should do something more, but not sure what, Jenny looked to Marge, hoping for a suggestion.

Marge stared down at the sheriff with disbelief before lifting her stunned gaze first to the pot still in her hands, then to Jenny. Without uttering a word, she sat the pot on the table, stepped back away from the sheriff, rolled her eyes back, and sank neatly to the floor.

"Marge!" Setting the dagger beside her now-empty cup on the table, Jenny knelt by her friend's side and briskly rubbed her hands and her cheeks to revive her. "Marge, wake up."

Marge stayed out cold.

Worried she might have struck her head when she fainted, Jenny felt around for a gash or a knot, but found neither. "Marge, wake up."

Again she rubbed Marge's cheeks and hands.

Finally, Marge moaned but still did not open her eyes.

"Marge, I said to wake up," Jenny tried again.

This time, Marge obeyed. Still sprawled neatly on the floor, she fluttered her eyes a moment, then opened them, first to look at Jenny who still knelt at her side. Then beyond.

"Uh-oh." Marge's eyes rounded in her still-pale face.

A chill skittered down Jenny's spine when she turned to see what drew Marge's attention. There, standing directly behind her, was the sheriff. And he had the dagger again.

Holding it, poised to strike with one hand while gingerly touching the back of his head with the other, he commanded her to get up.

Jenny's heart shattered into a million painful pieces. Suddenly she doubted she would ever live long enough to become Chad's wife.

"I said, get up!"

Jenny tried to obey, but her legs proved too weak. She

had been through too much in these past few hours. She made it about halfway, then fell back again, almost landing on top of Marge. "I can't."

"Then I'll kill you where you sit," he said, pulling the dagger back to gain added momentum, then thrusting it forward.

Closing her eyes, Jenny rolled to one side, hoping to duck out of his way, just as the sound of gunfire split the room, causing her a second of confusion.

A dagger that shoots?

Forcing an eye open, she dared a quick look at her attacker, surprised to find him now facing the back door, blood pouring out of his shoulder only inches above his badge.

In a final moment of black rage, Wade charged toward the back door like the wounded animal he was just as Chad stepped inside, his revolver still drawn.

He fired again.

This time Wade fell back, nearly landing on Marge, who had pulled herself to a seated position.

Marge looked at the sheriff, unblinking, then at where he had lain before, then at Chad who had come over to make sure Wade wasn't getting up again.

"Glad to see you," she said with a half-smile, then rolled her eyes and sank blissfully to the floor again.

"Not as glad as I am to see you," Jenny said, finally finding the strength to stand. Bracing an arm against the table, she watched breathlessly while Chad felt of Wade's chest. Had they both been forced to kill that night?

"He doesn't deserve it, but he's still alive," Chad said, immediately taking the sheriff's belt off and using it to tie his hands behind him. As soon as he had the sheriff secured and a folded towel stuck inside his shirt to pad some of the blood, he stood and opened his arms to Jenny. "Looks like it is now officially over."

He held her a long moment, then drew in a deep breath.

Slowly, he pushed her away, his face suddenly stricken. "I guess you'll be leaving now."

Smiling at him with all the love in her heart, Jenny went immediately back into his arms. Already lifting her face for a kiss, she uttered the same words she'd heard so many times herself.

"Guess again, stranger."

Epilogue

Jenny sat on the padded stool Chad had made for her so she could still spend a few hours each day in the developing room and not cause any harm to the baby. Although there had only been that one incident in which she had suddenly become very light-headed and nearly fainted, on the whole she was handling her pregnancy very well.

Especially for a woman of her age, as Marge was always so quick to point out. Between Marge, Chad, the doctor, and Nora Simmons, who had returned to work for her only days after the wedding, Jenny found herself always under somebody's watchful eye.

"Aren't you about finished in here?" Chad asked, leaning indolently against the doorframe, having just come in from work. "Nora already has supper on the table."

"I'll be there in a minute. I just want to get the sealant on these photos I took this afternoon."

Curious as usual, he came to stand behind her, resting his hands possessively on her slender shoulders. "Whose did you take today?"

"I took some of the new sheriff and his wife," she answered, holding one out by the edges for him to see. "She wants me to try to have them ready in time to send one to her mother for the woman's birthday, which is the end of next week."

"How far away does her mother live?"

"Far enough I'll need to have them ready for her first thing in the morning to get them there on time."

"Well, just don't you overdo. I don't want you nearly passing out again and scaring the life right out of me."

"Don't worry. I won't overdo. I'm not about to risk hurting the baby." She touched her rounded stomach lovingly. The baby was the main reason she had given up freelancing with Tyler's repaired book camera and had set up a portrait studio instead.

Fashioning it after Tyler's old studio, only using one of his smaller cameras instead of the Rochester, she had given up her love of travel for staying home and taking family-type photographs.

Because Janeen had believed her to be Tyler's illegitimate sister, and was so grateful to her for having helped bring Tyler's murderer to justice—and after hearing Jenny knew photography—Janeen had insisted Jenny take everything inside Tyler's studio except for some of the photographs.

Jenny accepted the gift graciously, but to everyone's surprise, she dismantled the Rochester shortly after she and Chad were married. Although Jenny knew she would miss her cat, and her brother's annual visits at Thanksgiving, she did not want to take the chance of accidentally being sent back to the future.

Instead, she had taken one last long look at her old apartment, the cat long since having deserted his shelf, then lovingly took the camera apart and put the pieces away in a special box.

"Just see that you don't," Chad responded lifting her hair so he could kiss the back of her neck. "I don't want to risk losing either of you."

Jenny watched while he sauntered out of the darkroom, into the studio he had built for her with his own two hands. Because of all the bitter memories linked to Tyler's house, they had decided not to buy it from Janeen and live there.

Instead, they had built their own just a little over two blocks away, very near the river.

Smiling happily, Jenny brushed on the last few strokes of sealant, then slid off the stool and stretched her aching back muscles, glad now she had given up following in her great-grandfather's footsteps. Although it had been fun, continuing his daring exploits for her first year there—and even though it had made Chad want to pull out his long, gorgeous brown hair—she'd had enough of such dangerous exploits and was more than willing to give it up for the baby.

Finally, she would be a mother. Odd, she'd never realized just how much she longed to have a child until she met Chad. But now, it was exactly what she wanted.

Turning out the lamp, she stretched again, then stepped out into the studio where she now performed a far less strenuous form of photography. Smiling, she remembered the week Janeen had visited them. Janeen had returned to Black Rock with her new daughter, Victoria, long enough to visit and sell Tyler's horse plus a few of the larger household items she had not had Chad ship back East.

She stayed until Wade Mack was convicted for the murder of her husband, then went right on back to Philadelphia. But she had kept in touch since, wanting updates first on Jenny's work, and then on her pregnancy after Chad let it be known he was to be a father.

Now, with the baby only weeks away, Jenny was happy to stay very close to home, spending only a few hours a day taking and developing the family photographs, and looking forward to the day when she could photograph her own Chad holding their first born child.

A child she hoped to name Tyler.

SURRENDER TO THE SPLENDOR
OF THE ROMANCES
OF ROSANNE BITTNER!

UNFORGETTABLE   (4423, $5.50/$6.50)

FULL CIRCLE   (4711, $5.99/$6.99)

CARESS   (3791, $5.99/$6.99)

COMANCHE SUNSET   (3568, $4.99/$5.99)

SHAMELESS   (4056, $5.99/$6.99)